Mister Star

MISTER

Mister Benne

Mister Lawso

Mister Dixon – Book 3

Mister Stark – Book 4

Mister Lane – Book 5

Mister Marshal – Book 6

Mister Steel – Book 7

Mister Reed – Book 8

Mister Stitch – Book 9

Mister Lyric – Book 10

Mister Riggs – Book 11

BREANNE BERGIE

Editing: EJL Editing

ONE

First Impressions

I was early.

Again...

I even stopped at the cafeteria to get a coffee, and I was still ahead of schedule. Arriving early seemed to be my normal routine here at Lakeshore University. It was the only university I considered attending because I want the best and today was the moment I waited for.

I blew the wavy long black wisps of hair out of my face and adjusted my textbooks in my arms. I held them clenched tightly against my chest and my hand grasped my warm coffee. The order was black because I needed something strong to wake me up for the day. It was an important day and a crucial lecture for my business management class. I had to be on high alert and function properly to comprehend all the information given because a very important man gave the lecture.

I heard a noise at the end of the quiet hallway and turned around, but no one was there. A frown spread across my face and my nose crinkled with curiosity. No one was ever here this early except for me, and it was so quiet that if a pin dropped, it would echo through the hallway.

I shook my head at the nonsense and whispered to myself. "No one is here."

I blew the hair out of my face again, but dropped a textbook. "Shit..."

I bent down to retrieve it and had a hard time managing all the books I wanted to have for this lecture. I had to balance them within my clenched arms and reached out for the fallen textbook. The textbook tucked between my fingers. I placed it back where it belonged and stood up with a spin. But some of my coffee spilled on the floor.

Nothing the cleanup crew couldn't handle.

Suddenly, I bumped into a firm form as warm liquid spilled all over my hands and onto my beloved textbooks. There was no time to react except for a curse word that filled the hallway from my mouth. I stared down with displeasure at my coffee stained, soaked books and then at shiny black dress shoes.

"You should watch what you're doing, young lady," a stern voice said as it echoed down the hallway and sent a shiver down my spine.

His firm tone gave me daddy vibes, but as my displeased eyes worked their way up his business suit, my mouth almost fell open when they landed on his face. A wise face with deep and dark eyes that burned into mine. The look of amusement toyed inside his depths, but his features remained cold and I knew exactly who he was.

Mr. Daxon Stark.

The powerful billionaire CEO of D.S. Industries and the same man who came to give a lecture today. He was the owner of the top-ranking company in the entire world and he stood before me with my coffee spilled all over my textbooks. The same man who I'd looked up to for years. I'd tossed and turned in bed because I knew he'd be here today. And by the look on his heartless face, I'd blown my first impression.

"I-I didn't think anybody else was here," I stammered under his dark stare and blinked repeatedly.

"Well, that's very unfortunate for you." Mr. Stark growled with annoyance as he ran a hand through his salt and pepper hair, but pointed towards my wet textbooks. "Maybe now you've learned your lesson, young lady."

I couldn't speak.

No words came out of my mouth after the mess I'd made of this entire situation. Tears stung my eyes, but I wouldn't dare let him see me cry. He was Daxon Stark for Christ's sake and he didn't tolerate self-pity in his business. I wanted to impress him and I was afraid the chance was all shot to hell.

"If you'll excuse me, I have a lecture to get ready for," Mr. Stark said as he fixed his collar and flashy blue business tie. "I hope you enjoy it, princess."

Just before he broke eye contact, I saw a hint of amusement in his eyes and it toyed with my nerves. It caused my cheeks to burn crimson as I watched him walk away and enter the lecture room without a glance back. All I could do was stare at the door after his departure in disbelief.

A career in business has always been the right path for me and it was a dream I wanted to achieve. Lakeshore University was my ticket towards making that dream become a reality and Mr. Daxon Stark has been my idol since day one. I can't remember a day where I didn't fawn over every single business magazine I could find with his face plastered on the front of it. But he wasn't just famous for his business, he was a popular billionaire bachelor.

Every magazine wanted him as their top story with his face on the cover. Daxon Stark was forty-seven years old, but every woman wanted him and he had a reputation for being a playboy. He may be wise, but he was definitely also easy on the eyes. After meeting him up close and personal, I definitely agreed, but I was afraid I'd blown my chance.

Chatter filled the hallways, and footsteps echoed around me. I gazed down at my wristwatch, wet with coffee, and muttered to myself, "Let's get this over with."

My morning had been once full of excitement and new beginnings, but now was rife with self-disappointment. I may have a dream, but I needed to stop being such a clumsy fool. If I was going to get anywhere in business management, I had to pull myself together and focus on my goal. Mr. Stark had taught me something valuable. Even if he didn't realize it. I had coffee spilled all over my beloved textbooks, but I would still move forward.

I followed behind classmates who probably didn't even remember my name and blended in nicely as I made my way towards a seat. My eyes searched the front of the room, but no dark eyes or salt and pepper hair were in sight. Mr. Daxon Stark was nowhere to be found, and I breathed a sigh of relief. He had put me on edge with his harsh attitude, but I wouldn't let him mess with my dream.

The lecture room quickly filled up with students and their conversations. It was almost time for the lecture to begin. The lights dimmed, but the front of the room remained lit.

Mrs. Heard, our primary teacher, went towards the podium and fumbled with some papers. She cleared her throat and tapped the microphone. A sharp buzz filled the room and students turned their attention towards the front.

"Good, now that I have your attention, we can begin," she chimed as she pointed over towards the chairs in front of her. "Mr. Dylan Stark will give today's lecture. The president and chief operating officer of D.S. Industries. Let's welcome him to the stage."

I was left in shock by the turn of events and the introduction of Dylan Stark. I had no idea Mr. Stark even had a son, or that his son helped him run his billion-dollar business. It was a piece of information I missed. Either I was so caught up in Daxon Stark's brilliance, or it was possible he kept Dylan out of the public eye. But the media was cutthroat and the odds of that were low.

I was too consumed by his dad.

Sure, Mr. Daxon Stark was rich, famous, single and extremely good looking for his age, but that wasn't what drew me to him. I was drawn to his intelligence and the way he had built his company from the ground up. Everything about his brilliant mind fascinated me, and I had to learn more. He was easy on the eyes, but Mr. Stark has other attributes I was far more interested in. Especially if his skills helped me figure out my big dream.

The auditorium filled with a welcoming applause as Mr. Dylan Stark took to the podium and adjusted the microphone to reach his height. His father was about the same height as him. He was not that much older than me and I wouldn't doubt we were the same age. He cleared his throat, but didn't appear at all nervous as he smiled a mouthwatering smile and pushed back his brown hair. His gaze fell over the audience and my heart leapt into my throat. Mr. Dylan

Stark was a heartthrob and a complete hunk. Not to mention he was filthy rich because of his dad.

"It's a pleasure to be here. I'm Dylan Stark and I'm thrilled to be leading this lecture today for all eager business-minded alike." Dylan introduced himself and fixed his black tie. "There will be many of you who take this lecture seriously and for some of you it will be a stepping stone towards another path in your life."

His serious eyes gazed over each one of us, and I could swear I felt him look deep into my soul. His message was clear and his dark eyes made the statement firm. This was a make it or break it moment and I intended to hang on for the journey.

"The business world is ruthless. It's cutthroat, cold and calculated. Each step forward could be a step back. One day, you could be on top of the world and the next lost in space." Dylan said as his tone appeared wise and in charge. "But one thing I've learned is that perseverance is the key to success and after that it doesn't stop coming because you've finally broken through in the business world."

I twirled strands of hair between my fingers and got lost in the lecture. The talk of the right attitude, business and money. His wisdom at such a young age, and his voice completely took me. The depth of tone was rich and smooth like chocolate. The layers melted inside my ears and created a heavenly tune. I could get lost in the sound of it for days and never come back.

I bit the pen cap between my teeth and wished I could bite into him just like every other woman in this auditorium. Dylan Stark fascinated me, and he left me in awe. His brilliant words were just like his father's and I was sure he learned so much from the best. I know I had, and I was not even related to him. I would give anything to be close to these fascinating men and see a glimpse inside their world. But I was a nobody business student and everything I did would have to start from the ground up.

Just like Dylan's father.

Minutes turned into an hour, but I didn't realize until I glanced down at my watch when Dylan took a sip of water. He excused himself for a moment and I watched as his Adam's apple bopped in his throat. The liquid cleared a path for his voice to return, but he gestured over towards the chairs in front of him before he continued.

"I would now like to introduce you to someone who started D.S. Industries. Many of you may know him for his tremendous success in the business world and his motto to always be on top. Not to mention his face on every magazine cover." Dylan chuckled as the crowd did the same and I admired the sweet sound of it. "My father, Mr. Daxon Stark of D.S. Industries."

Mr. Stark's salt and pepper hair caught my eye as the crowd applauded. He was poised and ready to take charge. He fixed his tie, got to the front of the podium, and shook his son's hand. I saw him whisper something in Dylan's ear. I wished I could hear every word as Dylan kept a straight face, but left the front of the room.

It was Daxon Stark's turn to be front and centre, and after my first impression, I knew this would be strictly about business. There was no room for error in Mr. Stark's eyes and his intense glare roamed across the room. The heat fused and everyone would surrender to it. They would follow his every command because Daxon Stark was the leader. He knew it; he breathed it and he lived it. No one was better than him, and he made sure everyone in the room understood.

"Thank you, son, for the introduction, but Dylan explained the business world like a professional. He has lived in the eyes of it all from birth and I've ensured he knows everything there is to know. The world of business is a lonely place and you have to learn how to adapt on your own. You need to have the patience and perseverance to keep your business afloat. If you don't, then your days are numbered. There are always more eager businesses in the world that would kill to have what you do. So, once you're on top, you'll do anything to keep it that way." Mr. Stark said as his deep stare overlooked the audience and he glanced down at his expensive wristwatch. "But there's not much more for me to say. Time is money and money is time. If you have questions, I'll be happy to answer them for you here at the front."

And with that, the most critical session of my life ended.

The lecture could be repeated, and I could stay lost in their world forever. I could mesh into their world repeatedly, but Mr. Stark's wise words hung in the air. Time is money and money is time. If I wanted to earn money, I had to invest my time. My internal clock was dead set on meeting Mr. Dylan Stark.

But I'd have to meet his bossy dad all over again.

TWO
Charmer

It was now or never.

My textbooks clenched to my chest, I gazed down at them and frowned. The coffee had dried, but the stains and ruined pages were visible. I walked to the nearest garbage bin and tossed them inside. I dusted my hands of the beloved textbooks, but knew this opportunity was far more important. First impressions were everything and I might have blown it with Daxon Stark, but I sure as hell would not blow it with his son.

Today, I had dressed to impress and hopefully it paid off. I briefly fixed my hair and pushed the wavy wisps aside, but tugged at my purple skirt suit. I pressed my lips together, clasped my hands together and took a deep breath.

Here goes nothing...

My index fingers fiddled with one another as my nerves set in, but I pushed my worries aside and stepped closer to Dylan Stark. I placed my hands at my sides to stop the nervous twitch and tried to appear as confident as possible. At the moment, observing Dylan was my only option because another student had his attention and I patiently waited. I watched him gesture with his clean masculine hands and I could imagine the smell of fresh soap. He smiled at her, and kept eye contact.

That was, until they locked on mine over her shoulder.

Instant heat flushed my cheeks as his deep gaze burned into me with curiosity. He broke eye contact, and I'd nervously lick my lips. But his eyes caught the action and grabbed my attention once again.

"It was nice to meet you..." Dylan Stark told the student as he shook her hand and never broke eye contact with me. "Please excuse me."

The student simply nodded her head and stepped aside. Dylan paid no attention and set his focus on me. The dark depths of his eyes lit up as he came closer and I could see the different shades of brown in his eyes. Electric sparks flew through the air, goosebumps rose over my skin and the hair stood up on my arms.

His face lit up, and his eyes narrowed together. "Have we met somewhere before? You just caught my eye and something about you seems so familiar?"

"I-I don't think so..." I stammered with uncertainty and opened my mouth to speak, but no other words came out.

"I could swear I've met you prior to this?" Dylan frowned as he let out a soft chuckle and ran his hand through his hair. "Doesn't matter, anyway."

"Why do you think we've met before?" I asked out of curiosity.

"You just have a beautiful face that I can't take my eyes off of." Dylan gave a small smirk as his deep gaze ran across my face. "I'd remember this kind of beauty anywhere."

"Well, beauty is overrated, but brains..." I giggled softly and tapped my forehead. "I've got that."

Dylan chuckled, and the smoothness of it lingered in my ears. It was rich, wholesome and a sweet sound any girl could get used to. A smile beamed across his face and made me weak at the knees, but I held my composure. I couldn't fuck this opportunity up. I would bet the inconsiderable amount of cash I had in my bank account that Mr. Dylan Stark was flirting with me. The son of the famous billionaire, Mr. Daxon Stark.

"I take it you gathered my name from the lecture?" He asked as he extended his hand and looked down at mine.

"Um, yes, and what a lecture it was." I beamed as I extended my hand and he took mine in his grasp. "You're very business minded for such a young age."

"Twenty-four, to be exact." Dylan smiled as he still held my hand and his thumb slowly moved over my skin.

"Excuse me?" I asked, puzzled by his remark.

"I'm twenty-four years old." Dylan answered as his smile left his face and I missed it already. "I'm good at business, but sometimes I suck at conversation."

I giggled like a crazy school girl, but cut it short when a pair of dark eyes caught my attention over Dylan's shoulder. They were the same as Dylan's, but cold and distant. They didn't linger with amusement this time, but conveyed a threat loud and clear.

Stay away from my son.

I plastered a huge smile on my face just for him and turned my attention back towards Dylan. I didn't know what his problem was, but I would not let him stop me from this opportunity. Dylan was interested in me. I was bright, eager and willing. Even if he was just flirting, we could still talk business, and it would help me get closer to my goal.

"We're actually the same age." I breathed as I gazed down at our hands intertwined and didn't let go.

"Well, I'll be damned..." Dylan whispered as his eyes locked with mine again and he licked his lower lip. "So, what's a beautiful woman like you doing in business management?"

"It's always been a dream of mine to run a company from the ground up." I replied as I bit my lower lip and tingles ran up my spine.

"And what's your name?" Dylan asked with curiosity.

"Celeste Lovette." I breathed as the air sizzled around us, and he drew me to him.

"Lovette Industries, I like the sound of that." Dylan whispered with wonder as he looked off into the distance and his wonderful brain worked. "I can see it all now."

I giggled, he chuckled, and our gazes locked. "I love the sound of that."

Suddenly, a throat cleared. "Am I interrupting something?"

"Oh, dad, this is Celeste Lovette, a business student here at Lakeside University." Dylan beamed as he dropped my hand and the connection calmed. "Isn't she lovely?"

Mr. Stark roamed his eyes over me, from my wavy black hair all the way to my high heeled black shoes. His gaze burned and sizzled through my dress. It left me exposed. The intensity of him loomed over me with powerful force and my breath caught in my throat.

"Hm, lovely, indeed." He simply muttered under his breath and made sure I heard every damn word.

"Do you have any advice for her?" Dylan asked with eagerness.

"There's no time for leisure with business." Daxon Stark replied as his gaze fumed into mine, but I held his stare. "Remember, son, this is strictly business. No time for pleasure."

He turned his attention towards his son, and they exchanged looks. The air grew still, and an awkwardness took over. I don't understand how one clumsy mistake could make a man act so cruelly. Even though I idolized him, he was an asshole in person.

Mr. Stark turned his icy eyes back towards me, but the amusement was back in them and it toyed with me. He wanted to play whatever sick little game he had up his expensive sleeves, but I wouldn't have any of it. I turned away from his dangerous dare and gazed down at my hands.

"Now, if you'll excuse me, I have business to deal with." Daxon Stark glared at me as his gaze burned and he turned his attention to the next eager student.

I smiled shyly down at my hands and took the hint to leave. I couldn't bear to look up into Dylan's eyes with the embarrassment that coursed through me. My heels turned, wispy black hair flew into my face, but his hand caught mine.

I stopped at his physical warmth, stunned, and gazed at his stunning good looks. His eyes shone with something I couldn't describe, but it was far from pity. He didn't speak a word but simply pushed his business card into the palm of my hand.

Moments passed before he released my hand and I stared down at the card. The turn of events shocked me and it had me lost for words. His father was blatantly clear and didn't appear to be someone that anyone should mess with. He was powerful, overbearing and rich.

"This has nothing to do with business, but you've captivated me with your beauty. I'd like to wine and dine you. I want to show you a glamorous time." Dylan whispered, and his eyes never left mine. "Please call me sometime, sooner rather than later."

I gazed at him with reluctance and caught sight of his father over his shoulder. "But your dad doesn't seem to agree."

"Forget about him, Celeste. My father is always about business, but there's more to life than just work. You're an intelligent woman and I'd love to show you just how beautiful you are."

My body temperature rose at his words and my cheeks turned crimson. My entire being was on fire and he lit the match. The flame within me crackled with chemistry and I couldn't deny it.

I tapped his business card against my hand and playfully smiled up at him. "You're quite the charmer, aren't you, Dylan Stark?"

"Oh, you know it." He smirked wickedly towards me and licked his juicy lips.

I returned his smirk and turned my back to him. I didn't promise to call him, but left his imagination to play a wild game. Dylan Stark's eyes burned into my backside as I walked away lost in wonder, but a second pair of eyes also burned with something I couldn't describe.

And they were his father's.

THREE
Change of Plans

I bounced back to my dorm at Lakeside University with an extra skip in my step. The early morning had been gloomy, but now the skies had opened up and everything was brighter. I was not sure if it was because of Dylan Stark or just Mother Nature's mysterious way, but I didn't care.

I went into this life-altering lecture wanting the billionaire CEO Mr. Daxon Stark to change my life, but unexpectedly his son had. His wise words about business and his charm had swept me off my feet. His impressive mind and his extremely handsome looks had drawn me to him. I still had a dream I wanted to achieve, and it was my top priority. I shouldn't lose sight of that, and that's why I was hesitant.

Should I call billionaire Dylan Stark?

The question ran through my mind as I stepped into my co-ed dorm and stared down the white hallway. The smell of fresh paint filled my nostrils as I strolled down along and my heels clicked on the tile. Signs were up with the reminder of wet paint, but they painted it last week. No one had come by to remove them and I broke the rule as I ran my hand along the dried paint.

I smiled to myself as I remembered Dylan's charming words and my cheek heated at the remembrance. He had made quite the first impression, but his dad was another story. My smile turned upside down as I remembered our accidental collision and his condescending attitude. How dare he treat a student the way he did? I should go to the board, but what good would it do?

Mr. Daxon Stark was a famous billionaire CEO and in his eyes, I was a nobody. I was the dirt on the bottom of his new expensive shiny shoes that he could just kick aside. I was one of his many fans, who he clearly disregarded and didn't give a shit about. It would serve him right if I dated his billionaire son and ended up in his personal space. Another struggle I'd deal with and a reason to accept Dylan's proposal of a date.

I slipped my key for dorm room fifty-five into the keyhole and pushed through the door. Perfume replaced the smell of fresh paint and it hung strongly in the air. I waved my hand in front of my face and my best friend popped into sight.

"It's like a fruity cloud in here." I mumbled as I put my keys down on the table and walked inside.

"Oh, you love it." Paisley beamed as she clapped her hands together and came into my close circle.

She placed her hands on my shoulders, and her bright blue eyes shone into mine. They were like the ocean and sometimes I swear I could see waves within them. Especially when she gets angry. Don't get on a redheaded, blue-eyed chick's bad side. Not this one. She will eat you alive.

"So, how did it go?" Paisley asked as she shook my shoulders and smiled brightly at me. "Did you get to meet your idol and genius, Mr. Stark?"

"Oh, I got to meet him all right. Him and his poor attitude." I grumbled as I rolled my eyes and sighed with irritation. "I bumped right into him and spilled my coffee all over myself."

She burst out in laughter, but immediately stopped when she saw my unimpressed expression. "Oh, right, not funny? Clearly, his fame and fortune has gone straight to his head. But is he as gorgeous in person as he is on the cover of a magazine?"

Paisley's question caught me off guard. "I-I don't really know because I..."

"He's that gorgeous, huh? I knew it! A dashing silver fox." Paisley interrupted as she let go of my shoulders and her hands covered her heart.

A silver fox?

I wouldn't classify Mr. Daxon Stark as a gorgeous silver fox. He was just a self-centered asshole. Yes, he had magnificent eyes any woman could lose herself in, a powerful body inside a dashing business suit and hair any woman could grab onto. But his personality was shitty and his money has gone straight to his head.

"Forget Daxon Stark..." I mumbled as I waved my hand in the air and held Dylan's business card in front of my face. "And say hello to his son."

"What?" Paisley exclaimed with shocked surprise as her hand covered her mouth and her eyes grew wide. "Mr. Stark has a son?"

"Right? I was just as surprised," I added with excitement. "I guess I've been so focused on Daxon Stark and his success that I missed the president and chief operating officer of D.S. Industries."

"No way!" Paisley shouted. "Mr. Stark's son helps him run D.S. Industries? Is he cute?"

I fanned my face with the business card and fell onto the bed. "He's absolutely amazing, like a dream come true."

Paisley stalked forward and snagged the business card out of my hand. "Mr. Dylan Stark... How the hell did you get his business card?"

I sat up with my arms behind me and smirked. "Dylan Stark gave it to me, himself."

"What?" Paisley cried out with disbelief and confusion took over her face. "But why?"

I stood up and walked over to the window with my arms crossed. "He wants me to call him and take me out on a date."

I kept my back to Paisley, but I heard the screech of excitement leave her lungs. A smile crept over my face, but soon faded. I had zero faith I even stood a chance with Dylan Stark. He was born rich, extremely gorgeous, and could have any woman he wanted.

But why would he want a nobody like me?

"You need to call him right away, Celeste." Paisley announced and spun me around to face her with her hands on my shoulders. "What the hell are you waiting for?"

I let out a long sigh, and it blew right into her red locks. "He's way out of my league, Paisley."

Her eyebrows wrinkled together, and she shook her head. "No, he's not, if he gave you his freaking phone number! You're gorgeous and all the men want you. You just don't give them the time of day because you're always focused on school."

It was true.

I had always been focused on finishing school and one day owning my own business. I didn't want to lose focus on my goal. But now Dylan Stark has entered the picture and he could change everything.

The way he looked at me—his hunky handsome looks and those gorgeous eyes. It might be all I needed. But I was uncertain I was right for him.

"I don't know, Paisley..." I groaned as I frowned and looked down.

"Well, you won't know until you give him a chance." She argued as she held the cell phone within eyesight and his business card. "You should call him."

I scrunched up my face with uncertainty, but took them. "Okay, I will give it a shot, but get ready for utter failure."

Paisley's squeal filled my ears, and we sat down on the side of the bed together as I dialed Dylan's Stark's number. I held the phone with uneasiness, my nerves on edge, and listened to each ring. One, two, three.

But on the fourth ring, his rich tone charmed through the phone line.

"Hello, this is Dylan Stark." He answered, and I melted under his spell.

He sounded so professional, upfront, and powerful. I was intimidated, nervous, and ready to hang up. But he'd wonder who was on the other line.

"Go on..." Paisley whispered in my ear with encouragement and poked me in my side.

"H-hi, this is Celeste Lovette. We met earlier at the business lecture at Lakeside University. I hope I'm not interfering with business matters." I stammered with jitters and my stomach turned.

"Oh, no, you could never do that, Celeste." He said as his husky tone took over the phone and my legs grew weak.

My cheeks blushed, and I fumbled with the conversation. "I-I was calling... I-I mean I was..."

Suddenly, his laughter filled the earpiece, and my palm hit my forehead. I was an utter failure and sucked at this shit. He deserved confidence but I was a mumbling wreck. I completely blew it and waited for him to hang up.

But his voice came back on the line. "You're calling to accept my dinner invitation this evening?"

"T-this evening? But that's in a few hours. I don't even have anything to wear. I..." I grumbled in a nervous mess.

"Don't worry about that. Text me your address and I will send you something to wear. A beautiful woman like you deserves extravagant things." Dylan breathed as his voice charmed me and I was in disbelief by the turn of conversation.

I looked over at Paisley, who held her ear near the cell phone. A huge smile spread across her face as she squeezed my shoulders with encouraging excitement. His forward behavior and willingness to continue shocked me. I couldn't believe he wanted me.

"Oh, you don't have to do that, Mr. Stark." I mumbled with flustered delight.

"Yes, I absolutely do, and you will accept my gift because you deserve it. But please call me by my first name." Dylan Stark said and his tone held power. "I hate being called Mr.

Stark. It belongs to my father, and we're two very different people."

Idiot.

"Oh, yes, Mr. Stark... I mean, Dylan." I fumbled and hated myself for being out of practice with men.

"Good, now that sounds so much better." He chimed, and I could imagine a smile spread out across his handsome face. "I will pick you up at quarter to five and wear that bright shade of red lipstick you wore earlier. It really brings out your eyes."

And then he hung up with a loud beep in my ear.

I smiled and touched my fingertips to my plump lips. I pulled them back and gazed down at the red lipstick smeared on them. My heart swooned, and I'd be sure to touch it up just for him.

But Paisley's shrill of excitement filled the dorm room. "Oh, my god, Celeste! Can you believe him?"

"No, I can't believe any of this, but I have a hunky date in a few hours and I better get ready." I beamed with delight. I was on cloud nine and texted my address to Dylan Stark.

FOUR

Swept Away

The water trickled down on me and the warmth was a cozy blanket protecting me from the cool air outside. The steam filled the bathroom and created a thick mist. I must've been in here longer than I thought.

Suddenly, there was a loud knock on the bathroom door and it startled me, but I knew exactly who it was. I smiled and put down the soap. But I grabbed the shower curtain and wrapped it around myself before the door swung open.

"You're going to look drop dead gorgeous in this, Celeste!" Paisley squealed as she couldn't contain her excitement and held a very expensive hanger in her hands.

I peered through the mist at the black velvet hanger draped from her fingertips. My eyes roamed over a gorgeous black spaghetti strap dress that glistened in the light. Tassels hung down as Paisley shook it back and forth with her jaw wide open. If I didn't know any better, I'd bet she already tried it on.

"Well, what the hell are you waiting for? Try it on!" Paisley exclaimed as she reached over, turned off the shower, and handed me a towel.

She gave me a fluffy pink one. It was like feathers wrapped around my body. I let it sink into my skin and dry my wet flesh as I took the extravagant garment from Paisley's much too eager hands. I gazed over it with disbelief as the tassels swayed and the light hit it just right.

"I can't even believe this is real right now." I muttered as I shook my head and my wet hair clung to my shoulders.

"Well, you better believe it." Paisley giggled and looked down at her wristwatch. "Because he's going to be here in less than thirty minutes."

"Oh, my god!" I exclaimed with shocked excitement and stepped out of the shower.

"You better get your ass moving!" Paisley teased with encouragement and smacked her hand against my ass.

I squealed with laughter and she left me to get ready. The door closed behind her and I let the towel drop to the floor. My eyes landed on the sexy pair of underwear I picked for this perfect occasion. The thong I bought for a date I thought could never happen to me, but had come my way. The lacy black fabric hugged each thigh as it went up my legs and rested in place. It was form fitting, but out of my comfort zone.

I picked up my bra that matched, but shrugged my shoulders and tossed it aside. I didn't need a bra for this glamorous dress. I grabbed the dress with excited hands and lifted it over my head. My body shimmied as it fell over me and hugged me tight. It was the perfect fit and displayed all my curves.

"Holy shit..." I mumbled with disbelief under my breath.

I couldn't believe he got my size right, and it was everything I could ever imagine for myself. I never thought I could experience something so beautifully expensive with so much luxury at the hands of a handsome and extremely wealthy man. One that I never expected would have laid eyes on me and loved what he saw. His gorgeous deep brown eyes made me melt at his feet. But the same eyes had seared into me with an intense power during the lecture and warned me to stay away. Deep eyes that burned into my backside and made me shiver with uncertainty. The eyes of his silver fox father. He could leave any woman kneeling at his feet and pleading for more.

But not me.

Dylan Stark was the only one I had eyes for with his gorgeous looks and he was on his way to get me. He should be here any minute and here I was, daydreaming about his daddy. Dylan's father and Daxon Stark got under my skin.

"Get a grip and get your ass in gear..." I mumbled to myself and grabbed my brush.

I combed the bristles through my long, damp waves as they curved nicely down my shoulders and bounced with each brush. I applied a bit of makeup and my plump lips smacked the bright red lipstick together. It was his favorite thing about me and I didn't want to disappoint him. He was a man of power and wealth I had never known, but I was excited to experience his world. Even if it was just for one date.

There was no way a handsome and extremely rich man like Dylan Stark could ever fall for me. My hopes were low going into this and expected little at all. I was an undergrad with no business experience and just a dream. I had under two hundred dollars in my bank account and once he got to know the real me, he'd run in the opposite direction. Dylan Stark could have any woman and he wouldn't want me.

Suddenly, there was a knock at the door, and it startled me, but excited me. It broke me from my negative thoughts as I ran my hands through my hair one last time and smiled at my reflection. The one I couldn't wipe off my face since I met Dylan.

"Celeste? Someone is here for you." Paisley said as her tone teased with eagerness.

I exhaled and looked into my deep brown eyes. "You can do this, Celeste..."

I grabbed the doorknob, braced myself for what was on the other side, and opened the bathroom door. I found an unfamiliar man dressed in a suit and bow tie wearing a black hat in my dorm room. Paisley eyed him up like he was an expensive piece of meat and I held back my laughter.

"You must be, Celeste." He started off with a charming smile as he held red and white roses in his hands. "Mr. Stark is waiting for you out in his limousine."

The limousine driver extended the gorgeous flowers towards me. My heart swelled, but Paisley stepped forward and swooped in. I pouted as she took a big whiff of the extravagant scent and waved her hand at me.

"Go on and get out of here. I've got this and will put these beauties in some water." Paisley admitted with a moment's hesitation.

The polite limousine driver extended his arm towards me. I shyly smiled and grabbed my heels. They hugged my feet as I fastened them in place and took his arm. He walked me away, but Paisley's warm giggle followed me down the hallway and mixed with whispers. My heels clicked along the tiled floor as students stopped and admired my beauty. Gossip poured down the hallway of the university dormitory and I'd never be the same student again. I was the centre of attention and it was all because of Dylan Stark.

I continued to follow the polite gentleman's lead. We walked out the entrance and there was a limousine pulled up right in front of the dormitory. My eyes went wide at the sight before me and never in my wildest dreams did, I imagine being swept away in such luxury.

Eyes peered into my backside, and I knew everyone was watching. My nerves had settled as the reality of the situation sunk in and I knew at any moment I'd see him. I didn't picture this kind of attention, but I could get used to this.

The back door of the limousine opened, and a flashy shoe stepped out. A long leg followed as my eyes worked upwards and I found he wore a black suit that matched with my pretty dress. The perfect combination and my eyes landed on his gorgeous smile as it shined straight at me. I couldn't turn away even if I wanted to.

Mr. Dylan Stark's eyes roamed over me with a glint of awe and flames flickered with desire. A lust that was all for me and I couldn't figure out why, but right now I could care less.

He ran a hand through his slick black hair and over his jaw. "You look amazing in that dress."

But all I could do was smile like a damn fool.

His eyes twinkled at me, and I loved the way he made me feel. A fire burned deep inside the pit of my belly and threatened to explode at the hands of this very man. The way my mouth watered at just the sight of him and I couldn't get enough. My heart beat a thousand miles a minute at every word that came out of his glorious mouth.

Everything was right, even though it shouldn't be. He should be with a woman within his business and someone more experienced than me. Not a nobody in university and uncertain of where my future headed.

"Maybe this was a mistake and I..." I mumbled as my nerves got the best of me and I had second thoughts.

"What? No, Celeste..." He interrupted as he stepped forward without hesitation and the limousine driver dropped my arm. "There's no mistaking this and the connection I feel towards you. Meeting you happened for me and I want this."

He stood inches away from me as he brushed the back of his fingertips along my cheek and my belly quivered. The connection was there all right, and it sizzled to life. I could just imagine the gossip and pictures being captured at this very moment. And his father's stubborn, handsome face entered my mind.

"I don't know..." I mumbled with uncertainty.

"Come with me and let me show you what your life could be like." He breathed as his fingertips left my cheek, travelled down the nape of my neck, along my arm and my fingers intertwined with his.

It was absolutely magical.

I peered into his eyes, and they stared into the depths of my soul. They spoke to me of promise and a tale of all I could have. Everything that could be mine if I was his. All I never thought I could have, but suddenly seemed possible and I followed him. Mr. Dylan Stark took me away in that limousine and never looked back.

FIVE

One Year Later

My hand shielded the sunlight as I peered out at the blue tones of ocean. The scenery was everything I needed. I inhaled the fresh scent of water as the sun beamed down upon me and my wavy waves blew with the cool breeze. My toes dug into the sandy beach and curled into the warmth. I may live in the city, but the beach life was for me.

I scanned across the light blue of the ocean as the waves gently crashed ashore and mixed with the wet sand. The current pushed it up to reveal the many wonderful treasures one could find as people strolled along the beach. But my eyes wandered back out to the darker blue tones that didn't rest and crashed within the water.

The jet skis whisked along the deep water, people parasailed from the sky above, motorboats whizzed past and sailboats slowly made their way across the ocean. It was a sight I could get used to and never leave, but Dylan had flown us away for the day on his private jet plane. I wasn't sure how much time we had left.

Not much if dear daddy had anything to say about it.

I shook my head at the annoying thought and tried to push him out of my mind. I wanted to enjoy the day, but Daxon Stark haunted my thoughts with his demanding, wicked ways. No matter where I went or what I did, he was there. Ever since I followed this path in life, Dylan's father was right there. Everything was always about the business and my fiancé helped run it.

I gazed down at my big diamond engagement ring and it sparkled with the light. The sun's rays hit it from all angles and made it shimmer like the extravagant piece it was. I twirled it around on my finger because it moved easily with its gigantic size and peered out at my fiancé.

He strolled through the water near the shoreline as beads of wetness fell down his gorgeous body and dripped back into the ocean. His beach body mixed in magnificently with the scenery. His tanned skin made women beg to run their hands on it and ripped muscles from head to toe. He was everything any woman could dream of. Dylan may be a filthy rich businessman, but he was breathtaking, and he was all mine.

I smiled at the thought and knew he'd take care of me for the rest of my life once we spoke the words, "I do." Since we left on our date and our only date, I had never looked back. I got to live an extravagant life full of money and whatever my heart desired. Dylan made it all happen and promised me to never work a day in my life. It was a far-fetched fantasy, and I was reluctant at first because I had my dream. I wanted to run my business one day, but I was afraid it might never happen. And there was Dylan offering me everything.

What woman doesn't want to live a lavish life of luxury?

I was a young woman struggling to get through university with hardly any money in my name. I had dreams, but they all went out the window as soon as I met Dylan Stark. My dreams had now changed, and I was living a life I never imagined. I could live it with a man I loved. A man I could raise a family with and a business that would eventually pass down to our children.

But not if Daxon Stark had anything to say about it.

Ever since he found out about our blossoming relationship, he had been a thorn in my side. A constant reminder lurking in the shadows and watching my every move with distrust. He tried to sabotage every little thing I did, but kept it hidden from his son.

I'd never forget dear daddy's stern warning after we announced our engagement. The way I withered under his powerful stare and pondered his distaste for me, wishing it could be different. We were going to be family, and all he wanted to do was hate me.

A cell phone rang, and it had been Dylan's. He was a gentleman and excused himself from the table to address a business matter. His father had given us lovely congratulations, but it had all been fake. His eyes followed his son as he left the room and we were all alone.

But then his deep brown haze glared my way.

His distrustful daggers pierced into me as he rose from his seat and the chair squeaked on the floor. My eyes landed on the business suit jacket as it hung from his chair where he discarded it, but landed on his white dress shirt. He left it unbuttoned at the top as he moved towards me and my mouth went dry. His dominance loomed over me as he pulled at his blue tie and it hung loosely from his neck. Veins ran down it as his pulse throbbed in his throat and the madness was all directed at me.

He leaned in with a hand on the table beside me and a day's worth of stubble stared back at me. The mix of salt and pepper within it. I licked my lips and my insides quivered. His other hand gripped the back of my chair, but he startled me when he shook my seat. His wicked grin grew within my eye shot and his shirt dipped low enough for me to get a good view of his chest hair. My mouth was no longer dry and watered at the sight. But my irritation grew with his never-ending rudeness.

He let in a deep breath as he sniffed my black locks and let out a low groan. "Oh, princess..."

I closed my eyes for a brief second as I shivered underneath his powerful wrath and couldn't help the desire coursing through me. It mixed with hatred and forged a war inside of me. A battle I could never escape with him this close to me and I couldn't understand it.

He chuckled slightly. It crawled over my skin and my eyes shot open. "You may have my son wrapped around your pretty little finger, but not me. You will never have my company. I will die before it ever happens, young lady."

The sudden room temperature changed, and I wasn't sure if it rose because of his closeness or his rude attitude, but I had enough. If it was war he wanted, he got it. He chose the wrong woman to mess with. I had enough bite for his never-ending bark.

I peered up into his deep gaze with the same distaste he showed me. "I wouldn't dream of it, Mr. Stark, but our future children might."

My lips curled into a smirk I knew he'd hate and he pushed off of my chair with frustration. He let out a low growl from somewhere inside his wickedness, and I knew I had won this battle.

He flattened his tie, straightened his back and snapped. "We'll see about that, pretty young thing."

Mr. Daxon Stark hated me, and I couldn't stand him.

That day proved to be the beginning of a mistrustful relationship and it wouldn't end soon. He was a grouchy thorn that would prick me at any opportunity he got. He was the prick who wanted to see me out on my ass and as far away from D.S. Industries as possible. But unluckily for him, I wasn't going anywhere.

SIX
Beach Day

Music flowed through the air and surrounded me as I stretched out on my stomach and my skin soaked up the sun. I could hear laughter and chatter as people went by. The beach Dylan picked wasn't a secluded location, but I didn't mind.

The rays heated my flesh and sizzled as time passed. I untied my bikini top and knew I wouldn't have a tan line. It was all part of the plan. Being lazy and relaxing on the beach was what I loved to do most. But just being here was a much-needed treat.

Suddenly, sand kicked up in my face and I gazed up to see long legs run away from me. I brushed the sand off and made a face. Anger bubbled to the surface, and I wanted to tell him where to shove it. People should watch where they were going. But my fiancé caught my eye, and the rage faded.

His toned beach body flexed with each movement as his eyes caught mine and I couldn't look away. He had me trapped with each step as he made his way towards me and ran his hands through his wet hair. His pecks glistened in the sun, abs of steel rippled down to his torso and his swimming trunks hung loosely on his hips. Women watched him as he passed by, but he didn't pay attention to them.

He was all mine.

My mouth watered and wanted him. He could read it in my eyes and once he was by my side, he smiled wickedly down at me. There was no denying him.

"Hey, handsome." I breathed as I pointed towards my bare back. "Want to help me with this?"

"Oh, I absolutely do." He grinned and got to work.

He bent down beside me and ran his fingers slowly up my skin. They started right above my bikini bottom and worked their way up. Inch by inch created an intoxicating desire to have him, and I knew he wanted it, too. He grasped each string in his fingers and tied them together while my breathing hitched into overdrive.

Sometimes this man drove me wild.

Once he finished, I slowly turned over and peered up at him with my head resting in my hands. His eyes roamed over my body and I was completely naked under his stare. They went higher until they met with mine and desire flared inside of them. I looked down towards his swimming trunks and his lust for me. Most importantly, I knew what he wanted without even asking. He wanted my mouth on his cock.

"Well, tiger, what are we waiting for?" I asked as my eyes shone wickedly up at him and I rubbed my hand on his dick.

I didn't care who was looking. People could watch if they dared. He was all mine and I could do what I wanted with him.

"I have no idea, but I think my girl's hungry." Dylan growled as he scooped me up into his arms and laughter escaped me.

I clung to his neck as he walked us inside our beach cabana. I smiled as he set me back on my feet and he closed the curtains for privacy. The sunshine was very dim inside as the slight breeze blew against the curtains. Dylan turned his attention back towards me, but looped his fingers through his waistband and pulled them down. It revealed his oversized cock that stood at attention for me, and my mouth watered more at the sight.

He was massive, manly, and magnificent.

I licked my lips as he stood there, and I moved closer. My head tossed to the side and my black waves of hair flew with it. It created a seductive dance and his cock throbbed. He groaned as I came closer and I knew he couldn't wait to get his hands on me. But I took my time.

With each step, he grew hotter for me and I loved him withering under my control. My smile grew into a passionate smirk and I couldn't wipe it off my face. Until he couldn't take anymore, launched forward and his lips crashed onto mine.

The sudden kiss took me by pleasant surprise, and I whimpered into him. He wasted no time, parted my lips and dived inside. His hands were in my hair and my hands clenched his bare chest. He swirled his tongue with mine and tasted me like he couldn't get enough. My breasts pressed against him and I wanted to be naked, but I knew he didn't want that. He only wanted my mouth.

His hand found mine and pushed it down until it rested on his dick. I wrapped the thickness of it inside my hand and stroked him just the way he liked it. He groaned into me and nibbled my lower lip. Sweet juices flowed out of my pussy and I wanted him inside me, but I knew that wasn't happening. This would have to do.

Suddenly, he grabbed my chin and broke the passionate kiss. My body hummed with electricity and begged him for more, but he was through with it. He looked down at his rigid length and let his spit leak down until it hit his cock. My hand rubbed against the wetness and my breath quickened.

"Get down there and suck my cock, little pussycat." Dylan hissed through clench teeth as he placed his hand on my head and pushed me down.

I didn't resist because I knew exactly what he wanted and I was ready to take all of him. My hand continued to stroke him as his spit helped with the journey and the tip of his dick met my gaze. My tongue left my mouth and licked it, but gave it a little swirl. I peered up at him as he gazed down at me, full of red fervent desire. A passionate greed took over him like it always did, but I never resisted my man.

"Come on, take it, beautiful." He breathed from above me with impatience and his hand urged me forward.

It grasped my hair into his fist and my eyes remained locked with his as I wrapped my lips around his massive dick. My lips sucked him inside my mouth and back out again as he groaned from above me. My pussy grew wetter with each suck, and I wished he'd slam his cock right between my juicy pussy lips.

"Oh, yes..." He whispered and pushed me deeper until his cock met the back of my throat.

I gagged, and he released me, but I sucked the side of his thickness. My tongue flicked along it in a sensual dance and I continued to do the same for the other side of his ridged length. Each flick led to a nibble, and he loved every moment. The sweet play with his dick and the attention to every little detail. He pulsated, quivered, and breathed heavily. I stroked him, licked, nibbled, and sucked.

But he couldn't get enough.

He placed both of his hands in my hair and, without hesitation, pushed me into him. My head bobbed to his rhythm as my lips wrapped around his cock and he pumped himself into my mouth. He fucked my face as his balls hit my chin and my eyes watered when his tip hit the back of my throat. My hands cupped his ass cheeks as he slammed into my mouth with each thrust and set my world on fire. He didn't let up and panted above me. But I knew he was close.

His climax built with each gag and every thrust. He was a wild beast about to explode and I was ready to receive his gift. His dick throbbed in my mouth and it leaked a bit of premature juice. It mixed with my saliva and made his journey smoother towards release.

"Yes, take it like a dirty little girl." Dylan breathed from above as he thrust deep into my mouth and his body trembled. "I'm going to give you a nice pearl necklace."

He thrust once more, and I gagged until he released me. His cock came out of my wetness and he stroked himself wildly within his grasp. But I closed my eyes as he gave me his gift and his creamy juices spilled across my neck.

We breathed heavily until he was spent, and I looked up at him. I licked my lips of the remaining mess upon them and he ran the pad of his thumb across my lower lip. He reached over and tossed me a complimentary towel from the hotel.

"You better clean up that nice necklace I gave you, darling." Dylan smirked as he found his swimming trunks and put them back on.

I did as I was told and patted the towel across my neck. It soaked up his liquid he ejaculated on me and I threw it aside. He stepped forward and pressed his lips against mine. My toes curled into the sand and I wanted more.

"That's my good girl." He breathed as his lips brushed mine and we parted. "We will leave for the city in an hour. My dad expects me back in the office tomorrow morning."

I frowned up at him. "Why do we always have to be at your father's beck and call? I was hoping to stay here for a few days and have more time for ourselves."

He reached out, brushed my cheek, and caressed my pouty lips. I sucked his finger inside and swirled my tongue around it. I treated it like it was his cock and I couldn't get enough, but all I wanted was for him to fuck the shit out of me.

"You know my dad, time is money and money is time." He replied as he popped his finger out of my mouth and moved away from me. "Get everything packed and we'll be on my jet plane in an hour."

He walked out of the cabana and left me alone with my horny self. I couldn't believe him and wished he wanted more time with me. But we had to always make time for dear old daddy.

Mr. Daxon Stark always got his way.

He was edgy, greedy, and takes what he wants. I grew tired of living under dear daddy's thumb and I couldn't wait for it to change. Once we were married, hopefully that would be the day.

I laid back in the lounge chair and sulked with disappointment. Here I was, once again, with no orgasm. My hand reached over to my beach bag and pulled out my handy vibrator that I needed for times like this. I took it everywhere with me because it was my only means of experiencing a release. I never get to experience it with Dylan because he always finished before me. Unless he stuck it in my ass and hit my beloved g-spot. Other than that, our relationship has been one sided sexually, and it was something I never understood. I tried not to complain because he provided me with everything and gave me a life I had never dreamed of.

"Oh, well, we meet again..." I sighed as I turned on the vibrator and it hummed to life.

Dylan's deep, dark eyes came to my mind. I closed my eyes and ran the vibrator over my nipples as they peeked against my bikini top. The sensation coursed through my body and tingled across my skin. I ran my fingers over my lips and licked them until they were wet. My fingers moved over my stomach and down to my clit, where I touched myself. My nub moved around with my fingertips and created a pleasurable dance that brought me closer to what I sought.

I reached inside my bikini bottoms and put my fingers inside my wetness. The juices were still there from earlier and spread inside my walls. I moved my fingers in and out until I quivered for more.

But it wasn't enough.

I moved the vibrator down to my clit and circled there. My breath quickened with each motion and a moan of pleasure escaped me as I pictured his eyes roam over my naked body. They would swirl with flames of desire and a hungry need only for me. He would want me, take me and devour me. He'd give me everything I needed and never leave me unsatisfied.

My release built higher and higher as the waves crashed outside the cabana. I was lost in my own world and my imagination as he took me to heights that I longed for. But as my climax exploded and took over me, I could only see Dylan's father watch me while I met my peak.

SEVEN

D.S. Industries

The plane ride back to the city was tiresome. I didn't want to go back. There was no point in bringing the subject up again because Dylan's mind was set. He always has to please his father and daddy seemed to come first.

Why?

I never understood it. Either he needed to please dear daddy or it was daddy's way. His way or the highway. In this case, Dylan Stark would be out on his own. No money from daddy, no fancy cars, no penthouse, no maids, nothing. Dylan Stark would have to start from the ground up just like I had to, but I gave up on my dream. He'd still have his father's name to help him along, but I knew it'd still be a challenge.

But why does he want to live under his father's shadow?

The constant commands and to do lists. He was second best to his father and could never be his own man. Who wanted to live like that?

I certainly wouldn't, but here I was every day living through it for the past year. I only put up with it because of Dylan. He was my fiancé, the man I would spend the rest of my days with, and he had given me everything.

Including this fancy penthouse connected to D.S. Industries.

I stretched my arms after I had a quick nap and smiled brightly as I gazed around. The penthouse was gorgeous and Dylan had lived the bachelor life here before I moved in. It needed life added to its plain existence, and I spruced it up to my liking. More colored plants and a woman's touch. It was far too empty and plain before I got here. More of a busy working man who just brought a woman here to fuck on the side.

Now it wasn't.

It was home.

I tossed my wavy hair to the side and put my heels back on that laid on the floor at the side of our bed. I glanced back at the empty pillow and wished Dylan was here, but he was hard at work. And I needed this time to catch up on sleep.

I stood up and straightened out my purple dress. I headed towards the bathroom to touch up my makeup before I headed out the door. My heels clicked along the hardwood, and I gazed at my reflection in the mirror. My deep eyes stared back at me with different hues of brown, and they all swirled together. Small wispy pieces of hair fell over my rosy cheeks from sleep and I pushed them aside. I touched up my red lipstick and puckered my lips together until it was just right. My eyeshadow needed to be refreshed because I smeared it on my pillow.

Once it was complete, I fluffed my hair one last time and grabbed my handbag from the counter with everything I needed inside. The front door opened with ease and I locked the door behind me.

D.S. Industries loomed overhead as I made my way towards the front lobby, and the sunshine glared behind the enormous building. It created a bright glow around it and made it look like the gateway to heaven. It would be if it weren't for its owner, Mr. Daxon Stark. More like a gateway into the fiery depths of hell after being around him for so long.

I used to idolize the shit out of him, but after I got to know him, it grew into hatred. The same hatred he felt towards me, and it was his own doing. The person he was on the inside was cold and distant. He only ever had time for his business, and it always came first. The business side of him mixed in with his personality and I could never see him change it. I couldn't imagine anything could.

"Good morning, Ms. Lovette." The secretary at the front desk of D.S. Industries wore a proper smile and greeted me.

"Good morning, Gracie." I smiled in return at her pleasantness, but knew it was all an act for Mr. Daxon Stark.

If she didn't and he found out, she wouldn't have a job. Gracie was a sweet, but shy woman and took whatever crap Daxon threw at her. She was a blonde-haired beauty with sharp blue eyes and she had so much potential. She shouldn't deal with Daxon around the clock. Gracie deserved far more respect than Mr. Stark gave her.

She nodded her head at me, pressed her lips together and gently tugged at her short black dress that Daxon ordered her was the proper fashion. I returned the nod and headed for the elevators as I fidgeted in my knee-length dress. I pushed the button, and the elevator dinged, signaling a not so busy day at D.S. Industries.

I boarded it alone and tossed my hair to the side as I pushed the button for the fiftieth floor. I gazed around at the large elevator and the mirrors all around me. My eyes looked around until they fell upon me and my reflection stared back at me. They found my handbag, and I remembered the cake cards inside. The reason I was here.

I pulled them out just as the elevator sounded for the fiftieth floor. Mr. Daxon Stark's office was on this floor along with Dylan's. He had to be right by daddy's side at all times and Daxon made sure of it.

I wanted Dylan to go cake tasting with me and he couldn't because of work. Dylan should attend and we should be able to do this together like a normal engaged couple, but it was daddy's orders. I should at least be able to see my man before I went out shopping for our wedding cake.

I looked down at the cake flavors in my hands and stepped out of the elevator. Not watching where I was going as my mind wandered to wedding cakes, wedding dresses, colors, centerpieces and party favors. I wanted Dylan to go over some cake flavors before one of many cake appointments this morning. I hoped to squeeze it into the schedule if he was still here.

Suddenly, I collided with a rock-solid form. I was a few feet away from the elevator and a grunt escaped the person I ran into. The cake cards fumbled within my hands, but didn't tumble to the floor. Thank god for that.

"You can never watch where you are going, princess." A deep, rich tone huffed with annoyance.

I gazed up with embarrassment as my cheeks flushed bright red into Daxon's dark haunting stare and it made my skin crawl, but not in a bad way. A way I shouldn't feel, but I couldn't help it. His greedy gaze didn't stop at my eyes and roamed down my body. The temperature turned up another notch and my breath hitched under his glare.

Mr. Daxon Stark was a silver fox and even though I couldn't stand him, he was sexy as fuck. He was the daddy I shouldn't be tempted by, but my body cried out for him. I shouldn't want anything to do with him, but with him this close, I couldn't escape the reminder. I hated him because of his hatred for me and that was the way it should be.

His rudeness towards me fired up everything inside, but his unwillingness to know me puzzled me. He never gave me the time of day or even bothered to try. I had given up long ago and switched my focus to more important things. If my future daddy-in-law wanted to be my enemy, then so be it. Two can play his wicked game.

I cleared my throat and grabbed his attention. "I'm here to see Dylan before he gets too busy with work."

"You're too late. He had an emergency business meeting to attend earlier this morning." He grinned as his clean-shaven mouth perked up and he gazed down at the sample cards in my hands. "What's all this?"

I grinned back at him with sass. "Wouldn't you like to know?"

He leaned in closer, and my toes curled at the smell of his expensive cologne. "I actually would, since it is about my son."

His nearness flustered me. My heart pounded in my ears and I cleared my throat. "Well, if you must know, it's different flavors for our wedding cake. He was supposed to give me an idea of what he likes since he can't attend because you have him on a tight schedule."

His hand reached out to touch the cards, but our fingers brushed in the process and tingles of red, sultry heat ran through me. His deep eyes locked with mine, my breath caught in my throat and I needed to wet my lips.

But it was a huge mistake.

His eyes darted towards the movement and fell on my plump lips. I saw the flames ignite and flicker within his deep depths. It made my pussy pulsate.

Daxon quickly pulled away and flattened his tie. "Well, that's a shame."

I swallowed the passion down my throat and glared up at him. "Yes, it is, isn't it, Daxon?"

He simply stared at me and wouldn't respond. He completely ignored the fact he couldn't let his son live a life that didn't revolve around him twenty-four-seven. Dylan had a life now with me and he just couldn't accept it.

God, I hated him.

"Right, well, I don't have time for this and our cake appointment awaits." I beamed as I returned his ignorance with a flick of my hair over my shoulder and turned my back towards him.

He didn't deserve my time of day.

I strolled over towards the elevator and pushed the button to leave the fiftieth floor. All I felt was his eyes burn into my backside and I couldn't help but wonder what he thought. The brain waves that made him work and be the cold-hearted man he was.

But I couldn't care less.

He was a rude, mean and an ignorant prick. I hated him and he hated me. But he tormented me in ways I had never known before.

The elevator doors opened as I stepped inside and hit the main floor button without another thought. I wouldn't look up to meet his eyes because he didn't deserve it from me. I gave him the cold shoulder and treated him the same way he always treated me. Nothing but distrust and hate.

The elevator doors were almost closed when I heard his smooth and rich tone breath. "His favorite cake flavor is chocolate fudge."

But the elevator doors collapsed shut and reflected my shocked face within its mirrored walls at his sweet gesture.

EIGHT

Dress of my Dreams

"Hurry! We don't want to be late." I breathed as I patted my best friend's shoulder and my keys jiggled.

I put them back into my purse and looked down the busy city street. Enormous signs hung outside each shop as we rushed past them and looked for a particular boutique. A famous one and one of the best. The most expensive wedding designer in the entire world. She'd provide me with the best options of bridal gowns for our big day. It would be an extravagant event, and Dylan wanted the best.

"Well, we better get our asses in gear!" Paisley shouted as she grabbed my hand and we giggled.

"There it is. Look, up ahead!" I exclaimed with excitement and pointed in the boutique's direction.

Our heels scurried across the pavement, and we entered through the front doors. We didn't even have to touch them as they moved on their own and the glass circled. We followed the doors path, and it led us through. But our eyes lit up in awe as soon as we walked through those front doors.

The company painted the walls with deep purple and white wedding gowns hung off of each mannequin. Lace, crystals and satin met our eyes. The light inside was bright enough to reflect the glare of each glimmer of those wedding dresses, and my vision twinkled with delight at the sight.

This place was amazing.

We slowly strolled forward as wedding gowns clouded our thoughts and let go of each other's hands. I spun around with a smile on my face and thought I was in heaven. Dylan was right, this is the best there was and my fiancé always wanted everything perfect just for me.

Suddenly, a chipper tone broke me from my thoughts. "How can I help you?"

I gazed over at a young woman behind an enormous desk. She was the receptionist. She greeted us with a smile that appeared fake. A sleek black dress flowed around her knees and she had pulled her hair back in a neat ponytail.

"You can help us by showing us more of these magnificent dresses." Paisley beamed brightly and pointed towards me. "My friend is getting married."

The young woman peered over at me and squinted. "Do you have an appointment?"

I jabbed Paisley in the side, and she giggled. "What?"

I responded with a bright smile. "Yes, I have an appointment at one in the afternoon to try on some wedding gowns for my wedding day."

"And your name is?" The receptionist asked in a stuck-up tone that struck a nerve and she wandered behind her desk.

Her big black heels clicked along the tile and the black fabric swayed against her legs. She tapped her black manicured fingernail against the polished desktop and awaited my response. She appeared rather annoyed, and it struck a chord with me. Hopefully, everyone around here wasn't this rude.

I cleared my throat, smiled with attitude and flicked my hair with sass. "My name is Celeste Lovette and my fiancé is Mr. Stark himself."

The young receptionist smirked and raised an eyebrow at me. Her bright blue eyes flickered down my body and back up again. She continued to tap her fingernails against the desktop and it got on my nerves.

"Look, do I have an appointment or..." I rambled with annoyance.

She clicked her tongue and interrupted me. "Mr. Daxon Stark is getting hitched, is he? I never would've thought it was possible. Especially with someone like you."

"Wait, a minute..." I glared with shocked disbelief. "Now, what's wrong with..."

But then I stopped.

It surprised me, and Daxon's face popped into my mind. I couldn't ever see that vile man get down on one knee and propose to any woman, let alone me. Mr. Daxon Stark was selfish, business oriented and his ego ran the show.

"O-oh, no, not Daxon Stark. My fiancé is his son, Dylan Stark." I fumbled with my words and regretted not being more specific.

This was a big day for me, and I didn't want to think about Dylan's heartless father. He should be the last thing on my mind and far out of reach. I didn't need his cold distraction to ruin my day.

The rude receptionist broadly smiled and gazed down at her computer scene. "Now, that makes sense. I can't imagine him ever getting married with the lifestyle he leads."

She stopped the annoying fingernail tap and touched the screen. Her eyes lit up, and she looked back at us, but smacked her lips together. She came around the desk and her ponytail wagged behind her with an upbeat spunk.

She pointed her long black fingernail at us and smiled. "Right this way, ladies."

Paisley leaned in close and whispered. "She's a snobby bitch, isn't she?"

I rolled my eyes once the receptionist turned and replied. "You get used to it around here. With the rich and famous, money talks."

We followed her lead as our heels clicked along the expensive tiled floor and I was so excited I had Paisley by my side. She took a couple of days off from school to come down and visit me. I picked her up at the airport in the morning and Paisley was a guest at our penthouse for her stay. There was enough room with an endless amount of space and numerous guest rooms besides our master bedroom.

We rounded a corner and an older lady with greying hair came into view. She gazed our way as the click of our heels caught her attention. She had a taste for high fashion and was elegant, with flashy rings on every finger. I concluded she was the appointment I was waiting for. She was the best wedding designer on the entire globe.

Dylan wanted me to look perfect because our wedding day would be the biggest event of the year. It was the most gossiped about topic in the media and he wanted me to look the part. Dylan wanted his glamorous bride to be the center of attention. I'd make sure I was.

And Paisley was here to help me say yes to the perfect dress.

"Celeste Lovette is here to see you, Sandra. She's Mr. Dylan Stark's bride to be." The snobby receptionist said as she stepped aside and did her job.

"Ah, yes, I've been waiting for you to arrive." Sandra beamed towards us and nodded her head with approval. She clapped her hands together with a wave. "Come now, let's not keep the dresses waiting."

She led the way towards a private area and into a room with hundreds of wedding gowns hanging from racks. Some had a clear plastic covered overtop of them while others didn't and displayed their true beauty. But all I saw was white.

Skylights were overhead, with sunlight beaming through, and a dressing room was off to the far side. There was a small stage in the centre of it all and it attracted my attention. It held mirrors to catch every angle of a dress. The perfect dress would hug me tight and I knew this was where I'd find the perfect dress for me.

Sandra wandered to a spot at the rack with a long row of wedding gowns, picked out three, and handed them to me. "These are the best dresses for the style you envisioned for your wedding day and they are my absolute favorite. Please, go try them on and come out when you have your perfect dress."

"This is so exciting!" Paisley exclaimed as her voice echoed within the big room and she pushed me towards the fitting room. "Hurry up and go find your dream dress."

I beamed brightly and didn't wait a moment longer as I made my way towards the dressing room. It was purple inside, with a bright chandelier overhead and a tall mirror inside. The enormous mirror captured every inch of me, but my excited face reflected at me.

I unhooked one of the wedding dresses from the velvet hanger. It was a dress with white satin and a flowered lace design overtop. I quickly discarded my clothing in rushed excitement and tried it on. It flowed over me. It wasn't the one. I took it off and eyed the next one with a wide ball gown bottom. It had a princess appeal to it and it was the perfect fit, but again, it wasn't my wedding dress.

"Okay, save the best for last." I exhaled with impatience and hoped this was the one.

It easily came off of the black velvet hanger and the gown fell over the top of my head. The dress hugged me in all the right places and my eyes sparkled at the sight. The dress gleamed in the mirror and I looked up as I met my deep brown eyes. They glistened with tears and should be tears of joy. But they were drops of memories from long ago as they fell down my cheeks and I remembered my mother.

My mother had gotten married at a young age, and before she gave birth to me. She had loved her husband so much, but he hadn't felt the same. He had left her shortly after they got married, within a matter of only months. My real father not only left her, but abandoned me, and I had never known him.

I was always the child growing up with daddy issues. Every Father's Day was a complete embarrassment at school and other kids teased me for not having a dad around to call my own. Almost every holiday was a reminder of what I'd never have, and it was a hard pill to swallow. But my birthday was the worst, and I never liked to celebrate it.

It wasn't the balloons, birthday cake or the fact I grew older each year. I hated it because it was the day my real father walked out of my life and never came back. It was the day he left my mother, admitted he didn't love her and broke her heart.

My mom was never the same, but she raised me the best way she knew how. Until I graduated from high school and she had a mental breakdown. She ended up at the hospital on suicide watch and later a psychiatric institution. She never came back from the hurt and betrayal my father had left her with all those years ago. It ate her up deep inside until she had her collapse with reality.

I wiped the tears from my face at the memories and inhaled a deep breath. I blew it out and plastered a smile on my face. The remembrance was hurtful all over again, but I stuffed it down and moved forward.

Just like I always did.

I ran my hands over the white satin fabric as the crystals gleam with the chandelier light and I was so incredibly lucky to be here. The past was just that, and I had so much to look forward to in the future. A future with my handsome and wealthy fiancé.

Soon to be my husband.

I nodded at myself in the mirror and opened the door as I strolled out to the center of the stage. I was ready to show off the wedding gown I believed was the perfect one. My eyes met with Paisley's and they lit up at the sight of me.

Her eyes glistened with tears, and a hand covered her mouth. "Oh, my gosh, Celeste, you look radiant."

I took one step and then another as I climbed up the tiny stage, but there was some commotion behind me. Sandra held a long wedding veil in her hands and placed it neatly within my black, wavy hair. The veil matched the wedding dress with the same lace, crystals, and white shimmer.

I turned to look at myself in the mirror and couldn't believe my eyes. Beauty peered back at me and one I never thought I'd see. Myself in a wedding dress, but not just any dress. My very own wedding gown.

Tears pricked at my eyes, and I met Paisley's thrilled stare in the reflection. "This is it, Pais. This is the one. It's the wedding dress I'm going to wear when I walk down the aisle and marry Dylan Stark."

NINE
Business Meeting

The afternoon had moved along nicely after I purchased my wedding dress. I had to come back two months before the big day to have it fitted, and so did Paisley. We found the perfect maid of honor gown for her with matching crystals. Everything about it was glamorous. Sandra had suggested it because it was in style at the moment and would be stunning beside my wedding gown.

Paisley tried it on beside my wedding dress and no one's eyes were dry. We cried happy tears at the unforgettable moment and relived stories of the past. But her constant friendship always stuck by me and I was grateful I had her by my side.

I peered over at her sitting on the couch beside me with her feet tucked in underneath her and a Kleenex box in between us. She leaned her head against her hand with her elbow resting on the arm of the couch and she sobbed at a cheesy scene from the movie The Wedding Planner. Jennifer Lopez won my heart every time as she stole the groom's heart and never gave it back. Not that he wanted it back, anyway. He was hers and she was his, even if they didn't see it until the very end.

We decided this would be suitable for the occasion and we were in the mood for anything to do with weddings. I watched as they danced and kissed in the park under the tree with a late-night movie playing in the background. The scene was perfect for a romance and the kiss was full of passion.

"God, I wish I could find a man like that." Paisley sighed as she admired the happy couple and the movie ended.

"You won't if you keep falling into every guy's bed on the first date." I teased and threw a piece of popcorn at her.

Paisley made an offended face and threw the popcorn back at me. "Oh, is that right?"

She dodged for a handful of popcorn and a food fight broke out. We hysterically laughed as popcorn littered the couch and showered the living room. It reminded me of old times back at the dormitory where anything goes, and it was just the two of us. I was so thankful to have a loyal friend like Paisley by my side, no matter what happened in life.

Suddenly, the front door creaked open with the jiggle of keys and we stopped midway through, launching another piece of popcorn. Dylan stood by the door as it slowly closed behind him and he eyed us both. His brown hair was off to the side, like he ran his hands through it several times. He was frustrated, and I knew his day at work had been a tough one. Dear daddy had hooked into him and pulled at the line as much as he could.

"Hey, darling..." I muttered with embarrassment and pulled popcorn from my hair as it fell to the floor.

I strolled over to his side as my cheeks burned bright red and leaned in close. He smelled of cologne as my lips gently touched his cheek and left a slight peck there. As I pulled my head back to look at his handsome face, a frown laid in its place instead of an adoring smile. He reached out, and I waited for his sweet caress, but he grabbed a piece of kernel from my hair.

"Can you clean up this mess?" He glared with annoyance, ignored my affection, and looked over at Paisley. "Did you forget we have dinner plans with my father in one hour for an important business meeting?"

I blinked my eyes several times at his rudeness and pulled away from him. "I must've forgotten."

He walked away from me and over towards the countertop in the kitchen. His cold shoulder was nothing new after a long day of work by his father's side, but I never understood his harsh treatment of bitterness with me. I didn't choose for him to work for his dear daddy. If it was my choice, Dylan would do something else, and I'd never have to see his father again.

"I need you ladies to be looking your best because a client will be there." Dylan breathed as his voice echoed. He placed his briefcase on the countertop, turned away, and walked further into the penthouse. "Well, don't just stand there. You know my father doesn't like tardiness."

My face burned brighter with embarrassment from his behavior and I frowned towards my friend with an exhausted sigh. "Well, we better get ready for dinner because dear daddy awaits."

Paisley simply scrunched up her face and asked. "Is he always like that?"

I rolled my eyes and led the way to the bedroom. "Only for his father."

***

I smoothed my bright red dress, tousled my hair, and laid my hand on my fiancé's thigh. The smooth fabric glided on my hand as I caressed him and squeezed him with tease. I smiled up at him, but he pushed my hand away and Paisley watched from the other side of the limousine.

I knew Dylan was tense, and he always was for these functions. It happened when his father was involved and I couldn't blame him one bit, but he was being a prick. Plus, he embarrassed me in front of my friend and it got on my last nerve.

"Lighten up a little, darling." I mumbled and kept my voice low.

"It's hard when I'm walking right into the pit of a fiery dragon." Dylan growled under his breath.

Normally, on a limousine ride to a business meeting, I'd suck on Dylan's cock. It gave him the stress relief he needed to function with his intimidating father around, but Paisley was here. So, it threw him for a loop and would help explain his inappropriate behavior. But I still didn't deserve his crap attitude, and neither did my best friend.

He had some sucking up to do.

I huffed and sat back in my smooth leather seat with my arms crossed. The limousine bounced from a speed bump and I gazed out the window at the fancy restaurant. The bright white lights beamed back at me and created a shimmer on the window of the limousine.

The vehicle stopped out front, and the driver came around to open our door for the arrival. He wore a neatly kept black suit with a black top hat and it had a straight brim. Dylan exited the limousine first and didn't offer me his hand. The kind driver did, and I nodded to the sweet gesture as he offered Paisley his hand next. She took it and beamed up at him with a flirty tease.

If she could, she'd probably fuck him in the back of the limousine right about now and I giggled at the thought. She let go of his hand, ruffled her hair with her hands and smoothed out her dress. She flashed him one last flirtatious smile and batted her eyelashes with approval, but the driver got back into his ride.

"Oh, he's just playing hard to get." Paisley teased as she took my arm within hers and we followed behind an impatient Dylan. "But your fiancé is being quite the jerk."

"Shh, would you keep your voice down?" I whispered and made a face as I leaned in closer. "He always gets his balls in a bunch when dear daddy is on his mind."

"Well, he better make up for his rude behavior later." Paisley playfully winked at me, and I felt my cheeks blush.

I simply flashed a shy grin, but knew exactly what she meant. He should grant me mind blowing sex and an explosive orgasm. But little did she know, I usually ended up with my vibrator.

"Right, let's get this over with, ladies." Dylan breathed over his shoulder as his eyes set on his father and he led the way.

"Are you ready to meet the famous world class grouch and owner of D.S. Industries?" I muttered under my breath, but only Paisley heard me.

"Do I really have a choice?" Paisley asked in a sarcastic tone and shrugged in defeat.

I giggled, but the laughter caught in my throat as soon as Daxon Stark's deep stare glared at me. A heat rose from my tippy toes tucked inside my high heels and travelled to my cheeks. His eyes burned with mistrust, but as his gaze travelled down my body, something else mixed inside it. It was something I couldn't describe, but figured it was his downright hatred for me.

His eyes left me and wandered to my friend, who still had her arm wrapped around mine. His eyebrows narrowed and his eyes squinted as he glared at her with uncertainty. He smoothed his black business tie and clicked his tongue against the roof of his mouth.

Oh, shit...

"I didn't realize we were expecting guests?" He glared with distaste and got out of his seat.

"It was a pleasant surprise when I got home." Dylan replied as he took his seat and didn't offer me mine.

Bullshit...

Dylan's been nothing but an asshole since he got home and my blood was about to boil over. Paisley must've felt the tension and squeezed my arm, but let me go with a reassured smile. I returned it and walked to my seat beside Dylan, but to my surprise, Daxon held the chair out for me. I gazed at him, stunned by his gesture, and he nodded towards my seat as his brown eyes toyed with mine.

Oh, I get it.

He simply played the part of a devoted daddy-in-law for the matter of his business. His pride and passion. Well, two could play his wicked game.

"How kind of you..." I breathed with sass, plastered on a fake ass smile and lowered my voice even more. "Daddy Daxon is at it again."

I sat down in my chair beside Dylan while his father leaned in close and he pushed in my seat. He glided me into the table with minimal effort as I imagined his biceps with them flexed under his expensive suit and his aftershave surrounded me. The masculine scent drew me in and made my womanhood clench with need. But it was his warm breath on my neck that made me shiver with temptation.

"You better not ruin this for me, young lady." He growled in a whisper only I could hear.

And I whispered in return with sass. "I wouldn't dream of it, daddy."

He let out one last growl from deep in his throat and pushed off of my chair. My breasts bounced a bit from the force and I held in a gasp. I didn't want to create a scene. I gazed around the table and the client's kind eyes locked with mine.

"Is there a problem, Mr. Stark?" She asked with uncertainty and her confusion squinted back at us.

Daxon cleared his throat behind me, made his way back to his seat, and pressed his tie against his chest. "No, just another situation I never see coming when my son's beautiful fiancée is around."

The client narrowed her eyebrows together and frowned at me. She looked from Paisley towards me and it lost me for words. The shock was still in my system from his nearness, and his mistrust for me always threw me off. I looked at Paisley with a nervous grin and she knew all too well the tension fumed from me.

Paisley blurted out with a bright smile on her face. "This is just an eventful meeting that's been bound to happen."

The client broke out in a smile and laughed at her comment. The awkwardness in the air subsided as I laughed right along with her and others joined in. It was a forced situation for me, but Paisley's fast thinking saved the day. I mouthed her a quick thank you when no one looked my way and she secretly winked in my direction.

Crisis averted.

I exhaled all the tension I once felt, but it built back up as soon as Daxon's eyes met mine. They pierced into me with a forewarning. Don't fuck this up or I was going to pay the price.

From across the table, I raised one eyebrow at him and pressed my lips together with anger. I gave him the cold shoulder and ignored his overbearing rudeness. I focused on anything but him and when I glanced at him, I could tell it worked like a charm. He ridged his jaw with tension and his hand moved through his silver fox hair with unease. The bright strands caught my eye in the light and the smoothness of them made me want to run my hand through it.

I shook my head at the thought and enjoyed the accomplishment. The satisfaction of getting on dear daddy's last nerve and I loved every minute. He definitely deserved it.

I basked in the success and created a conversation with the client. Her name was Beverly, and she was an older woman with a very kind aspect to her. She was quite delightful and nothing like Daxon when it came to business, but I noticed a fabulous diamond wedding ring dangled from her finger. She spun it around her ring finger and it would glimmer with the light.

"So, how long have you been married, Beverly?" I asked as I rested my chin on my palm and warmly smiled her way. "It's absolutely breathtaking."

Beverly smiled with the glow of love. "It's been twenty long years, but the best of my life."

"Marriage is a special gift and it should be taken seriously. It's a bond you have for the rest of your life and when it's broken, it's like a piece of you is gone." I breathed with passion as the words escaped my mouth because of the twinkle of happiness in her wise eyes, and it made me hopeful.

Beverly tilted her head to the side, lost in her own thoughts, and breathed. "Yes, and not everyone these days can understand that. You're quite the gem, Celeste. My husband and I have had our fair share of rough times, but we've stuck through it because we wanted to be together."

I sighed with awe. "And that's the greatest gift. A love that can't break."

My gaze broke from Beverly's as she laughed in delight at my words and they fell upon the deep, dark pair seated beside her. I became trapped in Daxon's stare when it should be my fiancé's. They swirled with so much emotion I couldn't read him, but I couldn't break away. Lost in him and his upheaval of chaotic disruption that always threw me sideways. A heat that burned between us as the air sparked with static and a flame burned to life.

But she disrupted the moment when the client raised her glass.

"Let us raise a toast." She gazed from me toward Daxon with a wise smirk on her face and raised her champagne glass high in the air. "To unbroken love stories."

But my eyes got lost in Daxon once more and my lips parted with a response. "To unbroken love stories."

As I clicked my glass against Beverly's, my lips formed a smile and a shudder ran through me. I broke eye contact with Daxon and felt his son's hand caress my thigh. I looked at him as he smiled with admiration at me, but all I could see was his father's face.

TEN
Fantasy

The limousine ride back to our penthouse was an awkward one. Paisley wasn't her normal spunky self because of the tension between me and Dylan. I was still fired up from my fiancé's behavior this evening and he had some explaining to do. Dylan remained quiet in his seat and consumed by his phone. He would wait for a phone call from dear old dad on the business deal. His mind was set on that.

I cleared my throat and shifted in my seat. The air was so tense and tight that my throat closed in. I swallowed hard and rubbed my hands together in my lap. The sweet melody filled the limousine and was the only thing that held me together. It saved me from opening the door and leaping out into oncoming traffic.

But Daxon's face at dinner unnerved me.

His eyes haunted me, taunted me with thoughts I never thought I'd want. His much too gorgeous lips curled up into a daring smirk and made me want to smack it back into nonexistence. The way his body spoke to me was of sheer disregard, but there was something else I never thought I'd see.

Thankfulness.

Mr. Daxon Stark, my dear father-in-law, was thankful for my presence and it made me even tenser than this awkward limousine ride home. Daxon had this way of crawling under my skin and consuming every fibre of my being. He did it to toss me away, but it only pushed me to stay. I wasn't one to back down and let a rich prick like Daxon Stark ruin my life.

Dylan's phone chimed with a text message and the light from the touch screen shone against his face. A light smile played across his lips and I pondered if daddy was on the other line. He let out a soft chuckle, and I knew it wasn't the case. Dylan and his father didn't share a light-hearted relationship filled with laughter. It was more on the serious side and always about business. Everything came down to it with Daxon Stark and there was no way around it.

"Who is that, darling?" I asked sweetly, as I straightened my back and raised my eyebrows with interest.

Even though I didn't give a shit and was still smoking like a thick smog.

"Oh, just a co-worker and I exchanging a word about the business deal."

Bullshit.

I knew better than that. Dylan never smiled or joked about his career. He was just like his father and dear daddy had groomed Dylan just the way he wanted him to be. Ruthless, calculated and cutthroat.

Dylan had always been secretive, and I knew it from the beginning. He painted me a picture of what my life could be like and he made it come true. Except the parts of him left locked with hidden secrets and wouldn't let me have the key. It left me stumbling around in the darkness and trying to find the light. A light that I knew shone so brightly with a truth he kept buried from me and didn't want anyone to see.

I was around all the time with this lavish life I lead and I paid attention. There was more going on and I knew it. I had no idea what, and I knew some answers were on his phone. But I was not that kind of person.

Everyone had a right to their privacy. Even my fiancé. I just hoped I didn't have to pay the price for whatever secret he kept hidden.

The streetlights played along his face with the colors of red, green, yellow and blue. His brown hair shone as each color touched it and shimmered across his smooth skin. His gorgeous eyes remained locked on the phone as his fingers tapped in a message and I wanted the words to reflect on his face. But he didn't look at me and the limousine came to a halt.

I was happy he didn't because I'd have questions to answer. He'd see my curiosity, and I'd give myself away. The tension within this ride had been too much for me, and I needed some fresh air. I needed to clear my head.

I grabbed my purse and was the first one out the door as soon as it swung open. I didn't waste time and Paisley followed behind me. Someone immersed Dylan in his text message and was the last one to leave. I couldn't care less at this point and just wanted this evening to be over.

"Are you okay?" Paisley asked as she touched my shoulder, but I couldn't look at her.

"I'll be better in the morning after a good night's rest and this dreaded evening put behind me." I admitted as my heels clicked along the tiles and my penthouse door came into view.

"It wasn't all that bad. The food was delicious and Beverly was sincere." Paisley said as she tried to ease the tension and kept it positive. "And your future father-in-law wasn't so bad. He was more like a big grizzly bear trying to protect his business, which includes you."

I giggled softly. "Um, ya right. The only thing he cares about is his company and he's made it very clear he wants me to be as far away from it as possible. Mr. Daxon Stark trying to protect me? I'll believe it when I see it."

I unlocked the door as my keys jiggled together and pushed it open. My purse dropped onto the nearest chair and I discarded my heels in a hurry. I just wanted to get this night over with and crawl into bed.

"Well, there was definitely something there between you and Dylan's father. Some sort of lingering tension, but I don't think Dylan noticed it." Paisley said as she waved her hand and took off her shoes. "So, maybe it's just me?"

Paisley's words struck a chord with me, and I remembered his closeness. The smell of him as it lingered in my nose and made my toes curl. His body heat mingled with my own and set a new temperature within the restaurant. His touch as it burned over my skin and set my being on fire. But I cleared my unnerved thoughts as I shook my head and pushed them aside.

"It has to be. There's no way that man will ever like me and I've grown to hate him. So, the feeling's mutual." I smiled sarcastically and shrugged my shoulders.

"I wouldn't be so sure about that." Paisley sighed as she stepped towards her bedroom and flashed me a playful smile. "Hate can always bloom into love."

"I think you had too much to drink." I laughed as I rolled my eyes and tried to ignore her comment. "But I guess

I'll see you in the morning. If you need anything at all, just knock and I'll come running."

"Okay, sounds good and love you bunches." Paisley said as she puckered her lips together and blew me a quick goodnight kiss.

My eyes landed on her closed door as the room filled with quietness and it felt empty. I looked towards the front door, but my fiancé was nowhere in sight. My gaze landed on the clock and I wanted to go to bed, but he kept me awake. He should've been right behind us and I pondered what kept him.

Minutes ticked by and finally the door opened, with Dylan walking through it. He held his beloved cellphone to his ear and smiled from ear to ear. The door fell shut behind him and he clapped his hands together in one swift movement. The loud sound made me jump. His brown hair fell into his face and he brushed it back as he laughed happily, but I knew exactly what was happening.

Daddy was on the other line to celebrate another success.

One more business deal down and a billion more to go.

His eyes locked with mine as he hung up the call and stuffed the cellphone in his pocket. "We did it, baby. We closed the deal."

He loudly clapped his hands together repeatedly and fist pumped the air. I usually love success, but this one wasn't memorable. It had been tense from the very beginning and it was all thanks to my fiancé.

"Congratulations on pleasing your father once again, darling." I snapped, unimpressed, and strutted towards our bedroom.

I didn't bother looking back at him for his reaction, because I could feel his eyes burn into my backside. The bedroom door slammed behind me, but I couldn't give a damn. All I wanted was to sleep away this nightmare and forget it had ever happened.

I unzipped the back of my dress, and the expensive garment fell from my shoulders as it tumbled to a heap on the floor. My feet stepped out of it and walked away from this mess of a day. I sighed and reached down for the elastic pantyhose that hugged my thigh. I pulled it down just as I heard the door click shut and I knew Dylan had greeted me with his presence.

I could feel his eyes roam over me within the darkness, and tingles lingered along my body. Heat fumed in my toes and burned all the way up my back, but I continued to get undressed in front of him. My pantyhose fell to the floor along with my dress and I reached around to unhook my bra, but his hands met my fingers.

"You were amazing with Beverly tonight." He whispered into my ear as his warm breath lingered there and my breath hitched. "We should thank you for this deal."

Suddenly, his words brought meaning and as his lips touched my shoulders, another set of lips caressed my skin. I imagined them trailing up my arm and a moist tongue lingering along with my goosebumps. Kisses plastered along my heated flesh and those lips teased my other shoulder.

Dylan unhooked my bra, and I became lost in them as it fell to the floor. Hands wrapped around my waist as they held me close and I felt their need for me. Dylan's hard cock pressed into my ass and my legs quivered with want. My entire body shivered with desire for them as Dylan brushed my hair back and tugged it until my head fell backwards. Lips that were not his found my exposed neck and grazed their teeth against the tender flesh. His hot breath ran up my neck, and I let out a gasp as he nibbled there.

He teased, taunted, and tortured me with lust. Dylan caressed, played, and tempted me with desire. And I became their combusting flame that flickers wildly within the darkness.

Those lips ran up my cheek and his tongue licked me there. He left a lasting impression before I caught his face in the darkness. My eyes adjusted to it and his face looked just like Dylan's, but a wiser version. Deep brown eyes burned into mine with need as he stared into them and captivated me. His fingers drew a line up my skin until he cupped my chin and pulled me in. But he captured my lips in a greedy kiss and everything in me melted for him.

His tongue parted my lips, and he dove inside. The wetness of him swirled with my own and we danced a dangerous dance. He nipped my lower lip and slightly pulled back as his lips left mine, but his teeth still held my lip. He let it go as his hand caressed my cheek and I opened my eyes.

It was Dylan kissing me and not the wiser man. He was gone, and only Dylan was with me. He was the only one who consumed me and taunted me. Dylan had been the only one with me while my fantasy ran wild and I envisioned two. Two men thanking me for all I did for D.S. Industries. Two men who happened to be father and son.

Oh, my god...

What the hell is wrong with me?

The back of my legs hit the bed and stopped me from falling. I blinked several times as my mind reeled at the thought of a threesome with my fiancé and my soon-to-be father-in-law. I hated Daxon and everything he stood for, but I lost myself in some sexual fantasy that involved him. Dylan's words must've gotten to me and I just became lost in some silly fantasy.

But oh my god was it ever good.

"Are you playing hard to get?" Dylan breathed as his hands met my hips and he pulled me closer. "Because I can play along."

"No, but Paisley is right in the next room and..." I lied as I didn't need my soon to be husband knowing I just had a sexual daydream about a threesome with his father.

He feathered kisses along my collarbone and chuckled softly. "Since when has that ever stopped you?"

He was right.

My hands laid on his chest and nuzzled back. "It hasn't, but your embarrassing behavior was uncalled for this evening."

His hands cupped my breasts, and the pads of his thumbs caressed my nipples. They formed into aching erect buds under his tantalizing touch and he circled until he pinched them. Tingles ran down to my cunt and I wanted to give in, but I was reluctant.

"Come on, Celeste..." He pleaded with me. "You know how tense I get with client meetings and having an unannounced visitor just threw me off."

I pushed him back with anger. "And that unannounced visitor is my best friend. She's going to be a big part of our wedding."

I glared at him, but he still came closer and caressed my wavy locks that fell into my face in the heated moment. He played with their curls and pushed them back behind my ear with ease. He ran his hands up and down my arms with a caring motion that soon calmed me.

"I'm sorry I was such a dick, but let me make it up to you." He promised as he spun me around and gripped my hands behind my back with his rich, husky tone in my ear. "Make up sex is always the best."

I didn't fight it because sex with Dylan doesn't happen often. It usually came down to me, pleasing him and ending up with my beloved vibrator. Any pleasure for myself I'd gladly take, and this was my shot.

His hard dick rubbed against my ass cheeks and I returned the favor. His cock fell between my plump ass cheeks and I clenched them together. I created a hold that he loved as I ran my cheeks up and down his throbbing cock. My pussy became wet against my thong and I ached for him to move it. I wanted him to enter me and slam into me until there was no return.

It turned me on to no end as he pulled back and pushed me forward until my chest hit the sheets. The softness of them against my face, but his harsh hand slapped against my ass.

"Oh!" I cried out as he did it again and my pussy dripped for him.

He wasted no time and pulled aside the string from my thong. The tip of his mushroom head dick rubbed against my pussy lips as he lubricated it and got ready. I moaned from below as he teased me and I loved it, but I remained still. I left him in full control because I needed him so badly and wanted him to consume me.

"You'll take it like a good girl." He breathed from above me and I was at his complete mercy.

Suddenly, his dick entered my cunt and pulled all the way out. I clenched the bed sheets in my grasp and got ready for more. He slammed back into me again, but this time, he didn't stop. He pumped at a fast pace, and I cried out for more. As it bounced to his beat, he grabbed onto my ass cheeks. The sensation rose and my climax grew as he dove into me.

My girlfriend in the next room didn't matter anymore, and it never did. I was wild and untamed, but he knew it. It didn't matter who was around and mind-blowing sex was all I needed. I didn't give a shit who heard my cry of pure pleasure. Not even if it was dear daddy.

Daxon entered my mind as he slammed into me and I couldn't help the thoughts that came next. His dark eyes dived into my soul and his gorgeous lips curved into a wicked smile all for me. Salt and pepper hair that was so smooth I could run my fingers through it. His edgy attitude sparked a flame inside me and never burned out. Not to mention his extremely fit body with muscles for days.

"Oh, god, yes!" I cried out as my release came closer and my fingernails dug into Dylan's arms.

But Daxon remained with me as Dylan pumped into my pussy and I pushed my ass against him. I gave him my pace and he let me ride with it. The sound of my ass slapped into his thighs as he drove into me and got one step closer.

"Yes, just like that..." Dylan groaned from behind me and he picked up pace. "Oh, fuck!"

Suddenly, I felt his body go rigid with his seed filling me and he was spent. He gasped for air from behind me and released my hands from his grasp as my body fell onto the bed. I shivered with the need to release, but it never came. Dylan once again went before me and left me with nothing.

"See, baby, I told you..." Dylan breathed against my ear and kissed the back of my head. "Make up sex is the best."

And he headed for the master bathroom, turned on the shower and left me to my release with his seed dripping down my leg.

ELEVEN
Compromised

"This will be perfect." I whispered to myself as I admired the thin piece of red fabric and held it up against my body with excitement.

The see-through lace design was perfect, and the red color would match my lipstick. Dylan loved my red ruby lips, and I wanted to seduce him. This sexy lingerie would do the trick.

I brought the garment up to the cashier and laid it on the checkout counter. The cashier looked at it and smirked as she chewed her gum in a vigorous motion. The annoying sound burned my ears and made my eyes twitch with each smack of her lips. They darted towards her shimmering lip gloss and I couldn't look away as she rang through my purchase. She placed the sexy garment into a fancy box and sealed it up.

"That'll be $208." She muttered as her teeth chewed the gum and she held out her hand to take the cash I owed.

I gave her the exact amount because I wanted to get as far away from that sound as possible. It was a nightmare for my ears to endure. I thought they might start bleeding at any moment from the unbearable sound and it would surprise me if she had a job in the morning.

I grabbed the box and walked out into the mall. My heels clicked along the tiled floor and I caught sight of a little card store. This was one final touch I needed to add to Dylan's seductive surprise, and I scribbled a message for him. Then I made my way towards D.S. industries.

The surprise wouldn't be complete without a stop at his office to leave the gift in plain sight just for him. Since our make-up sex last night didn't quite go in my favor, I'd take matters into my own hands. I'd gift him with a sexy surprise and a message to help spice up our evening. The chances of me climaxing were higher with me in control.

I smirked as Dylan's workplace came into sight and I had an excited spunk in each step. I was on a mission to seduce my husband to be, and no one was going to stop me. Not even dear old daddy.

"Good afternoon, Gracie." I beamed in a cheery, upbeat fashion and held up the box. "I've got a gift to drop off for Dylan. Is he in the office?"

She flashed a bright smile and pulled at her tight black dress. "No, he's at a meeting right now and doesn't want to be disturbed."

Sounded just like him.

"That's perfect. This will be a surprise when he gets back." I smirked with my devious plan in mind and headed for the elevator. "Oh, one last thing, Gracie?"

"And what would that be, Ms. Lovette?" Gracie asked as she blinked her eyes and tilted her head to the side. It showed I had her undivided attention. A quality that I was sure Daxon taught her or else she'd be out on her ass.

"Is Dylan's father in the office?" I asked with uncertainty and held my breath.

The last thing I needed was to run into Daxon. I didn't need a scolding stare burning into my backside or his sarcastic behavior getting on my last nerve. And I certainly didn't need Mr. Daxon Stark finding out about my plans to seduce his son for the evening. None of that was on my schedule for today.

"No, Mr. Stark is out for lunch." She smiled gracefully and shook her head with her ponytail waving from side to side.

"Great, that's just perfect. Thank you, Gracie." I exhaled the breath I'd been holding and pressed the button for the elevator.

Within a minute, it chimed, and I climbed on board. It carried me up towards the fiftieth floor as my nerves got the best of me and I wasn't sure why. Sure, I was on a top-secret mission of seduction, but there wasn't anything to be worried about. Dylan was in a meeting and daddy was out for lunch.

What could go wrong?

I shook myself just as the elevator doors opened and walked onto the fiftieth floor. I held the box against my chest and carried on forward. But stopped dead in my tracks.

Oh, no...

I peered through the double doors, and everything didn't look right. The carpet was new; the desks were bigger than I remembered and the room smelled of fresh paint. I went in further towards the other office and it, too, didn't look the same. Everything has changed.

Each office was unrecognizable, and I had no idea which one was Dylan's or Daxon's. The makeover was so fresh that the paint was probably still wet. There were no nameplates and no pictures. Absolutely no way to figure out which office was Dylan's. But after closer examination, I found a note with Dylan's name on it attached to a desk. This had to be his office.

The plan must go on because this girl wanted an orgasm.

I raised an eyebrow, closed the door, and pressed my lips together with determination. I tiptoed over towards his office chair, swiveled it out, and placed the box on top of the smooth leather. Sneaking around put me on high alert and I wanted to get out of there as fast as possible. Everything was going according to plan, and I didn't need to get caught in the act.

I tucked the chair back into place and hurried towards the door, but halted on the spot. There was commotion on the other side of the door and my eyes went wide. I could hear a female giggle and a low, husky voice, but I couldn't be sure who it was. It didn't matter because their footsteps were headed this way.

'Oh, shit!' I mouthed out loud and backed away from the door with moments to spare.

My eyes landed on the office closet and it was the closest thing for me to hide in. I hurried over towards it with fear of being caught and got inside. But I had to leave the door slightly ajar just before the unwanted company stumbled into the room and my mind went crazy.

It was Daxon!

And he was in a heated embrace.

They kissed wildly as his lips fumbled to caress more of her skin and he pressed her up against the closed office door. Her moans filled the room as his hands ran up her thick thighs and he cupped her butt cheeks within his grasp. He didn't hold back as he devoured her and her hands ran wildly through his untamed hair. The salt and pepper strands glistened with the light as he flicked the switch and pulled back.

"I want to see every inch of your pretty youthful body." Daxon growled as he got back to work and didn't waste time.

And was she ever young.

She was probably my age, and that fact made my pussy throb. Or maybe it throbbed from the way he touched her, kissed her and consumed her. Either way, I couldn't look away from the sexual frenzy that ensued. The small crack through the door gave me a front-row seat. The bachelor billionaire Daxon Stark about to fuck the daylights out of a woman no older than me.

My breath hitched as he pulled her off of the door, but his lips never left her body and he brought her over towards his desk. His back was towards me as he ripped open her blouse and devoured her perky mounds. He claimed them as his mouth took each round nipple and his tongue teased. She threw her head back in pleasure with her hands clenching the sides of his desk and I bit my lower lip.

The sight of him in his greedy glory did something to me deep inside, and my panties felt wet. The sweet juices had a mind of their own, and so did my aroused body. In this naughty moment, I didn't look at Daxon Stark like my future father-in-law. I viewed him as eye fuck candy and I wanted his hands all over me.

"Oh, fuck, Daxon!" She cried out as he moved his hard cock against her pussy and his mouth travelled down.

She willingly spread her legs as he kissed over her navel and continued lower. He pulled down her skirt as it fell to her heels and her thin thong pulled aside. His head moved as he licked her clit, and she moaned for more. My cunt pulsated at her pleasure, and I gripped my thighs together. I tried not to pleasure myself at the sight of them, but he had me fired up. I couldn't deny Mr. Daxon Stark really knew how to please a woman.

"Oh, god, yes!" She cried out as she gazed down at him and he ravished her juicy pussy.

Her knuckles were white and his breath labored as she clung close to the brink. She moved her hips as he ate her up and didn't miss a bite. But all too soon, he stopped and snapped the elastic back into place.

She unbuttoned his black dress shirt with a devious smile and ran her hands over his extremely fit chest. His shirt remained open, and he undid his belt for her. But he grabbed her waist and spun her around in one swift movement while she cried out.

He bent her over, and a sensual purr escaped her pretty lips. His hands found her wrists, pressed them together behind her back, and he buckled his belt tight around her wrists. He bound her in place as his pants fell to his ankles with his briefs followed close behind and my eyes burned into his firm behind.

Daxon's ass was pure perfection. An extremely fit buttock any woman would love to get her hands on. And right now, that woman was me.

"I'm going to fuck you and give you a nice present straight from D.S. Industries." Daxon groaned as he fisted his cock and smacked her plump ass cheek.

She squealed with pleasure and looked back at him. Just as she did, he slammed his cock into her and her body jolted. He held the belt upwards as he barreled into her from behind and the force made her back arch. Her tits bounced freely with each rough pound as she begged him for more, and he gave her what she wanted. His ass clenched with each thrust and the tight muscles worked. I couldn't turn away as I watched with lustful wonder and wished it was me.

The fast pace kept up until she cried out her climax. He groaned a release and spilled his seed all over her backside. He jerked his hand against his thick dick until he was spent and squeezed her plump ass one last time. Daxon stepped back and bent over, so I got a good glimpse of his balls and my hand covered my mouth. Pleasantly surprised to see Mr. Daxon Stark's well equipped.

Daxon clothed himself and rounded his desk to grab some tissues. He placed them in his lover's hand, who was still bent over half naked on his desk, and undid his belt from her wrists. Her one ass cheek was bright red from the pleasured pain he inflicted, but she didn't seem to care. She cleaned off her back and stood up with a look of satisfaction. Fixed her clothing and went in for a passionate kiss. But Mr. Stark turned his head to the side so she could simply kiss his cheek and she did as instructed.

As always, Mr. Daxon Stark would have his way and she appeared to be his latest quick fuck conquest. She had willingly fallen for it. It didn't appear to bother her one bit as her heels clicked against the floor. Not one word was spoken, and she left his office.

I watched as Daxon tightened his belt and went around to the head of his desk. He showed no shame in what he had just done, and he was a powerful man in all his glory. But my cheeks burned with heat at the thought of it all, and I willingly peered on from the shadows.

If Daxon Stark ever found out I gawked at him fucking his latest lover, I'd never hear the end of it. I'd never live it down, and he'd be sure to let me have it. I wouldn't be surprised if he...

Oh, no!

My seductive gift!

Daxon went to take a seat, but the box caught his eye. "What the hell is this?"

I sat within the shadowed office closet with mortified panic and I covered my mouth to conceal my shriek of shame. I couldn't be caught doing the unthinkable. He couldn't find out what was inside that box!

He picked up the gift not meant for him and read the card stuck on top. "A special gift for my fiancé to unwrap later."

His eyes narrowed with curiosity as he looked at the door and back at his chair. He ran his hand over his salt and pepper stubble with uncertainty, but reached for the box. His hand lifted the lid slightly, and I knew I had to do something.

"Don't you dare open that!" I cried out in panic as I revealed myself from my hidden space and pointed at him with anger.

He didn't have the right to open it, because I didn't mean for it to be his. I was to give myself up to be tortured now or wait for it to happen later. I'd rather take the chance and get my seductive gift back.

Daxon stood there in disbelief for a moment as he held my box, but his eyes soon narrowed and a wicked, sexy grin curled across his face. He bit his lower lip and nodded his head as everything registered, and he realized the extent of it. His expensive black shoes slowly walked towards me and the box lid remained closed. He still didn't know what was inside, and I wanted to keep it that way. I'd do anything to keep it from him.

Daxon stopped in front of me and held the box out towards me. "Well, well, well... What do we have here, princess?"

He looked down at the box, and I went to snatch it out of his grasp. He was too fast and grabbed my wrist. I went to take it with my free hand, but he dropped the box on the floor and grabbed my other wrist. He wrapped them together within his powerful grasp, and I gasped in surprise. He didn't stop there and removed his belt. I watched wide eyed as he tightened his belt around my wrists and my stomach fluttered with a hungry need.

I was one hundred percent turned on.

"Did you like what you saw?" His husky voice asked as he pulled his belt tighter with his teeth and his greedy stare never left mine. "You shouldn't be snooping around my office like a naughty little girl."

Once he had me tied up, he gripped the belt in place and I couldn't escape. He bent down and followed his command. Daddy was in complete control, and he knew it. I had nowhere to go and no place to hide.

He had me on my knees in no time, but I had to watch on in horror as he reached for the box once more. I shook my head and tried to move my hands, but he was much too powerful. Daxon removed the lid from the box and revealed my hidden, seductive secret.

My red lace lingerie.

He held it up and admired the sexy garment. It would hug every curve, but barely covered up my body. It had no bottom and was meant to be screwed in. And the way his deep brown gaze darkened; I knew he envisioned me in it. It sent a wave of electric energy coursing through my being and my breath hitched.

"Is this for me?" He teased with torment, and I held his sarcastic gaze.

"In your dreams, daddy." I snapped back, just to get a reaction out of him.

But it worked.

Daxon licked his lips with annoyance and bit his bottom lip. "You're a very naughty girl, Celeste and daddy should teach you a lesson."

I shivered when my name rolled off his tongue. Or maybe it was from his promised punishment. But either way, I was here for it.

The red lace lingerie fell back into the box and he pushed it aside. The motion made me gasp as my wispy hair sucked in and out of my mouth. My breath picked up pace as he pulled me closer towards him and into his energized bubble. His charismatic face was only inches from my own, and he closed his eyes as his nose inhaled the scent of me. He smelled my wild scent along my cheek and up into my hair.

My flesh heated with his nearness and my eyelids closed. I was lost in his world as his warm breath touched my cheek and caressed my dry lips. I licked them and felt his breath touch the wet flesh. His desirable breaths mingled with my own as I heard them.

He was going to kiss me and I shouldn't let him, but I couldn't help myself. His tortured punishment was almost too much for me to handle and I shook on my knees. Daddy was teaching me a lesson, and he enjoyed it way too much.

"I'm a monster..." He whispered in agony as his fingertip grazed my bottom lip. "But what does that make you, princess?"

"Your darkness." I whispered as my voice sounded unrecognizable and my eyes snapped open.

Daxon stared at my willing mouth, but his eyes locked with mine. His lips formed into that cruel grin once again, and I realized he was toying with me. But I gave in.

I fell for his trap and into his wicked game. He took me for a ride to see if I'd be the first to break and he'd have me out on my ass. Far away from his business and his son.

Well, he didn't win this time.

"Fuck you, daddy." I said with anger.

He raised an eyebrow at my sassy comment and pulled his head backwards. He bit his lower lip with frustration, but it curled into a sexy grin. "It would be my pleasure, princess."

He undid the belt and my hands fell free. I wasted no time and grabbed the box from the floor. I rose off of the floor, but he grabbed the box once again and I halted.

"Let me go, Daxon." I warned him.

He peered down at the bright red contents spilling out from the sides and locked eyes with me. "Promise me one thing? Cry out for daddy when you wear that for him later."

I clenched my teeth together with frustration and only flashed him a glared warning. My wavy hair flew through the air as I spun around with fury. I stomped my heels out of his office. I was a little girl lost in her temper tantrum. Daddy's cruel punishment got under my skin, and his laughter followed me into the elevator until the doors shut.

TWELVE
Risky Yacht Business

Several days had passed since my encounter with daddy dearest and he ruffled my feathers. My surprise for Dylan hadn't gone to plan and Daxon had ruined it. After him screwing his latest conquest and him catching me in the shadows, I threw the entire gift right in the trash. It no longer held memories for Dylan and me to create. His father had tarnished it with the memory of him and that perfectly delicious ass.

My skin grew hot at the very thought of it as the ocean breeze blew against it and tried to cool me down. Wispy black hair tickled my cheeks, and I was glad I put my dysfunctional hair in a messy bun. My hands rested in my lap against a pale blue sundress and I adjusted my sunglasses on my nose.

We crowded the small boat with Paisley, Dylan, Daxon, the driver, and me. We headed for an important dinner to close another business deal. But this one required a spontaneous vacation that D.S. Industries paid for and some time away from the busy city.

I looked around at Paisley admiring the view, Dylan seated beside me, and my gaze fell on Daxon. I couldn't look away. He locked his deep brown gaze on me, and everything about it made me tremble inside. I saw his tease, taunt, and torment he held all for me. Then there was the hate he had for me. A fiery dysfunctional passion burned deep inside those wicked eyes.

He still pissed me off with his behavior in his office and the passionate torture he put me through. I had expected him to go straight to Dylan with my mistrustful actions, but he didn't. I could've sworn Daxon would do anything to get rid of me. To get me as far away from the family business and out of his son's life. He had caught me watching him have sex and it should do the trick.

So, why hasn't he talked?

I was certain he had a grand scheme up his sleeve and he'd wait for the right time to strike. The perfect opportunity to take me out of the equation and have his way. I smirked at him and gave him a gentle wink to let him know I was thinking about him. Just to get on his patience and it worked. He gave me that familiar lip lick, followed by a bite of his bottom lip.

I didn't give him the time of day as Dylan grabbed my attention and squeezed my thigh. "This is an important deal. The Brava family runs a tight business and you need to be on your best behavior."

His stiff warning unsettled me and I simply nodded so he couldn't hear the worry in my voice. Dylan remained unreadable, but I knew a business deal always put him on edge. And this one was a big one. Enough to travel hours away from home to seal the deal.

I looked over at Paisley, who rolled her pretty blue eyes when Dylan wasn't looking, and I softly giggled. She knew how to lighten the mood and I was grateful she would endure the torture. At least for a couple of hours.

Suddenly, I heard Daxon clear his throat as my gaze darted in his direction and he glared at Paisley. He had caught our inside escapade. His stern warning blazed my way with the look of irritation on his face and he bit his lower lip with annoyance. It was a common trend he had with me, but I simply ignored the rude measure.

My attention landed on far more important matters, and that was the enormous yacht beside us. The bright blue paint hit the sunlight and the rest of the yacht was a pearl white. It shimmered with the sunshine and stood out on the clear, open ocean. Our tiny boat bounced as it pulled up beside it and settled on top of the water. I stood up and pressed my hands against my dress as it flowed down to my knees. Dylan took my hand and helped guide me onto the yacht's deck, but into the hands of an older gentleman.

He took my hand, greeted me with a welcome kiss on my knuckles, and I blinked with surprise. "Welcome aboard. It's a pleasure to meet a wondrous beauty."

I blushed, took my hand back and fumbled with my hands. "Thank you, it's very nice to be here, Mr...."

"Mr. Michael Brava, the man we came to do business with this afternoon." Daxon said as he introduced the gentleman we came to see and firmly shook his hand. "This is Celeste Lovette, my future daughter-in-law."

Mr. Brava was much older than Daxon, with a bald spot shimmering with the sunshine and he eyed me up from head to toe. He held a wooden cane with expensive carvings engraved on it and didn't lean his body weight against it. He appeared to be steady on his feet, and I wasn't sure if he actually needed it. It was a look to complete his fashion statement or the support he required.

A younger gentleman joined us and cleared his throat. “I’m Nicholas Brava, Michael's son and dinner is ready if you’d like to join us?”

“Don’t mind if we do.” Paisley announced as she stepped forward and held out her hand. “I’m Paisley, Celeste’s best friend.”

Nicholas’s eyes locked on Paisley’s extended hand and I expected him to shake it, but he bowed to kiss it. His lips tenderly grazed over each knuckle, and his eyes pierced into hers. Paisley never wavered from his majestic spell, and she beamed with delight.

“Right this way, Paisley.” Nicholas urged as he stood up straight and held onto her hand.

My eyes widened as I followed their lead and Mr. Brava fell into conversation with Daxon from behind me. Everything came down to business with him, and I was just thankful he didn’t speak about Paisley’s flirtatious behavior. Maybe he didn’t even notice because he was always about work. But a man like Daxon caught on to everything, and I was sure there must be a plan behind his madness.

We wandered up some stairs, and it led us to an oceanfront view. Up on the top of the yacht was a fancy table all ready for our company. It was a beautiful view of the water for as far as the eye could see. It was a breathtakingly stunning sight, and I didn’t want to take my eyes off it, but a hand rested on my lower back.

"Please take a seat, Celeste." Mr. Brava said as he pulled a chair out for me and the pad of his thumb caressed my panty line.

I was uncomfortable and hesitant until my eyes fell upon Dylan's and he raised an eyebrow at me. He nodded towards the seat and found his own across from it. "Take your seat, darling."

I knew to do as instructed because the stakes were too high. Dylan was adamant about that fact and gave me full permission. I couldn't help feeling like a prized piece of meat Mr. Brava could dig his dentures into. And my husband to be gave me up for the grand prize.

I sat beside the crippling old man and pushed my pride aside. He quirked a wrinkled smile and nodded his head towards the servant. I wasn't at all surprised they were all females around the same age as me and wore tight white skirts that barely covered their ass. It was probably a specific touch asked for by Mr. Brava himself. But there was a job to be done and if entertainment for Mr. Brava was it, I'd try to bear through it.

Once this old man crossed the line, I'd be out of there.

"This looks delectable, Michael." Daxon said as he admired the first course served in front of him from across the table.

"Please, call me, Mr. Brava." He responded firmly and narrowed his eyes at Daxon. "We should remain strictly professional, except when it comes to the finer things in life."

Daxon simply nodded towards him as my stomach cringed and my throat tightened. I swallowed hard and knew Mr. Brava spoke of me. The very thought of that man's hands on me made my skin crawl, and I knew Daxon couldn't care less. He'd walk me on the plank and feed me to this old shark in a matter of moments.

Paisley piped in and broke the awkwardness. "Speaking of business, what's your role within the family business, Nicholas?"

Her eyes sparkled at him from across the table as she eyed him up and played with her hair. She paid no attention to her meal in front of her and only to this fine specimen before her. She wanted to move onto the last course and that was dessert.

"It's simply helping with business ordeals and to entertain the ladies." Nicholas flirtatiously said as he never broke eye contact with her and gave her a direct answer.

Paisley let out a giggle with a smirk of wonder and he lost her in his trance. Nicholas was playing his cards right, and she fell right into his passionate game. I knew that Paisley probably wouldn't be alone this evening and she could use a little fun on this mini vacation.

The first course contained a fancy tossed salad with tomatoes, cucumber, diced carrots and herbs sprinkled on top. A delicate light dressing drizzled over the top of the crunchy lettuce leaves. Each bite filled my tastebuds, but I was ready for some fine wine. I reached for the closest wine bottle and wanted a taste of the red liquid.

"No, let me do the honor." Michael insisted as his hand brushed mine and he took charge of the wine bottle. "Have a drink of the world's finest wine. It's exquisite, just like yourself."

I immediately removed my hand from his unwanted touch and felt the need to run. This man was no gentleman and gave me the creeps. But this was business, and I was a strong woman.

I gave a soft laugh and took my wine glass as he poured me my liquid courage. "Let's have a drink, shall we?"

I raised the drink towards my lips and took a sip. The smooth liquor ran down my throat with ease, and it was delicious. I didn't stop at a sip and had the rest. I was going to need it for the next few hours. His strong advances frazzled my mind and not in a good way. The wine would be my guide to tame my nerves for the rest of this ordeal.

That was, until his hand touched my thigh.

He caressed his thumb against my bare flesh and worked his hand into my inner thigh. "Celeste, you're quite the vibrant young woman and should be treated as such."

I raised an eyebrow at him and knew this old creep would not stop here. My gaze wandered across the table to my fiancé, who didn't even pay attention to Mr. Brava's forward advances and my impatience grew. My heartbeat loudly in my ears and my eyes fell upon the next man in line, who definitely paid attention.

My future father-in-law.

Daxon raised an eyebrow towards me, and he knew exactly where Michael's hand had gone. He just sat there and watched. He didn't speak a word as Mr. Brava's hand went higher towards my most intimate area. Not a peep as my lips pressed together, and I held in my anger. This older man was about to get his throat punched for groping me inappropriately, and I wasn't about to stand for it. But Daxon's eyes were a stern warning not to fuck this up.

Without hesitation, I rose from my seat and held in my rage. "Excuse me while I use the restroom."

I didn't wait for a response or make eye contact with anyone and immediately left the table. My skin crawled with disgust at his inappropriate touch, and I wanted nothing to do with it. They would not use me as some pawn just to get to their treasure. If this business deal fell through, I didn't care at this point. I was worth more than that.

I hurried down the stairwell and followed the way we came. It led me to the lowest level of the yacht and my breath heaved from my lungs with anger. Paisley's too taken by Nicholas to notice, my fiancé cared more about his meal and Daxon knew exactly what went on. But he didn't even care enough to stop it and devoted himself to his damn business.

Well, screw him.

Suddenly, a hand wrapped around my wrist and spun me around. "Where are you off to in such a hurry, young lady?"

I glared down at Daxon's hand and he let me go. "I excused myself for the ladies' room."

He pointed in the opposite direction. "Well, the restrooms would be at the back of the yacht. Not at the front."

And I snapped at him. "Why do you care what I do? It's no secret you hate me."

"Hate is a strong word." Daxon puffed out his chest and tapped his index finger against my lips. "It's more that I loathe you, but I won't have a pretty thing like you ruining my business deal."

He removed his finger in time before I bit it off. "Well, get back to it."

Daxon stepped closer towards me and it was the first time I noticed the top of his shirt was unbuttoned. His powerful chest muscles moved with each breath and the pulse in his throat pumped against his neck. His annoyance with me ran through his veins, and his powerful stance made me take a few steps back.

He bit his lower lip and his eyes ran down my body. "I can't do that without you. Mr. Brava has taken quite an interest in you and your exquisite trance."

He gave me chills, and I stepped back again, but held my head high. "Well, I'm not going back and you can't make me."

He came closer still, tilted his head to the side and narrowed his eyes. "Why do you always have to be such a brat?"

I glared back at him with determination and wanted to tease him a little. "What are you going to do about it, daddy?"

Daxon came up so close that his cologne filled my nose and his hot breath moved my wispy hair pieces. My eyes darted to his full lips and my tongue begged to lick him. He was too close and my body was crumbling at his feet.

"If you don't come back to the table and please our latest business deal, I'm going to take you over my knee and show you what daddy can do to a naughty girl like you." Daxon whispered as he licked and bit his bottom lip. "Come on, Celeste, you're used to pleasing men for money."

And I lost it.

I raised my hand with rage to slap him straight across his smudge face, but he stepped out of the way in time for me to miss. I lost my footing and fell forward. My hands reached out for something to grasp, but all I felt was air. I tried, and it was no use as a splash filled my ears.

A cold wetness consumed my body, and I knew I had fallen overboard. My eyes blinked underwater as my arms thrashed and pushed me towards the top. I broke the surface for a quick moment and shouted out, but water filled my mouth.

I pumped my legs as fast as I could and reached the surface again to cry out. "Help! I can't swim!"

My face dipped under the water again, and I couldn't keep my body up. The surface of the ocean was in sight, but drifted further away. My arms and legs worked, but all I did was fall down under. All I could see was the blue ocean as my lungs closed in and I was almost out of air.

Death creeped up on me and there was no one to save me. No one to pull me out of this ocean that wrapped its waves around me and wouldn't let go. It pulled me under and clenched my body as my lungs burned. The pain was unbearable, and I knew this was the end. The end of my fight left my body and I no longer tried.

I went limp as my body floated to the way of the water and my eyes blinked. The sunlight above me looked like a small tunnel surrounded by darkness. A darkness I wasn't ready to give myself to, but I had no choice. I wasn't ready to die, but death's door was wide open.

Suddenly, powerful arms wrapped around my waist and pulled me towards the light. My lungs were on their last bit of air and my mouth was ready to greet the water. Someone pulled me closer to the surface as the sunlight grew wider and the yacht came back into view. The surrounding strength tugged me towards the surface and was ready to break over the edge.

Just as we broke the ocean's deadly grasp, my mouth opened up and gasped for relief. My lungs screamed their welcome at the fresh ocean air. The powerful body that saved me held me close and swam me towards a ledge on the side of the yacht. Muscles flexed with each stroke along the water's surface, and I coughed to catch my breath.

"Grab onto the ledge, Celeste." Daxon breathed heavily and there was no mistaking his stern tone.

I was weak from the fight with water and didn't want to argue. I did as he instructed and held on with what little strength I had left. Daxon effortlessly heaved himself onto the yacht and reached out for my hand. I took it immediately as he pulled me up with him and I fell into his arms. I was too tired to complain.

I almost drowned. Daxon had saved me. He could've let me die, but he jumped in and rescued me.

The reality of it hit me hard, and I couldn't think straight. He could've had all his problems washed away with the ocean and never had to deal with me again. But here I was in his trembling arms with our wet bodies connected as one.

"Celeste? Are you alright?" Daxon asked with panic in his voice.

He brushed my wet hair from my face that had fallen out of the bun and tilted my chin. His eyes seared into my soul as

I laid on the yacht floor and his warmth surrounded me, but I still felt the chill. His thumb shook as he stroked my cheek and his eyes searched mine.

"I-I'm okay, just shaken up." I stammered as my teeth chattered together from the chill and everything trembled.

I expected to see his usual annoyance with me, but it was the complete opposite. All I saw was the same fear I had felt within his deep brown depths. The fear that I almost lost my life.

"Come on, let's get you warmed up." He breathed as he didn't waste a moment and stood with me in his embrace.

He carried me back onto the lower level of the yacht and I let my body lean into his warmth. I let him consume me because I wanted to feel whole again. And I knew when I was in his arms, he could make me feel like me again.

Suddenly, I heard Dylan's voice. "What the hell happened?"

Daxon peered down at me in his arms and repeatedly blinked his eyes. They narrowed and the look of his worst nightmare disappeared from them as he set me back on my feet. Dylan rushed to my side and covered me with his jacket.

"T-there was a misunderstanding and..." I tried to explain as my teeth chattered and my body vibrated. "I-I was clumsy and fell into the water, but your father rescued me. I-I can't swim."

"Oh, my god, are you okay?" Dylan asked with concern as he held me close and tried to warm me up.

Everything was a blur because I got lost in his father. I couldn't stop looking at him with my harsh new reality.

Something had shifted between us and it would never be the same.

Daxon Stark had saved me. I thought he wanted nothing to do with me. And all we needed was a near death experience to reveal the truth.

THIRTEEN
Trapped Together

Everything went by in a blur. I didn't even remember seeing the Brava family after everything that happened. Dylan showed concern for my well-being, but didn't question how I fell into the water anymore. Paisley was in shock, but Nicholas helped calm her back to reality and I knew she would stay the night. It didn't bother me because all I could think about was Daxon.

He was my hero when I never thought he would be.

Danger happened in the blink of an eye and he wasted no time diving into the water to save me. The water swallowed me whole, and he brought me back to life. He pulled me into the safety of his capable arms and shielded me from disaster.

I could still feel his thumb tremble with worry against my cheek. I could still see the look of fear in his deep brown eyes. The fear that he almost lost me. But I couldn't explain any of it because it was gone as quickly as it came.

Once the nightmare was over, he went back to his usual self. Dylan took over and his father had gone back to the distant look in his eyes. He avoided eye contact with me, and it stung. I shouldn't let him affect me this way. It was wrong to want more from him and I couldn't help myself.

The world he had let me into for those brief moments in time were the scariest of my life, but I had never felt so alive.

He let me in, saved me, and showed me his true self. Unlike this closed off man who couldn't stand the sight of me.

Dylan immediately ordered a boat for us to go back to the resort with no further talk of business. I was pleased to get off the yacht and put all this misery behind me. Between Mr. Brava's gross advances and my near-death experience, I had enough excitement for the day.

The boat ride back was a quick one and thank God for that. Daxon kept his distance all the way back to the resort. The awkwardness on the boat was enough to drive me mad. I'd take Daxon's annoyance with me over this dead silence. At least he acknowledged my existence. He wouldn't do anything except look at his phone and text an odd message. It was like nothing had happened and it was all just a bad dream.

But one I couldn't ever forget.

"I'm just thankful you are okay, darling." Dylan said as he swiped his keycard to enter our hotel room and his lips brushed my forehead. "The situation shocked Mr. Brava, and he apologized for the inconvenience."

The inconvenience was his disgusting behavior on his yacht. I never would've been in danger if it wasn't for his unpleasant conduct. I almost drowned thanks to that awful man and the circumstances that led up to it. The way he viewed a woman was inexcusable. A piece of prized fine meat that he just had all over his expensive yacht.

"Oh, I'm sure he was..." I muttered under my breath and bit my tongue.

"You should get changed out of those wet clothes." Dylan explained as he pointed towards the dresser and looked down at his phone. "I just have an important call to make."

I simply nodded my head and opened the drawer. It squeaked a welcome, and I pulled out a tight black dress, but a black lace caught my eye. It was the only piece of lingerie I bought for a special occasion. But after Daxon ruined my last surprise for Dylan, I was reluctant to wear it, but now I couldn't give a shit. I almost died, and it opened my eyes. Life was too short not to live it. I was getting laid tonight and I could use the company.

I smirked to myself at the little surprise I slipped on underneath my black dress and did up the zipper at the back. The oversized mirror at the dresser showed my hair was a mess, and I grabbed my brush to tame it. I ran the bristles through my wavy locks and it bounced to perfection. My hands teased it and I touched up my makeup in the spots that the water had ruined.

I could hear Dylan's voice and knew he still was on the phone, but I shouted I'd be back soon. I needed to get out of here and get some fresh air. The hotel room wouldn't help calm my thoughts. I knew business calls took long amounts of time and I just would not sit around waiting for it to end. So, I grabbed some cash along with the keycard and stuffed it in my lingerie breast cup.

My black high heels tapped along the hallway floor after our hotel door clicked shut behind me. The elevator came into view and I pressed the button. My eyes landed on a couple just down the hallway as he kissed her neck and she fumbled with the keycard to open the door. She let out a flirty giggle as he licked up her neck and the door opened. They tumbled inside and the door slammed shut behind them. I grinned at the thought of their wickedness and the lingerie under my dress.

I was getting lucky tonight.

The elevator dinged, it was here, and the doors opened. I stepped inside, but my grin disappeared when only one pair of brown eyes gazed back at me. They looked at me with surprise, but soon turned into that familiar wicked annoyance. It should be my fiancé's face looking back at me, but instead, it was his father.

I stepped back into the hallway. "I'll just get the next one."

Daxon blew out a breath of frustration, threw his arm out, and stopped the doors from closing. "No, princess, get on the damn elevator."

I glared back at him with a challenge. "Make me, daddy."

He stepped forward between the doors and bit his lip. The glare of displeasure shone in his eyes and he fixed his suit jacket. His hand loosened his tie, and he pressed his lips together. He did a number on me in my tight black dress. His eyes fucked me to the point I felt underdressed, but I wouldn't scurry away that easily.

"Shall I tell my son about our brief encounter the other day, where you watched me fuck my latest cunt and hid in my office closet?" Daxon dared as he fired a warning glare at me.

"You wouldn't dare..." I breathed with hatred as my nostrils flared at his threat, but I stood my ground.

"Oh, yes I would, young lady." Daxon breathed with a raised eyebrow and stepped back into the elevator. "Now, get on."

I let out an irritated huff, shot my nose up in the hair and got on his stupid elevator. I knew he meant business and when it came down to it, his word meant everything. If I didn't do exactly what daddy wanted, his threat would hold true. He'd have his way and I couldn't let him.

"Good girl, princess." He breathed in a husky undertone as he leaned against the elevator wall and crossed his arms.

I hated to admit it, but the look suited him as I glanced over and the elevator doors shut. The look of a man in control and dominated everything around him. He wasn't just wise, but he was cocky. Bullheaded and infuriating. But he looked so damn good.

Now, I was completely alone with him. My future father-in-law to be. Forced into this elevator with a man who was my worst enemy.

I turned my back to him and ignored his look of triumph. My reluctance to let him know he'd won this round made me hide it from him. He didn't deserve to see the look of fury on my face. So, he could look at my backside instead, but I was sure he was admiring the view.

My backside burned from his eyes as I looked at the buttons and saw he had already pressed for the main floor. My skin crawled with fiery tension and I knew his eyes caused it. I felt it from the back of my head all the way to my heeled feet. But the feeling would last extra longer on my plump ass.

As the elevator moved towards the main floor, I gave my hair a flick with my hand and ran my hand down my shoulder. It gently grazed my dress strap, and it fell from my shoulder. I moved my hair to the side, and it remained bare. Only naked skin exposed for his eyes and I swore I heard a groan escape his throat.

Two could play daddy's torturous game.

Suddenly, there was a loud bang, and the elevator stopped abruptly. I fell backwards from the force, but Daxon caught me in his arms. My wide eyes stared up into his with my head resting against his arm, and he held me close.

Too close.

His masculine scent lingered around me and my lungs breathed him in. My breath paused because I didn't want his aromatic scent to escape me. I wanted it trapped inside me forever.

His deep brown depths seared into my soul, and a hint of concern laid within them. His eyes narrowed together, and he was just as caught off guard as I was. This was the second time today I had ended up in his arms. It was the second time today I had never felt so alive in my life. And that very thought scared the shit out of me.

"I'm... I'm sorry, I..." I stammered as I found my voice and continued to look up into his eyes.

His face was bright with the silhouette of the elevator light behind his head. It made his salt and pepper hair very noticeable, but it was so sexy. His skin looked smooth, and I wanted to reach out to touch it. Run my hand over his late-night stubble and play with the hair at the nape of his neck.

"Don't apologize, princess..." He breathed as his warm breath touched my lips and his eyes searched my lips. "You're so damn good at teasing me."

The very thought I could make him squirm brought a grin to my mouth and his eyes took notice. A hint of mischief played within their depths, and I couldn't turn away. He caught me up in his spell and the curse he put me under made my lacy lingerie wet. My pussy ached for him when it shouldn't, but I stood no chance.

Wrapped up in him, he was my kryptonite.

Daxon made me weak. He made me vulnerable. He made me his.

I wanted him when I knew I shouldn't. This game he made me a part of was going to have consequences and I needed to put a stop to it. Fast.

"And what would your son think of that?" I shot back with an attitude and watched his eyes turn cold.

Reality set back in and I stood up. I fixed my dress after he released me, but my body grew cold without his touch. I ignored my body's reaction and looked around the compact elevator. My gaze fell on the buttons and wandered over towards them. I ran my hand along each one, but it was no use. The elevator wouldn't move and we were stuck here. I was stuck with him and there was no way out.

My throat closed in and I felt a panic hit me, but anger guided me. "We're stuck here. I'm trapped with you and it's all your fault."

"My fault?" He let out a shallow laugh, groaned as his hand ran over his mouth and pointed right at me. "This is all your fault, young lady."

His demeanor quickly changed, and the old dominant daddy was back.

"You're the one who made me get on this stupid elevator." I snapped back as my eyes glared at him and I stepped closer.

"And you're the one who snuck into my life when it was great without you." He argued as he licked his lower lip and his teeth played with it out of frustration. "You bring out the monster, me."

"Why do you have to be so cruel?" I asked with fury. "I don't know how you ever had a son. How could any woman put up with you?"

Suddenly, his eyes went blank. His shoulders slumped and all the fight left his body. He repeatedly blinked his eyes, and the color drained from his face.

I stood there stunned by the drastic change in him, and the elevator remained silent. We became lost in the silence as he just stared at me and me at him. Our staggered breaths were the only thing I could hear.

But then his shattered voice broke through.

"Dylan's mom died when he was two." Daxon admitted and his Adam's apple bobbed in his throat. "A drunk driver hit her and killed instantly."

He left me in disbelief and tears came to my eyes, but I blinked them away. "I'm so sorry. I didn't know..."

"How could you know?" Daxon said as he squinted his eyes and shook his head. "Dylan doesn't like to talk about it."

"I tried to ask him about his mother, but he always changed the subject." I admitted and touched his cheek. "He was so young; it must have been hard. You would've had to raise him all on your own."

He looked right at me as soon as my hand touched his skin and he laid his hand over mine. "It was unimaginable. The pain, grief and not just mine, but my son's."

His touch was intoxicating, and within this moment, it was just us. We weren't stuck; he didn't trap me; we were just together. Lost in this emotional memory that I just wanted him to heal from and pull him out of the loss he has felt all this time. Losing his wife and the life he could've had with her.

But she was gone.

He must've felt it too, because his eyes reverted to his icy-cold self and he pushed my hand away. "I swore off love. It only ends in disaster. I never want to face that again."

Suddenly, a gasp escaped me as the elevator kicked back into action and Daxon looked at me with distrust. His eyes seared into me until it stung and his guard was back up. A wall he put up between himself and happiness.

For that brief moment, I saw a man who loved someone so much it hurt and I never thought it could be from him. He let me in and tossed me back out. It made me understand him even more. It made me see how calculated he could actually be.

The elevator dinged for the main floor and brought me back to reality. The one where he hated me and I couldn't stand him. He finally brought a newfound truth to light, and the reality of it would bring aftershocks. I felt it deep inside.

I got off the elevator as Daxon's cell phone rang and he looked at the screen. He grabbed my hand and stopped me in my tracks. His urgency made me ponder who it could be.

"This is Daxon." He said as he got straight down to business and locked eyes with me. "Yes, I understand, and it's a pleasure to be doing business with you."

The phone call was brief and cut straight to the point. Daxon hung up, but his eyes remained locked on me. He didn't let go of my hand as his thumb pad stroked my palm and made me weak. This back and forth with him had me dizzy and I couldn't see straight. Let alone think right with him around.

"We got the Brava deal, and it's all thanks to you." He admitted as he squeezed my hand and pulled me back inside the elevator. "Your mishap on his yacht made him close the deal."

His words shocked me. The business deal went through because of my accident. Mr. Brava doesn't want any backlash. Poor business on his yacht would make the front-page news. He couldn't have that.

I smirked with pride. "He probably just didn't want me giving him a bad name after he felt me up on his yacht. It wouldn't look good in the tabloids."

Daxon chuckled, but let his hand fall. "I'm glad you're okay, princess."

He walked off the elevator without a glance back, and the doors clamped together. I couldn't move as his words registered and coursed right through me. His hot and cold behavior had me twisted up in knots.

But I went back to my room and would give Dylan the good news.

FOURTEEN
Someone Else

The elevator dinged for my floor and I stepped off with a whirlwind of emotions. I was not sure how long I was stuck in an elevator with Dylan's father, but it felt like an eternity. An additional barrier unraveled for billionaire Daxon Stark and it was unexpected. It was an experience I never saw coming, but I was glad it did.

It helped me understand him and the logic to his madness. The sad place he kept tucked away and hid it with darkness. A selfish, ruthless and driven man. He masked it all behind the company he built. His fortress, his business was everything. If it came tumbling down, so would the walls he built around his heart.

I took my keycard out and pressed it up against the scanner. The door quietly opened to the hotel room, and I strolled inside. The air in the room was hot, and a smell hit my nose. It caused it to wrinkle and I could recognize it.

The smell of hot sweaty sex.

I brushed the thought off and continued inside. They cut the living area off from the bedroom and Dylan was there. He must've gone back to bed while I got some fresh air. My heels dragged along the carpet and I made my way to the bedroom, but the door was wide open. The white bed sheets made movement, but I couldn't see anyone covered underneath.

"Dylan darling, I have some news..." I started, but my words fell short when the bed sheets flew back to reveal Dylan's shocked face. And he wasn't alone. "And apparently, so do you?"

I stared with disbelief at my husband to be with another man in our king-sized bed. A bed we hadn't even shared, but he was sharing it with another man. A very naked man.

"Oh, my god..." I whispered in shock with my hands out in front of me and angry tears hit my eyes.

Dylan's panicked face stared back at me, and he scrambled out of bed with a bed sheet pulled around his waist. I backed up and hit the dresser behind me. It startled me back to reality and this lonely nightmare. My fiancé was having an affair with another man.

"I-I thought you were getting some fresh air?" He breathed as he came closer towards me, but I backed up.

My back hit the doorframe next and tears fell down my cheeks. I tucked the keycard back in between my breasts and tucked my hair behind my ears. I was so upset my entire head felt like it was going to explode. The embarrassment coursed through me and it hardened me deep inside. He has been playing me for a fool this entire time. He never loved me and never could.

"I was going to until I heard the news from your father that you got the Brava deal and I was going to surprise you. But it appears I was the one in for the surprise." I glared at him through blurry eyes and looked at his lover.

The other man was extremely fit, just like Dylan. They tousled his hair from their lovemaking and a look of terror on his face. His green eyes were wide with shock as he stared straight at me. But I realized he feared me.

I looked back at Dylan, the man I was supposed to love and he was supposed to love me. He gave me a ring that was supposed to symbolize our love, but it was all a lie. And all I saw was red.

"I need to get out of here." I whispered and turned my back to him.

I headed straight for the door and his footsteps followed behind me. He repeatedly called my name, but I couldn't look back. He had betrayed me in the worst way. The thing that hurt the most was, I didn't even realize he was into men. I never saw that my husband to be was gay.

"Please, Celeste, please don't tell my father!" He cried out, and this voice echoed down the hallway.

I stopped dead in my tracks at the mention of Daxon. His face entered my mind and caused me to turn around to face his son one last time. Dylan stood in the hallway with his handsome face in so much distress. His eyes pleaded with me to keep a secret that I didn't want to. A truth that had turned my world upside down in the worst way imaginable and he wanted me to keep his secret.

"No one can find out I'm gay. My dad can never know. It could ruin everything. The future of the company is in your hands, Celeste." Dylan breathed heavily as he ran his hand down his face and turned around to go back inside.

The door clicked closed as it echoed down the hallway and scattered my heart. I was alone. Heartbroken, confused, angry, and bitter. Everything I thought I knew was over, and he expected me to keep it all to myself.

My teeth clenched together in anger, and my nostrils flared. I wanted to go back in there and tell Dylan Stark where to shove it. To let out all my rage on him and his lover, but I couldn't bring myself to do it. Instead, I bottled it up inside, wiped my tears away, and took a deep breath.

My eyes closed as I let the air swoop inside and fill my lungs full. It escaped through my nose and I opened my eyes. I turned away from this disaster and knew exactly what I needed to do. I needed to get plastered, and the bar was on the main floor. Everything about this day needed to be coated with hard liquor and I needed a whiskey on the rocks, stat.

My heels hit the floor, and I made it to the elevator. It took me straight to the main floor with no stops, and I was thankful for that. I didn't need any more interference after what happened. My future was told, and I was right where I needed to be with a glass of whiskey at my fingertips.

"Bottoms up..." I mumbled as I held the glass to my lips and the ice hit them with the smooth liquid running down my throat.

It was heavy, but not any heavier than my bitter heart. It pounded loudly with anger in my chest, and I wanted more than anything to make it stop. But I didn't know how.

Dylan had hurt me in the worst way possible and all I felt was revenge. I wanted sweet justice for all the times he snuck around behind my back. All those times, my senses tingled, and I knew he kept something from me. But I never imagined it could be this bad.

He was right, though. This secret he kept was huge. And it could destroy everything.

In a way, I didn't care. This could be my revenge to get back at him for everything he had done to me. But it would destroy Daxon.

His career was everything to him. His company was his life. And now I know why.

Could I put him through that misery?

Could I make him relive all the pain he'd locked away for years?

I groaned as my head hit the table, and the server brought me more drinks. More liquid courage to help me coat my bitterness and keep me from doing the unthinkable. It kept me from revealing the truth.

I stood up from my seat and chugged back the rest of my drink. It slammed back onto the table as I stumbled towards the bar and the anger hit me again. I just wanted to forget.

"H-hit me again, b-bartender..." I stammered in a drunken state and stumbled towards the bar.

Suddenly, arms wrapped around me, and I fell back against a solid chest. The smell of aftershave filled my nose, and I turned around, but expected to see Dylan. Instead, I stared up into a stranger's eyes and saw two of him. My world spun out of control. I let out a soft giggle and slapped my hand against his chest.

"L-listen, buddy, I'm just trying to get another drink." I said, as I raised an eyebrow and pushed against him.

"Woah, easy, sweetheart. I think you've had enough to drink." He said as he ran his hands down my sides and pulled me closer. "Why don't we take this party back to my room?"

He wouldn't let go of me, and his flirty gesture made me irritated. He smirked a gracious smile, but I wasn't up for a one-night stand. Especially not with him. He dared me with tease, but I wasn't into it. He just wasn't for me.

"J-just let me go, so I can get back to drowning my sorrows, okay?" I pleaded with him. "It's been a long day."

"Oh, ya?" He groaned as he thrust his cock against my thigh and squeezed my ass. "I know what else is long and hard."

"Ew, gross!" I cried out in protest. "Let me go, you creep!"

He chuckled, as I was no match for him in my drunken stupor and my hands thrashed against his chest. At least, I thought they did, but everything wouldn't stop moving. I tried to pull away from him, but my face kept falling against his shoulder. I just couldn't stay upright and the booze hit me harder than I expected.

"Come on, baby, we are going to have a good time." He said as I felt my heels move and follow in the direction he led, but I had no choice.

"I'm not interested! Now, let me go!" I pleaded with resistance.

Suddenly, his arms unwrap themselves from around me and I stumble up against the bar. The solid exterior held me up, and I looked over at the persistent asshole. But my fuzzy vision fixed itself and I saw two men.

One held up with his feet off the ground and the other in charge, with his powerful hands wrapped around the other man's collar. The asshole trying to take advantage of me was cowering at the hands of Dylan's father. But he was mad, very mad indeed.

"I believe the young lady told you she's not interested." Daxon said firmly through clenched teeth. "Do I need to bite off your ear and serve it to her on a platter so you can hear her better?"

"N-no, way man..." The stranger mumbled with fright and shook his head.

"Good, now fuck off." Daxon said as he threw him to the floor like he was a piece of shit and the guy peered up at him with fright.

The man got to his knees, but fell back onto the floor. Daxon's icy, stony stare didn't waver as the man stumbled to his feet in a hurry and scurried away. He left and didn't look back.

"Y-you didn't need to do that..." I stammered as the liquor took hold again and I stumbled in his direction. "I could've handled him."

But I landed in his arms once again.

His big, brawny and extremely fit arms.

"It sure didn't appear that way, princess." He breathed as he peered down at me and raised an eyebrow.

I squeezed his muscular arms with my hands and sighed. "You must work out every day. You've got the arms of a god."

He let out a chuckle. "Have you been drinking, young lady?"

I looked up at him with a matter-of-fact face, but it must've been silly. His face lit up with the most delicious grin and I could eat him up. I'd savor his taste and make it last a lifetime.

"Maybe just a teeny tiny bit?" I whispered and touched his hair. "How do you get your hair so perfect? The ladies must love it."

He shook his head and grinned. "Years of practice, my princess."

"Oh, I'm your princess now? Are you going to carry me away to my castle and lock me up inside?" I asked with tease.

"Something like that..." He mumbled and without hesitation lifted me into his arms.

"Oh!" I shouted out with surprise.

"Let's get you back to your room." Daxon breathed as he led the way, and I couldn't escape his embrace. "You've been out past your bedtime, young lady."

Panic overtook me as I remembered what got me here and why I was so drunk. I didn't want to go back to my room. I couldn't stand the sight of seeing them together again. And better yet, Daxon couldn't find out the truth.

"U-um... Wait!" I blurted out.

Daxon stopped in his tracks and didn't move a muscle. He peered down at me with questions and couldn't figure me out. My mind reeled, and I had to come up with an explanation. Fast.

"I don't want to go back to my room," I said.

"And why would that be?" Daxon asked as his eyebrows narrowed together and he was curious.

"Because I don't want Dylan to see me in this state. He'll be upset with me for making such a fool out of myself." I lied and hoped he bought it.

He blinked repeatedly, lost in thought, and I wished I could read his brilliant mind. The man I once idolized, and I was supposed to hate. But hate seemed to slip away and turn into something I didn't understand.

"Fine..." He growled with acceptance, but continued forward. "You will come back to my room and I don't want any argument about it."

I went to protest, but clamped my mouth shut. He wouldn't back down on his decision, and it was final. Daddy was in charge, and I let him carry me to his presidential suite. The most expensive suite in the entire hotel. I was going to spend the night with the richest man in the building.

My future father-in-law to be.

FIFTEEN

Presidential Suite

"Welcome to my suite, princess." Daxon breathed as he stood me up and closed the door behind me.

It didn't take long to get to Daxon's suite. It seemed to go by in the blink of an eye, or maybe it was the booze. But he carried me all the way there.

His warm body surrounded me, and I melted into him. His scent captivated me and made me want to stay in his arms. But his voice sang a sweet soothing tune and made me want to listen to him forever.

I almost forgot that he was my enemy. A man who I thought hated me and wanted me gone. But I saw a different side to Daxon within the last twenty-four hours and it made me almost forget the bad side of Daxon Stark.

I had to remember an egotistical man was still inside. He could creep out at any moment and get me with his twisted games. I wasn't sure if this was a good idea after all.

"Maybe I should just go..." I sighed with uneasiness and got ready to blot. "This isn't a good idea and..."

But Daxon grabbed my wrist.

"And where would you go?" He asked with concern.

I certainly didn't want to go back to my room. Not after I found my fiancé with his lover. The memories were still raw and hurt, but Daxon didn't need to know.

"I could just get my room and..." I tried to speak, but he stopped me.

"Nonsense. You will stay with me and that's final, young lady." Daxon said sternly, and the concern disappeared, replaced by his greed.

"You aren't the boss of me, daddy." I muttered with argument at his strict behavior and pointed my nose up in the air.

Suddenly, he jerked me close without warning and my breasts collided against his chest. My breath hitched and my eyes locked on his. I couldn't look away, no matter how hard I tried.

"Why do you always have to be so..." Daxon hissed as his eyes searched my face and he ran his finger along my chin. "Defiant."

"I guess you bring out the worst in me, daddy dearest." I snapped back, pulled my wrist out of his grasp and backed away. "I'm out of here."

I turned around to leave, but he raised his voice. "Wait!"

The instruction made me halt, and I knew I should continue walking, but I couldn't. I had to hear him out. Something in his voice begged me to over top of the usual dominance that flowed naturally from him.

He cleared his throat and softly said. "There's more than enough room here. You'd have a full bedroom to yourself."

The anger of his stern bark turned into a softness with his sweeter tone. It calmed me and made me smile to myself as I turned around to look at him. His hair disheveled, like he had just run his hand through it and he tried hard to put on a nice front. I had never seen him like this before, and it made me curious. Curious enough to stay.

"Okay, but I get dibs on which bed." I teased as I pushed past him, but heard a huff escape him.

Good, I still got on his nerves.

I smiled brightly as I wandered farther into the presidential suite. Lavish furnishings were in the living room area with a nice plush carpet for your bare feet. Grey and blue tones decorated the room. Big lights were set up in different places and an enormous flat screen television sat in the center of the room. But it was the vast windows that showed off the true view.

The ocean scenery laid out behind them with the moonlight gently grazing the water. It created a nighttime glow on the calm blue waters. The view was beautiful with palm trees and there wasn't a soul in sight. There was no one here but us. Our own private beach and it made my skin tingle.

No one would know I was here with my future father-in-law to be. It would be our little secret. And that scared the shit out of me.

"You can have my room if you'd prefer? It's a king-sized bed." Daxon offered as he pointed towards a bedroom and looked at me. "The other one is a queen, but I'm sure you'd want something far more luxurious."

His deep brown eyes burned into me. They traveled down my body and made me quiver. I felt naked underneath his stare, whether or not he intended to.

"I'm sure it will do for the night." I managed to speak and held my composure.

But his eyes did something to my insides.

"Very well then." Daxon said matter-of-factly and looked away from me. "The bathroom is adjoined and you might want to knock before entering. We wouldn't want another situation where you see me naked again, now would we, princess?"

Immediately, my cheeks burned bright pink, and my embarrassment rose. Daxon's magnificent ass came to mind, and I felt the temperature rise. The incident was between us, but I knew he wouldn't let it go that easily.

I clapped my hands together at the awkwardness I felt. "On that note, I should head to bed. I've got to sober up and all."

Daxon grinned as I walked past him, and he enjoyed my embarrassment. He thrived off of it and the little games he loved to play with me. I could get through this. I just had to spend one night in his suite and I'd sneak out first thing in the morning.

I got to the bedroom door and went to close it, but he stopped me. "Oh, one last thing... Don't forget to dream about me, princess."

I glared at him, and he let go of the door. I slapped it shut with a frustrated huff and his sarcastic laugh followed. The back of my head fell against the door and I cursed him to hell and back.

Damn you, Daxon Stark!

He frustrated me to no end with his whirlwind behavior. He was hot and cold. Good and evil. He was everything I shouldn't be attracted to, but couldn't help myself.

"Damn him..." I muttered to myself as I flung the covers back with frustration and buried myself in the sheets.

I covered my head and wanted to scream, but a smell overtook all of me. The smell of his cologne. It was the smell of Daxon.

"Oh, goddamnit..." I sighed as I took it in and he surrounded me.

I was in the bed he had already slept in.

Why didn't I think of this?

I was stuck here in Daxon's bed with the smell of him everywhere. The mix of his cologne and his fresh masculine scent. There was no mistaking it now that I had been so close to him. Too close.

Time passed as I laid there in my future father-in-law's bed and my eyes grew heavy. His scent wrapped around me like a warm blanket and relaxed me when I knew it shouldn't. His smell made me at home, but slumber took over and I drifted to sleep.

***

My hands reached out, but always came up empty. I ran as fast as my leg would go to reach him and he kept moving further away. I didn't give up as my arms stretched out and wanted to grab him, but never let go.

He kept stalking away with his back turned to me and his dark figure moved with ease. Bright colored balloons came into view with a birthday cake and lots of candles, but he never stopped. My mom went to hand me a present with a pretty red bow and all I wanted was him.

He kept moving with me in tow as a school classroom sprung to life and the teacher at the front of the classroom said. "All right class, let's make a special gift for dad."

But he never stopped.

He walked on into Christmas and a beautifully lit tree with presents underneath. Big bows on every single one and silent night played in the background. But he still wouldn't stop.

He kept going and flew into a dark street. Decorations were the only source of light for witches, ghosts, and ghouls. Orange pumpkins laid on doorsteps as people handed out candy to children dressed up for the special night of Halloween. But I reached for him and he vanished.

"Daddy!" I cried out and thrashed my arms about. "No, don't leave me! You can't go!"

Hot, wet tears fell down my cheeks as I grabbed for him, but nothing was there. I didn't want him to go. I just wanted him to love me.

My cries went unheard until I heard my name. "Celeste? Celeste, wake up!"

My hands were no longer empty, and I felt something touch my cheek. "Princess, please wake up. You're safe, you're here with me."

My eyes flew open, and I sat up in bed. Daxon kneeled in front of me. But his hand cupped my face.

"It's okay, Celeste, it's just a bad dream. It was only a dream." He whispered as warm breath caressed my lips and his forehead touched mine.

Strands of hair moved against my lips with each heavy breath I took. I felt like I ran a marathon, but I had only run after a ghost. A man I never knew and wanted so desperately, too. But I only ever got to see him in my dreams.

"You scared the shit out of me, princess." Daxon admitted as he caressed my hair and tucked it behind my ears. "I thought someone was attacking you, I thought..."

I placed my finger on his lips. "I'm so sorry. It was just a nightmare. A bad dream I can never escape."

He cupped my face in his hands and made me look at him. I dropped my finger from his lips and touched his cheek. His eyes showed nothing but concern. And it was all for me.

But a hint of his strictness played within their depths. "You can't scare me like that again, you hear me, young lady?"

Something changed in the air, and a heat flickered to life. It switched on and set the room on fire. The flames danced between us, but neither one of us wanted to put it out.

I licked my lips, and his eyes darted to them. "Yes, I hear you, daddy."

Lust blazed in his eyes, but he bit his lip with flustered passion. "You shouldn't do that, Celeste. You shouldn't call me daddy."

I bit my lip. "And why not?"

"Because I like it too damn much." He breathed as the pad of his thumb caressed my lips and I looked at his delicious mouth.

I knew I shouldn't. I knew this could never be. But he just tempted me.

"Well, that's too bad, daddy." I blurted out with tease.

I couldn't tame him and didn't want to. He wanted me and I wanted him. So, he let out a hungry growl and took what he craved. And his lips collided with mine.

SIXTEEN

Taste of Temptation

Daddy's mouth was toxic. A toxicity I couldn't resist as his lips greedily took mine. His tongue danced in sweet strokes and I returned the favor with tease. He loved it and groaned into me as the french kiss burned my insides. Flames erupted in me and worked their way down my body. It scorched deep in my belly and flickered to the most intimate part of me. It sizzled and my juices dripped to soak me.

Dear daddy turned me on like no one else and I didn't want it to end.

"I'm a monster for craving you..." He breathed heavily against my lips. "I shouldn't desire you, princess. You're my son's fiancé."

His lips left mine and our foreheads touched as his eyes locked on my engagement ring. It twinkled in the moonlight as his thumb caressed my ring finger and tingles ignited. He set everything in me on fire and I yearned for him. I knew I shouldn't and maybe it was the booze taking flight, but everything felt right. Nothing felt wrong about this, but I knew I wasn't sober enough to think straight.

But with him this close, nothing else mattered.

Only us.

I tilted his chin, and his deep eyes fell on mine. They drank me in and lust swirled. The flames of passion licked me in and my tongue stretched out. I licked his lips with possession and wanted him to be mine. Even if it was just for tonight.

I pulled back, but he grabbed the back of my head. "Tempting the devil, aren't you, princess?"

I moistened my upper lip. "I'll always tempt you, daddy."

He groaned and took my mouth in a flash of heated fury. Our tongues swirled, lips smacked, and teeth nipped. My hands crawled up his naked chest and ran through small patches of hair. His broad shoulders were magnificent and my claws dug in. He hissed and yanked my hair to the side with my neck exposed just for him.

He wasted no time and ran his hot tongue up my neckline. It found my sensitive earlobe, and he sucked it into his mouth. He played with it and tempted me while my hands locked behind his neck. He gave me everything I desired, and I knew he'd have me right where he wanted me. But I'd let him in a heartbeat.

I should resist, and I should put up a fight. I should hate him, but somehow it turned into a thirst for desire. And I fell for it one twisted game at a time. But he fell right along with me.

He pulled me up onto my knees as his other hand ran over my shoulder and down my back. It found the zipper at the back of my dress and he dragged it down. The sound taunted me and I moaned as his mouth continued to play. His tongue flicked and his warm breath tickled my ear.

"My, my, what do we have under here?" He whispered in my ear as he pulled the dress straps aside and exposed my lingerie to him.

He let the dress slide down my body, and it fell to my knees. He pulled back and drank in the sight of me. The black lace lingerie made my skin glow with the moonlight and stars lit up in his eyes. They twinkled with passion as he knelt in front of me and couldn't look away. I burned everywhere his gaze touched and he let out a thirsty growl. He licked his lip and bit it, but not out of his usual frustration with me. Out of pure undeniable arousal and his bulging grey sweatpants proved it.

I panted at the glorious sight of him and my messed-up hair framed my face. I bit my lip as we stared at one another in our lustful haze and his thumbs looped through his waistband. He pulled the elastic lower, low enough the waistline hovered just under his hips. A sexy trail of hair led down where I couldn't see, and I swallowed hard at the thought of what was under there. Everything in me screamed at me to stop, but my body wanted to pounce. I wanted to jump on him like a wildcat and be his dirty little pussy.

My eyes left the bulge inside of his sweatpants and flickered to his face. I already locked his eyes on mine as he watched my response and wondered if I wanted him. But I did so badly.

"Tell me to stop, princess." He breathed as he watched me and pulled his sweatpants lower.

But I wouldn't.

I couldn't.

I didn't speak a word as he pulled them further down, and the temptation to touch him was unreal. The need for his hands to be on me grew, and his massive erection popped over the top of his waistband. My eyes widened at his length and my mouth watered at the sight of him. Deep veins ran over his cock and the tip of his dick leaked pre cum as it gleamed with the dim light. I incredibly aroused him and I was dripping wet for him.

"Do you like what you see, princess?" He asked me with tease.

Everything about him was powerful, demanding and dominant. His muscular form loomed over me and his need to control oozed from him. But it made me his.

I slowly nodded my head with approval and bit my lower lip. My mind raced and the temperature in the room felt like it went up one-hundred degrees. My body was on fire for him and he reciprocated the same heat.

I watched as he reached out his hand, and his index finger grazed my plump lips. He ran it over my smeared lip gloss and my eyes locked with his. But I took his finger into my mouth.

I opened my wetness for him and guided his finger inside with my tongue. It swirled around his manly finger and my teeth gently teased. They bit down softly against his flesh and I sucked him in deeper.

My eyes glowed at him with lust and he held back his need to be in control. He let me gain it and play with him. Taunt him until he couldn't take it anymore. He let me guide my lips up and down his finger as he envisioned me sucking on his cock. I created a lubricated path with my mouth, but didn't touch him anywhere else. And I could tell the temptation killed him inside.

He groaned and pulled me towards him. I gasped as he swept me up in his heated embrace and I peered up at him.

He looked down at my mouth and trailed his finger along my lower lip.

"That's my good girl..." He groaned in a husky tone. "Open for daddy."

I did as I was told and got lost in his trance. I opened my mouth and watched as he puckered his lips together. His saliva made its way from his mouth into mine. The sweet taste of mint mixed with it as he spit in my mouth and the experience blew my mind.

"Get on your knees..." He breathed as his hand covered my collarbone and his need for power came back. "I'm going to fill that pretty little mouth until your body begs for me."

Suddenly, his grip tightened on my throat, and he pulled me towards his raging cock. His other hand cupped it and slapped it against my wet lips. But my reaction was to open for him.

My instinct knew what he wanted. It knew what he craved. And his thick dick slid up my tongue.

It hugged him as my mouth wrapped around his skin and he pushed deeper inside. So deep that he hit the back of my throat and my gag reflex kicked into gear. But he groaned as it tightened around him.

I took him all the way out of my mouth as his hand left my collarbone and sprawled out in my wavy hair. He grabbed the untamed mess in a ponytail and pushed his dick back inside. Back inside, the sweetness of me as he thrust his hips and my hands squeezed the bedsheets. I took all of him like a good girl and he filled me until I was full. His good girl turned dirty as my teeth grazed along the sides of him and he moaned with delight. He pushed me in deeper and let me come up for air, but it never lasted long. His massive dick would be right back where it started, buried deep inside my throat. Right where he wanted it to be.

Daxon Stark was in control.

And he fucking loved it.

I hummed against him and the vibrations crawled up his cock. He gripped my hair tighter and fucked my face faster with approval. I could take him and he knew that. He has met his match, but he still fought for power and I wouldn't let him win that easily.

I playfully bit down, and he pulled back with surprise. Saliva laid on my lips and I licked them clean as he tilted my head to look up at him. Our eyes locked, and he filled his with darkened passion. Lust all for me.

"So, you want to play dirty, princess?" Daxon hissed through clenched teeth. "Well, daddy can play dirty too."

And he slapped my ass.

It caused my mouth to open and let out a gasp, but he didn't waste time. He thrust his dick back inside and I wrapped around him. His thrusts were deep, but I could take it and he went slow so he could enjoy it. He breathed heavily from above me as his other hand travelled down my backside. He continued lower and his hand squeezed my ass cheek. I moaned against his cock and he rewarded me.

He moved the thong aside and ran his finger over my bare ass crack. He kept going until his finger met my juicy pussy and plunged his finger inside. I moaned against him and my hips had a mind of their own as they moved to his slow rhythm. He dipped it in and out with ease. But he enjoyed every minute.

He watched as my body begged for him, just like he promised. My pussy walls pulsated around his finger and he plunged another one inside. He pushed it deep inside me as I clenched down around him and pleaded for more. My entire being trembled as my mouth wanted to pick up the pace, but he held my hair in place. He made it long and drawn out.

He knew how to play dirty.

Suddenly, the sweet tease was over, and he pulled his fingers out of me. He unwrapped my hair from his hand, but grabbed the back of my head. The force made his cock slide out of my mouth and he replaced it with his lips. My senses went crazy when he lapped his tongue over me. He was a wild monster that no one could tame, but I loved it. He set me on fire and I never wanted it to burn out.

"Lay down, princess." He whispered against my swollen lips. "Daddy wants to savor you until you scream."

I did as I was told and kicked my black dress aside. I propped myself up on my elbows because I wanted to see every dirty little thing daddy was going to do to me. My bra straps fell down my arms, and he kicked his grey sweatpants aside. And he knelt naked on all fours in front of me.

His salt and pepper hair shimmered in the moonlight and his eyes blazed at me with passion from between my thighs. His eyes never left mine as he ran his tongue up my inner thigh. First the one side and then the other. He repeated it and ran his hand down my belly. Over my navel and towards my sweet place. He danced over my bare pussy and slapped my clit. I squealed for him and he circled it. He got it ripe and ready for him to take.

His tongue made one last sweet decent, and he plunged it inside of my cunt. I moaned as the pleasure hit me full force and his tongue swirled inside my walls. He played me like his musical instrument and I sang a sweet tune for him. Panting as he pressed his tongue inside me and moaning as he playfully bit my clit.

I held back my cry of pure bliss and bit my lower lip. I tried my best to hold back my release, but he built it higher to the brink. He toyed, teased, and taunted me.

His mouth sucked my pussy lips, and his tongue danced inside. He slapped my clit again and my ass rose off the sheets. The blissful force sent me closer to the edge, and he circled it once again. He continued his same intoxicating game, and my pussy was about to explode.

I was about to give into daddy, and he knew he was in control.

And there wasn't a damn thing I could do about it.

"Oh, daddy, yes!" I screamed out as my climax lost control and stars danced before my eyes.

He rode out my release with his tongue still inside me and my sweet juices met their maker. Strands of my hair sucked in and out of my mouth as he released his mouth from me. But a wicked grin laid in its place.

He rose over the top of me and hovered there. He peered down at me in complete control, and the grin left his face. Replaced with a serious side and he tilted his head to the side, but the head of his dick brushed against my pussy. I shivered at the feeling of him up against me and just wanted him buried deep inside. The need to have him was stronger than ever, but the look in his eyes held a question.

"Are you on birth control, young lady?" He asked as his eyes briefly left mine and roamed down my body. "Because I want to fuck the shit out of you."

I was always careful when it came to sex. I always used protection, but with his dick against my cunt, I couldn't think straight. He had my mind reeling with all the positions he could put me in, and I wouldn't fight it.

I'd give in.

I'd give myself to him.

So, I did the one thing on my mind and wrapped my legs around him. My hips swayed and teased him to avoid the subject. I would not let it ruin the mood. I wanted him to fuck me and I wanted him to fuck me now.

He grazed my lower lip with his fingertip and pushed behind it. At the same time, his thumb hooked in under my chin and he pulled me forward. Close enough that our mouths were only inches apart.

"I've been dreaming of this since the moment I first met you. I've stayed up late at night, fisting myself to the very thought of you." He growled as he released my chin and grabbed the back of my head. "You want my cock in you, princess? Well, daddy is going to give it to you."

And he plunged his massive dick deep within my depths.

"Oh, yes!" I cried out with pleasure. "Yes, daddy, do me!"

My cunt clenched down around him as his dick throbbed inside of me and he thrust without a single stop. Our twisted game had turned into an entangled lust. He groaned as he pounded into me and I grabbed onto his shoulders. My nails bit into his skin and he hissed with delight.

My tits jostled to his rhythm, and I cried out for more. My heartbeat wildly in my ears as my climax built higher for him and he fucked me like there was no tomorrow. His chest glistened with sweat as his thrusts never let up, and he closed his eyes for a brief second.

He took in our moment together and got lost in it. A moment he had been wanting and knew he shouldn't, but to hell with it all. The feeling of our bodies mixed as one, the smell of our wild sex and the sound of our moans.

I moved my hands into the back of his hair. The smoothness of it between my fingers and I played with it there. Mr. Daxon Stark was a sexy silver fox, and he was all mine for this moment in time.

I groaned as he slowed down his pace, but it was a sweet and steady rhythm. I bucked my hips to meet his speed, but he pushed further. Deep up into the hilt of me. So, deep into my core, I felt the sensation all the way to my toes.

I locked my hands together around the nape of his neck, and he lifted us off the bed. His magnificent cock still laid deep inside me and tucked into my warmth. He carried me as he kissed me and it swept me up in only him. He could take me to the hallway and screw my brains out. That's how much I didn't care.

I wanted to get lost in him. Lost in our sexual frenzy. Captured in us.

I felt a warm breeze hit my skin, and it gave me goosebumps. My backside hit a coolness, and he ran his mouth down my neck. The coolness was the window of the balcony and my eyes caught the sight of a full moon over the ocean.

But soon I saw nothing but white lights as he thrust into me once again under the moonlit sky.

"Oh, princess..." He growled against my ear as he bounced me on his dick. "You're so fucking tight wrapped around my cock."

I moaned in ecstasy and circled my hips on his dick. He pounded to the hilt, and my backside rubbed against the glass. I bit his shoulder, and he hissed at my tease. My teeth nibbled up his neck and found his earlobe. I sucked it inside my mouth and playfully bit down.

But I teasingly clenched it between my teeth and said, "And you're so fucking deep inside me, daddy."

He rumbled out a low, husky growl from deep inside his chest and lifted me off his cock. He switched it up and pressed me up against the balcony railing. His hand grabbed a fistful of my hair and he yanked it. My head jerked backwards and I let out a squeal of delight. But his hand connected with my ass cheek and stung sweetly.

"I'm going to bury myself in your sweet pussy, my dear future daughter-in-law, until you scream my name." He hissed in my ear and buried himself in me from behind.

"Mm, yes..." I moaned with pleasure.

He took me to new heights as he swirled his cock inside me and toyed with my spot. His big, massive dick thrusted into me again and again, but deep inside me. I clenched the railing with my hands and my mouth opened wide as my moan of pleasure filled the ocean night sky.

I couldn't believe he dared to screw me on his private balcony. The risk of anyone spotting us was real, and it turned me on immensely. Anyone could catch us in the act and as he fucked me from behind, I realized I didn't care. All I wanted was to be desired and daddy knew just how to please.

"Oh, yes..." I whimpered as my body shook with passion.

He slapped my ass and hissed in my ear. "I can't hear you, princess."

I smirked back at him, our eyes locked and electricity zapped between us. "Oh, yes, daddy."

And he let it all go and pounded my pussy as he said. "That's my girl."

Bright stars lit up before my eyes and my climax hit me out of nowhere. It rocked over me as I cried out for him just like he wanted, and I felt his dick pulsate deep inside my juicy walls. His seed spilled inside of me and he dove into my cunt with no regret.

"Oh, fuck, Celeste!" He groaned as he grabbed my ass cheeks and slammed into me.

He didn't stop until he was spent and I felt his liquid spill down my thighs. We breathed heavily as he pulled out of me and turned his back to me. I looked at him with my hair in my face as he stretched his arms out and held the back of his head. The moonlight hit his backside, and it was the most beautiful view I had ever seen. His perfectly sculpted ass kissed the light, and sweat glistened against his gloriously curved back. His powerful body begged for me to kiss him all over, but something was off.

He kept his distance from me as I fixed my fallen straps from our passionate sexual encounter and I said into the night. "Stay the night with me in bed, Daxon."

I watched as his body froze and his distance from me stung. We were once so close and now so far away. I hated the distance, hated to admit it to myself, but I wanted him with me. Snuggled into me and against me. I wanted to hear him breathe as I closed my eyes and fell asleep. I wanted him to be the last thought on my mind before I dreamed of him and only him.

He put his arms down and turned towards me. "I don't cuddle after sex, princess. Especially with my son's fiancé."

His words bit into me and chewed at a part of my heart. I wanted to argue and show my disappointment, but instead I hid my feelings. I stuffed them down and dug a hole inside of me.

I shook off my unwanted feelings and playfully pouted at him. "It would really help me fall asleep after the nightmare I had."

He let out a deep sigh and finally looked at me. The lust that was once there was now gone. Replaced with no emotion and he was unreadable. Cold, dark and distant.

He nodded his head and opened the balcony door. "Okay, but I have one rule."

I smirked and raised my eyebrow. "And what's that?"

"No cuddling." He answered firmly.

I walked up to him like I had won the battle and pecked his lips. "Okay, daddy."

He growled and smacked my ass. "And stop calling me that, young lady."

I bit my lip to conceal my squeal and smirked wildly as I walked back inside his presidential suite. My legs glided me back to the bed with ease and I felt like an enormous weight lifted off of me.

Sex with Daxon Stark was beyond good. It was mind blowing. He had rocked my world in a way no one ever had. But this had to be a one-time drunken mistake.

Intimacy with Dylan's father was never on my radar. He was supposed to be my enemy and my worst nightmare. But he had turned into the most fabulous sex come true.

If I wasn't plastered out of my mind, this would've never happened. I wouldn't have fallen into his trap and gave myself to him. I never would've had sex with my fiancé's father.

Or would I?

I laid down on the bed and a million unanswered questions swirled through my mind. The bed moved as Daxon laid down beside me and I looked over at him. He wouldn't look at me and stared straight up at the ceiling. Somehow, he had gotten his sweatpants back on while I was lost in my own thoughts.

I took a deep breath and closed my eyes to the silence of the room. The faint sound of waves crashing in the ocean and our breathing mingled together. I wished I could lay my head against his chest and hear his heartbeat. The one thing that made him alive and not this cold, distant man beside me.

Daxon Stark had let me in, but only briefly, and it was the best moment of my life. He gave me his world and one night to forget it all. But now it was time to get back to reality.

Suddenly, I felt a warmth against my hand. A brief, tender touch that sent warm tingles through me. His hand closest to mine gently brushed my fingers, and I took a chance.

I wrapped my finger through his.

He didn't flinch or pull away. Instead, he squeezed my hand and a small smile touched my face. He wouldn't cuddle, but holding my hand would do.

I listened to his steady breaths as I closed my eyes and felt connected to him. He may not hold me and love me, but he comforted me. And that was more than enough for right now.

Daxon Stark had a soft spot for me, after all.

SEVENTEEN

Morning After

The next morning, I woke up to a bright early light, and it hurt my eyes. My head ached, and I wished it would go away. I blinked my eyes and waited for my blurry vision to clear. For my mind to defog and I could think straight once again. But then it hit me.

Oh, my god...

I had hot, sweaty sex with my fiancé's father.

"Oh, no..." I groaned as I rolled over and expected to blush at him with embarrassment.

But I found no one beside me.

My head shot up off the pillow, but pain radiated in my brain. "Ouch..."

I squinted my eyes and tried to look around the room. The side of the bed Daxon slept on. The sheets were wrinkled from his body and I touched his side of the bed. It was stone cold. Daxon had left long ago, and I looked at the bedside table clock.

It was lunchtime.

"Oh, shit..." I mumbled to myself as I got up and scurried to find my dress.

I found it on the floor and picked it up. My feet fell inside of it and I pulled it up over top of my lingerie. My now very dirty lingerie, thanks to the passionate sex I had last night with Dylan's father.

I cursed myself to hell as I zipped up the back of my dress and my eyes fell on a notepad on the bedside table. They narrowed with curiosity as I went closer and noticed a message written on the white notepad with black ink. It was a note from Daxon.

'I've headed back to the city. Stay for as long as you want, princess.'

The message was brief and to the point. He left and probably wanted to forget last night ever happened. But my body hummed with remembrance of him.

The way his body felt up against mine. The sound of his low groans from deep inside. His kisses I could get lost in. His touch took my breath away.

Drunk and all, it was the best night of my life. The best sex. And it was hard to forget that.

But I had to.

I had to move on and I knew he would, too. He gave into temptation and had sex with his son's fiancé. It was something unforgivable. But it had to stay a secret.

It would be our dirty secret.

"I have to get out of here." I mumbled to myself with regret.

I stuffed the petty cash I had left in my bra and grabbed my key card from the table. I looked in the mirror at my sex crazed hair and ran my fingers through it. The waves of black hair were messy, but I couldn't tame them. They just bounced back in place and looked as wild as ever. I needed a shower to fix this mess and a cold one to tame my still aroused body.

I hated to admit it, but if Daxon was still here, I'd tease him for round two. Morning sex would be bliss and I knew it would be even better with him. After last night, his touch still lingered on me and I couldn't get enough.

But it wasn't an option.

Sex with Daxon Stark was a one-time deal. It was never supposed to happen and it never should've. It would never happen again.

Even though I caught Dylan in bed with another man, last night was an even bigger mistake. I got way too drunk, got caught up in the moment, and made the biggest mistake of my life. But my fiancé could never find out.

I was marrying Dylan and had to keep our secrets. Dylan obviously needed to keep a certain image for public appearance and I didn't need to blow my life to hell. He needed a perfect life with the perfect wife, and that was his plan all along.

Dylan gave off so many red flags, but I refused to see them until it was too late. Now, I was knee deep in this and I saw no straightforward way out. Not without hurting Dylan, his father, and the future of their company.

I walked towards the presidential suite's front door, and my eyes caught the ocean. People strolled by on the beach without a care in the world. Lost in the sand, sun, and waves. The same way I got lost in Daxon last night as he railed me on the balcony and anyone could've walked by.

What the hell was I thinking?

It was risky, reckless and selfish. Daxon was used to it, but I wasn't. I've never been that kind of woman and Daxon brought out the worst in me. But no more.

I'd go back to my fiancé. We'd fix things and pretend this never happened. I had to put my anger with Dylan aside and marry him. We needed to make this work because our worlds could crash and burn.

I blew out my frustrated breath and tore my eyes away from my mistake. I stalked out of Daxon's suite with regret and made my way back to our hotel room. The one place I didn't want to be, but I had no choice. It brought back everything that happened, and I just wanted to wash it all away.

Tears stung my eyes as I made it to our hotel room door and halted on the spot. I took a deep breath and took out my key card. My hand shook, and I had to hold it with two hands to gain my control back. I wouldn't let the mistake I made last night win, and I had to face the anger head on. I had to put it all aside and move forward. Daxon could and I could, too.

I pushed the hotel door open, and it groaned with a response. I didn't have time to process another thought as Dylan's worried eyes met mine and he leapt off the couch. He stepped towards me, but kept his distance. I knew his first reaction was to take me in his arms, but it was too soon for that.

"I was worried sick about you, darling. Where were you last night?" He asked as he held his cell phone in his hand and looked at me.

I wanted to look at him and say, 'I was with your father having mind blowing sex. Better sex than you ever gave me. The best orgasms because you never gave me any. I always had to rely on my vibrator and probably will still have to since you lied to me.'

But I didn't speak a word.

"I tried texting you, but I never got a response." He said with concern.

I simply opened my mouth to speak, but couldn't. Instead, I went towards our hotel bedroom and pulled my cell phone out of the drawer. I had turned it off, and I had forgotten it with all the secrets revealed yesterday.

"I left my phone here. Forgot it, I guess..." I mumbled as my eyes landed on the bed and I relived his lies all over again.

I took a deep breath and briefly closed my eyes. I turned away from the nightmare and opened them to my fiancé. His handsome good looks stared back at me with worry, but I knew deep down it wasn't for me. It was for himself and his reputation. His father's beloved company and everything he stood for.

I wanted to bolt and tell him to shove his lies where the sun doesn't shine, but I couldn't. Daxon's dangerously dark and handsome face came to my mind. I shouldn't give a damn, but deep down I did because he had let me in. He had shown me there was more to him than I ever thought possible. For me to turn his world upside down, I just couldn't do it. His company meant everything to him because he had lost the love of his life.

How could I ruin his life?

It was simple.

I couldn't.

So, I stared his son straight in the eye and fed him a bold-faced lie. "I stayed in Paisley's hotel room for the night because I needed to clear my head."

I wanted to step away, but I had to keep up the act. He had to believe I wanted this. He had to be convinced I'd go along with this plan even though we both knew he never loved me and never could. I had to lie to him, just like he lied to me.

"Look..." He breathed as he took my hands in his and begged me to understand. "What you saw yesterday was the truth, but I still care about you and always will."

The truth hurt. It stung like a thousand bees piercing my body and never letting up. My fiancé was gay, and I knew his love affairs wouldn't stop. He knew he could never love me because his heart belonged elsewhere.

But I pushed the brutal truth aside.

"I see that now, and your secret will stay with me." I said firmly and pulled my hands from his. "But don't you dare lie to me like that ever again."

My eyes glared into his with anger, and I wanted him to feel my wrath. I wanted him to know I was done with him pulling me along like a puppet on a string. If we were doing this, we'd be doing it my way now.

"So, you won't tell my dad..." He said with shock, but I cut him off.

"I won't tell dear daddy your secret. We will get married as planned and I'll go along with your lie, but on one condition." I interrupted sternly, and the control felt good.

"Okay, what's that?" He asked with curiosity.

"I can fuck whoever I want to." I said, and didn't blink an eye.

He took a step back and blew out his breath. He paced the floor in front of me and he got lost in thought. Dylan didn't look pleased by my condition, but I didn't give a fuck.

I was tired of being played and if I was going to be in a loveless marriage; I wanted my freedom, too.

He nodded his head as he looked at the ground and then at me. "Okay, you have a deal. But I don't like it."

"You don't have to like it, darling..." I grinned as I walked up closer to him and raised my hands. "You think I enjoyed being blindsided with my fiancé in bed with another man?"

He didn't answer me and raised his finger at me. "You better not let your affairs get out in the public eye or else..."

"Or else what, darling?" I said as I raised my eyebrow and pushed his finger aside. "I could just as easily bring you down with me."

He backed up, and his threat was harmless. Both he and I knew it. He had no means to tell me what to do any longer. I wasn't his puppet to string along. I'd be his fake wife, and that was it.

And I had a wedding to plan.

"Well, darling, we should pack and head back to the city." I said cheerfully and clapped my hands together. "But first I'm going to have a shower and put this dreaded vacation behind us."

I strolled into the bathroom with confidence, but deep down felt like it could break at any moment. It forever changed our relationship. We put the lie behind us, but now paved a dangerous game of cat and mouse. Secrets from way over our heads and I wondered who would make it out in one piece.

EIGHTEEN
Twisted Game

We got back to the city, and the weather was gloomy. Nothing like the bright sandy beach with sweaty warm weather. It gave me a chill as I pulled my coat tighter and held an umbrella over my head. The weather matched my mood after everything that happened, and I wished I could forget. I wanted to no longer remember his taste, touch, and smell. I craved it, but wanted to forget. He crawled into my head, borrowed there, and dug his way into every thought.

The truth ate away at me on the plane ride home and I tried my best to ignore Dylan's constant texting. I knew it was to his lover and couldn't believe I didn't notice sooner. The affair was always right there, staring me in the face, and I just ignored it. I brushed it off as he was working and too busy for me, but always there for daddy.

The man I just let fuck my brain out.

But Dylan could never find out.

My legs moved faster as we approached our penthouse, and I closed my umbrella. I went straight for the door, but Dylan beat me to it and pulled out his key. We had barely talked on the journey home, and I was grateful for it. But the awkwardness ate away at me because everything has changed.

Nothing would be the same, but that was life. A constantly changing world that always spun around and went on. Everything always moved forward and nothing stayed the same.

Dylan opened the door and let me through first. I dropped my luggage and wanted to stretch out on the couch from jet leg, but found it occupied. Taken by a red-haired cutie with bright blue eyes and freckles. My best friend.

"Pais? What are you doing here?" I asked with a big smile on my face and pulled her in for a hug.

Her warmth felt so good and a comfort swept over me. I was so glad she was here and a welcomed surprise. But I expected her to be swept away by Nicholas Brava on his massive yacht.

"I came home early." Paisley replied as she pulled back and pinched my cheeks. "I couldn't be away from my best friend for too long."

I giggled and pushed her hands away. "Well, I'm glad you're here."

"I thought you stayed the night in Paisley's hotel room?" Dylan asked with suspicion and pulled off his tie.

"She did?" Paisley wondered with curiosity.

Oh, crap...

It was time for a secret. Let the lies continue. Time for damage control.

"Well, I did, but Paisley wasn't there." I lied as I waved my hand like it was no big deal. "It was easy to snag a key card from the front desk and get into her room for the night."

"Hm, I'll have to remember that next time I go." Dylan said as his voice traveled down the hallway and he headed for the bathroom. "I should try sneaking into my dad's expensive presidential suite."

I let out a fake laugh as I heard the shower turn on and took a deep breath. I dodged a bullet when he bought the story. He could never find out about the affair. He could never know I slept with his father.

I turned towards Paisley, and she had her lips pressed together in thought. "What?"

She tapped her chin and clicked her tongue off the roof of her mouth. "You're lying, but the question is why?"

"Would you keep your voice down..." I mumbled as I pulled her closer and whispered in her ear. "What does it matter if I am? A little lie hurt no one."

"It does, if you spent the night with someone else?" Paisley hinted as she raised her eyebrows and waited for me to cave. "I never got asked to give back a second key card. I know you were never in my room, Celeste. So, the real question is, where were you?"

She wouldn't let up and I knew it. I had to give her something. I had to tell her the truth, but I didn't have to tell her all of it. No one was ready for it and I wasn't sure if I'd ever be. The truth made what I did with Dylan's father even more real.

"Okay, but you have to promise not to speak a word." I breathed and hoped this worked.

"Your secrets are always safe with me." Paisley beamed and took my hands in hers. "Now, out with it."

"Dylan and I got into a fight. I got drunk at the hotel bar and Dylan's father showed up. He saved me from an asshole trying to take me back to his room because of the state I was in. It was stupid and I never should've gotten that drunk." I sighed with frustration at myself and the situation, but continued with the actual truth kept concealed. "I was in no state to go back to Dylan after our fight, and I stayed with his father instead."

Paisley's eyes went wide with her mouth agape. "And what happened?"

"Nothing. I slept in his bed and he slept in the other room." I replied with a half-truth. There was more, but I couldn't let the entire story out. "That's it. I woke up around noon and he was gone back to the city."

She clamped her mouth shut and eyed me suspiciously. Her bright blue eyes squinted at me and searched my face for a truth she couldn't find. She was my best friend and knew it was there. I held my composure and didn't back down. She wasn't getting the truth from me today, and I didn't know if she ever would.

She chewed her bottom lip, let go of my hands and shrugged her shoulders. "Okay, if that's what happened, I believe you. But if the story just so happens to magically change, I wouldn't be surprised."

"What story?" Dylan asked as he came down the hall and dried his hair with a white towel.

He was shirtless with his pants on and it reminded me of him in bed with another man. The white towel reminded me of the white bed sheet wrapped around his torso and he followed me with fear on his face. The fear of me exposing the truth about him and his lover. He couldn't have all the problems and troubles. But we wouldn't even be here if he could've just kept it in his pants.

"Oh, just the story of Nicholas and our magical night together." Paisley answered with ease and backed up my story. "But unfortunately, that's all it will ever be. One night of bliss."

"I remember those nights." Dylan said as his eyes shot towards mine and he flashed me a smile.

I flashed back the same smile, but it was all fake. Fake happiness all for Paisley and it would help her not question me further. But I knew he remembered his lover and not me.

"Aren't you two lovebirds so cute?" Paisley beamed as she looked from Dylan to me and I knew it was a coverup, but went along with it.

I went over towards Dylan, smiled up at him, and pecked his cheek. "You hear that, darling? We're just so cute."

He gave a small smile, but looked down at his phone that dinged. The screen lit up when he pushed the button. He read the message and looked at me. "Dad invited us all for dinner this evening at the Lint Liquor. It's perfect timing to celebrate our successful business deal. I'm famished. Aren't you famished, sweetie?"

"Absolutely starving, darling." I replied as we went our separate ways and I headed for my walk-in closet.

I stared at the racks of fancy dresses and had a hard time choosing one. My hands ran over each one, but I couldn't pick. My thoughts were somewhere else and a place I got lost in.

Images of Daxon ran through my mind and the enemy I shouldn't crave consumed me. The remembrance of his magnificent body and the strength he held as he carried me effortlessly into his arms. The smoothness of him as he pounded into me and my world spun into an unknown.

A place full of red, fervent desire I never wanted to come back from and stay locked in forever. A passion that burned so bright it brought me to the stars and blazed me back down to earth. Back to my stone-cold reality and away from him. I looked down at a shimmering silver dress in my hands and was suddenly famished. But for something forbidden.

***

We wandered into the beautiful restaurant of Lint Liquor, and I was nervous deep down inside. This was the first time I'd seen Daxon after our night of passion and our time I couldn't forget. A forbidden encounter that never should've happened and never would again.

I clasped my clammy hands together in front of my glimmering silver low cut dress. It showed off my magnificent cleavage, and I dared it to catch his eye. I wanted him to remember, even though he shouldn't. I shouldn't want him to, but our wicked games rolled on.

"Do you have reservations for this evening?" The server asked as he looked down at his list and smiled.

"We do actually..." Dylan replied as he looked around and touched his fresh tie. "Reservations should be under Daxon Stark."

His eyes didn't even look back down at the list, and he nodded his head. "Right this way, sir."

We followed him to the back of the restaurant where it was more dimly lit with candles on each table. Shadows cast on the walls from the brightly lit flames and created a calm atmosphere. It was something I needed to settle my nerves as

Daxon came in sight and he looked way too good. His charcoal suit hugged his perfect form and his hair looked darker in the dimmed room. He appeared younger, and I pondered what he was like in his youth. I couldn't envision him on the football team at high school or as a nerd in the chemistry lab. He didn't quite fit in and I was curious, but look where curiosity has led me. Straight into his damn bed.

I tore my thoughts away from him and focused on getting a seat. A place beside my husband to be and to keep up the dotting fiancée act. For the sake of everyone and the company. Too much was at stake and I knew it. I couldn't let his wicked game get to me or his deliciously perfect body.

But my eyes fell on her.

A beautiful young woman who I recognized from a time recently and knew exactly where. She was no older than me and her striking appearance I'd remember from anywhere. Even from inside a closet, hidden out of sight. Inside my future father-in-law's office, while he had her bent over his desk and gave her the best time of her life. Just like me.

I glared in his direction, and he met my glare. His eyes burned into mine and I knew the game was on. He brought her here to make me jealous. I was no longer nervous with the uncertainty of him, but seething with hot bitterness. Mr. Daxon Stark had another thing coming, and he was about to get it.

I flicked my hair and turned my attention towards his hot date. "Who's this beautiful woman in our presence?"

Daxon raised an eyebrow and looked at the gorgeous woman beside him. "This is my date for this evening. I believe you've met her at my office, Celeste?"

I blushed bright red and I could've sworn he chuckled deep in his chest, but he held his composure. He had to egg me on with the fact I caught them in the act and the secret remained between us. But it didn't mean he couldn't torture me with it, and that was exactly his plan.

Her eyes looked at me with uncertainty. "No, I don't believe we've met."

"Oh, I'm sorry. I must've gotten it mixed up with a client." He apologized as he shook his head, but he knew the damage was already done. "This is Charlotte Kin."

"Well, it's a pleasure to meet you, Charlotte." Paisley said as she threw herself into the mix and nodded at her from across the table. "How did you meet, Daxon?"

We all took our seats. Dylan sat beside me and Paisley to his left. But I had to sit right across from Daxon and his gorgeous date. Not by choice, either.

Her cheeks turned rosy pink, and she looked towards Daxon. "Oh, it was rather brief at a nearby café and we just took off from there."

Right into his office, bent over his desk, and he gave her the best time of her life.

I looked down at the menu and beamed towards them. "Sounds like a fairytale wedding could be around the corner?"

Dylan chuckled, but choked on his drink as he sipped. Everything went quiet, and I looked up at the reactions I had just created. Daxon looked at me with the usual look of annoyance, and his date blushed even brighter. She blinked several times, surprised, and took a sip of bubbling champagne. She probably was going to need it.

"I don't do marriage." Daxon answered sternly as he bit his bottom lip and looked me straight in the eyes. "I make sure every woman I'm with knows that."

His gaze glared with certainty and I couldn't help but feel he directed his answer at me. The directness in his tone was forward and straight to the point. If anyone else knew we slept together, they would've felt it too. But I was in this alone and had to put up with his craziness.

"I was only kidding. Relax." I laughed as I brushed off the awkwardness and filled up my champagne glass. "You should have a drink, daddy, you look a little tense."

He grinned my way and secretly teased me. "Fill me up, young lady."

I did as he instructed as everyone laughed off the joke and I filled his champagne glass all the way to the top. Soft bubbles trickled the sides of the clear glass and shimmered with the candlelight. It gave a naughty mix with the twisted atmosphere we played. A game we found ourselves lost in, but I wasn't willing to lose.

"Gosh, my feet hurt from these dreaded high heels..." I mumbled as I rubbed my feet and wanted the fun to begin. "Mind if I take them off?"

I looked around at everyone at the table, and no one rejected. So, I unwrapped the sash from around my ankles and released my feet from the pretty silver heels. But in truth, my devious plan was right on track.

"What are you going to order, darling?" Dylan asked me as he didn't look at me and down at his menu.

"I think I'll just get a steak for this evening." I asked as I looked over towards Charlotte and eyed her slim figure. "A meaty steak is delicious, Charlotte. Don't you agree?"

I inched my foot closer toward Daxon's side of the table. Carefully bringing my foot underneath the table for no one else to see. My toes connected with his pointy shoe and I continued upwards. I moved my toes gently up his leg as I watched Charlotte, but I felt his eyes on me and didn't dare look at him. Not just yet.

"I'm quite famished and couldn't agree more, Celeste." Charlotte replied as she smiled my way and looked over at her date. "Aren't you famished, Daxon?"

I didn't stop and kept grazing my toes up higher. Slowly caressing his leg as I went further and my eyes locked on him from across the table. A hint of lust blazed inside his gaze as our wicked game played out and my foot touched his crotch. I rubbed my foot against his dick and his eyes flickered with red fiery flames.

I ignited a beast, and he wanted to be freed.

His cock rose within his pants, and the firmness of him made me wet. So wet, I could've touched myself from underneath the table, but Dylan was beside me and I couldn't risk it. Daxon didn't fight it or close his legs. He didn't resist and let me play, let me torture him the same way he tortured me. But only he and I knew it.

"Famished indeed." Daxon replied with a husky tone, and only I knew his body melted with desire.

I continued my taunt, but he tore his eyes from me and it took all he had to smile politely at his date. She smiled seductively back at him and twirled her hair in between her fingers. He looked at her with certainty and touched her hair. But it made my blood boil when he leaned in and kissed her.

My foot froze on his cock as he took her lips passionately and dove his tongue inside. I remembered his kiss and the skill of his masterful tongue. But his evil gesture made me see red.

So, I clenched my toes down on his dick and twisted.

"Ouch!" He cried out against her lips.

I carefully pulled my foot away as the table shook and the glass clinked together. I sat bewildered by the event, but I knew the reason for it.

"Are you okay?" Charlotte asked with worry and touched his shoulder.

"Yes, I'm fine..." He breathed as he adjusted himself in his seat and briefly glared my way. "Just a pain in my side that won't screw off."

He pretended to rub the side of his hip, but they both knew it wasn't that. It didn't throb with pain like his dick did. The only thing on this gorgeous man with a brain.

"Shall we order and get this celebration started?" I beamed as I cupped my head between my hands and put on my happiest face.

Daxon smirked at me from across the table and leaned in closer. "We shall, but it has already begun."

NINETEEN
Sorry I Missed Your Call

I dropped Paisley off at the airport early this morning and it was an emotional send off. I was going to miss having her around and having my best friend by my side again was what I needed. Her comfort, support and just to shoot the shit like old times.

Girl time was fun, but having her help with the wedding planning was amazing. With Dylan's long hours at the office, it was nice to have someone's input other than my own second guessing. She was a nice sounding board, and I was going to miss that.

There was still a ton to do and the wedding must go on. Even though it was all a fake ass lie. He doesn't want to be with me and I thought I wanted to be with him. But I jumped into bed with his father and it made my head spin.

And now I was confused.

I knew Daxon and I couldn't be anything other than family, but his touch still clung to my skin. The sound of his groan echoed in my ears. But his perfectly fit body made me weak, and it didn't help with him around all the time.

Moving away wasn't an option. Dylan had to be close for business. Dear daddy would want his son close. He couldn't afford any fuck-ups.

I paced the office floor as I waited outside of Dylan and his father's office. My skin tight blue jeans hugged me and a low-cut purple blouse added to the fancy touch. I felt pretty today and put on a necklace that dangled on my neckline. My hair was up in a ponytail to keep my hair in check on this windy day.

Dylan was late as usual and he'd meet me here to discuss the latest on our big day. A day I dreaded because of everything that has happened. My wedding day.

I held ideas of decoration in my hands and heard the elevator ding. Dylan had made it to go over the decoration samples and I plastered a fake smile on my face. The act needed to continue for the sake of everything, no matter how much my heart ached for true happiness.

But it wasn't him.

I frowned as a younger man with blonde hair stepped off of the elevator and files of paperwork were in his hands. He walked my way as a handsome smile lit up his face, but his shoe caught on the rug. He tripped and the files of paperwork tumbled onto the expensive carpet.

"Ah, shit..." He cursed himself as he bent down to retrieve the papers and put them back into each file. I strolled over to him in a hurry and bent down to help, but he raised a hand. "No, it's okay. I can clean up my mess. Your beauty would distract me, anyway."

I stood back with disbelief by his forwardness and blinked at him. "Excuse me?"

He looked up at me as his blonde strands fell back into place and a grin was on his face. "You heard me right. You're gorgeous, Ms.?"

This young man's ego was enormous, but it flattered me. Catching my fiancé with another man really put a damper on my confidence. It made me question everything, but not when I was in Daxon's arms. His very toned and powerful embrace that I...

This needed to stop. I need to forget about that night and move on. I had to stop daydreaming about a man I could never have because I was marrying his son. Dylan agreed I could screw whoever I pleased and this fine specimen could make me forget both Stark men. Even just for a few minutes.

"I'm Ms. Lovette and you are?" I asked with a flirtatious purr in my tone.

"I'm Greg. It's a pleasure to meet you, Ms. Lovette." He said as he stood up and reached for my hand.

I took the kind gesture, but my other hand held the decoration samples and I thought of my engagement ring. I tucked my ring finger further behind the photographs so it would remain unseen. What he didn't know wouldn't hurt him. Besides, he appeared to be a man who just thought about his cock.

The perfect distraction.

His dark emerald eyes shimmered at me with nothing but lust, and I reached out to touch his black dress shirt. "So, what brings you here, Greg?"

"Oh, I just have some important paperwork to drop off for Mr. Stark." Greg answered as he looked me up and down. "But you distracted me."

I let out a small giggle and played with his shirt collar. The fabric was smooth between my fingers and he smelled of fresh laundry soap. It wouldn't surprise me if he did his laundry every day. But maybe his mom did it for him. He was that young, after all.

Suddenly, the elevator dinged once again, and I had no time to remove my hand. I glanced over Greg's shoulder to see Daxon come into view with another woman. This time, she looked closer to his age and probably dyed her brown hair. She hung off his arm and her hair was all tousled like she just had the time of her life. I knew that look and experienced it a couple of days ago. Now, I did nothing but regret it. The regret surged to the surface and red furious jealousy kicked in.

He was flaunting another woman in my face.

His eyes locked with mine as he passed by, and I saw the same cocky grin on his face. He knew how to get under my skin. And my god, did he ever. So much that I tore my eyes from him and knew I'd return the favor. He wanted to play this twisted game, and I was up for the challenge.

"Well, everyone needs a distraction every once in a while." I said loud enough for Daxon to hear and placed my hand on Greg's chest.

He smiled and laid a hand over mine. "Well, as much as I'd love to continue this, Mr. Stark is here. I should get these..."

He stepped towards Daxon, but I put a hand on his arm to stop him. We switched positions and Daxon was now back in view with his latest fuck. They must've had a lunch date and were wrapping it up in front of his office. I watched over Greg's shoulder as she leaned in for a goodbye kiss and he took her mouth with passion. My being bubbled hot with anger and my lips pressed together. I clenched my teeth inside my mouth and wanted to stomp over there. I wanted to create a scene and break them apart because his lips shouldn't be on another woman. They should be on me, and I wanted it more than anything.

Daxon consumed me. It brought out the worst in me. This jealous, angry woman that wanted revenge and I was going to get it.

My hand tightened around Greg's arm as Daxon kissed her, but he had the nerve to look at me. His deep brown eyes seared into mine as his tongue swirled around in her mouth and made my toes curl. He wanted me to be jealous; he wanted to flaunt his woman in front of me and forget we ever happened.

She finally ended the dreadful kiss and breathed her goodbye. "I had an amazing time, Daxon. Call me soon."

She let go of him as he watched her go and she strutted her stuff straight for the open elevator. Her black high heels clicked the floor and Daxon's eyes roamed over her backside. He grinned at her and didn't break eye contact with her until those elevator doors closed shut.

And his grin faded.

That same old annoyed look came back to life on his face as his teeth bit his lower lip and he ran his hand over his stubble. He didn't speak a word and let his game play out. His latest cunt didn't know she was a part of it and my latest specimen was about to be thrown into the mix. Revenge was bittersweet.

I pushed my anger aside and smiled seductively up at Greg. "So, what are your plans for this evening, Greg?"

A smile returned to his face. "I'm not sure, but what did you have in mind?"

"Well, I was thinking..." I breathed as I pulled him closer and placed his hand on my hip. "We could start with some drinks and see where it goes from there?"

He was so close his warm breath fanned my face, and I could smell fresh cappuccino. I ignored it and kept my eye on the prize, even though the smell was overwhelming. I wouldn't let Daxon win this round and he was the one who would squirm.

"Well, that sounds..." Greg whispered close to my ear and touched my ponytail. "Very intriguing, Ms. Lovette."

My vengeful glare lands on Daxon, and I grin his way with power. His hands were at his sides and clenched into fists. The knuckles were white with rage and I knew he seared with jealousy. It oozed from him, and I didn't need him to admit it. His body language gave it away.

He stepped forward with frustration and tapped Greg on the shoulder. I stepped back and prided myself on a job well-done. Greg turned around, with confusion written all over his face. Poor guy didn't realize he was being played.

"Is that paperwork for me?" Daxon glanced down at Greg's files and back at his face.

"Yes, sir it is." Greg responded, and he looked at Mr. Stark.

Daxon grabbed the paperwork and gripped the man's shirt collar. He pulled him in so quickly it caused me to jump. His face was only mere inches from Daxon's, and the tension in the hallway thickened. Daxon was in control and for some reason, this jealousy he presented turned me on.

"Good..." Daxon glared as he pushed Greg backwards and fumed with anger. "Get the hell out of my office."

Greg didn't waste any time and hurried towards the elevator. I heard the door ding open, but didn't bother to look back. He was just part of the plan, and it worked out perfectly. The tension blazed between us as we looked at each other. His chest puffed out with every breath he took, and he looked like he wanted to take me over his knee. But it was time to face off with my worst enemy.

"You shouldn't be carrying on like this in the public eye, young lady." He warned as he stood right in front of me and his eyes blazed.

"And why is that?" I asked as I crossed my arms in front of me and challenged him.

"Because you're marrying my son!" He yelled as his voice echoed down the hallway and he ripped the pictures from my hand. "Does this mean nothing to you?"

He held the decoration samples up and slammed them down on a nearby table. The look of rage gleamed in his eyes and he frightened me for a moment, but I pushed it away. I wouldn't let him get his way. Especially when Dylan granted me permission to sleep with whomever I pleased.

Daxon didn't need to know that. It would only make it worse. And it appeared he needed a little reminder of the monster he truly was.

"It sure as hell meant nothing to you when you fucked me the other night." I snapped back at him.

I twisted the tables on him, and he was stunned. His reaction was like I slapped him across the face. The reality of what we'd done came back full force, and he pressed his lips together. His long body moved forward, and I had no choice but to move back.

"And that's all it was, Celeste, nothing." Daxon huffed heavily as he didn't stop his movement and cornered me in the hallway. "Nothing but a meaningless fuck."

My backside was up against the marble wall, and I had nowhere to go. Nowhere to turn, but into his arms. I couldn't think straight because all I breathed in was him. The sparks flew, and he captured me. Unable to break free, but I still had my voice.

"And I don't know who's better at making me come?" I urged him on with bitterness. "You or your son?"

Suddenly, my cell phone vibrated in my pocket, and it broke the spell. I reached for it while Daxon backed off and I looked down at the screen. It was Dylan.

"It's your son..." I mumbled as I went to answer the call, but Daxon snatched the phone from my hands. "What the hell, Daxon?"

"You want to know who's better at making you come undone?" Daxon breathed as he got close to me with an arm over my head and his elbow pressed against the wall. "Daddy is."

Without warning, he travelled the vibrating phone down my cleavage and I froze. He made the phone move lower over each nipple and they pierced against my blouse. They stood erect against the sensation and my breath shuttered.

"What the hell do you think you're doing, Daxon?" I asked, as I couldn't move and let him do his worst.

"You know exactly what I'm doing, princess." Daxon teased with a dirty tone. "I'm going to make you scream."

I reached out and clenched his shirt collar as he looked down at his wickedness and pressed his forehead against mine. His breath hitched as he brought the cellphone lower and his son tried to call me continuously on the other end. He probably pondered why I wouldn't pick up. But little did he know his father was pleasuring me on the other end.

The vibrations kept going as he pressed it against my pussy and had his way with me. He wanted to see me come undone his way and no one else's. He wanted me to cry out his name with his son's phone call.

"Oh, yes..." I breathed as his lips brushed mine and my climax built quickly.

My adrenaline raced at the thought of one wrong move, and the call could connect. My fiancé would be on the line and hear my pleasurable cries of lust for his father. It didn't scare me, it never confused me, and it just aroused me.

"Oh, yes, Daxon..." I moaned with passion as my hips thrust against the phone and the vibrations sent me spiraling.

I spun into a hole of red, fiery lust. The passion ignited through my flesh and burned deep inside. It bubbled and pushed its way out. My release climbed higher and higher.

He rubbed it against my clit even faster, teased me with it, and the vibrations stopped. Dylan must've given up, but Daxon didn't. His lips locked with mine in a heated frenzy, but the phone vibrated again. This time in different time increments.

He was sending me text messages.

They came quicker and closer together. The vibrations did me in, and I circled my pussy against the phone. I couldn't get enough. It came one after the other as Daxon bit my lower lip and I lost it in his arms.

"Oh, yes, Daxon, yes!" I screamed out as my shout of release echoed down the hallway and I climaxed on the spot.

Daxon let my lip go and whispered in sexual frustration. "I'll be the only man to make you lose all control."

He placed the cellphone in my weak hand as it fell to my side and I needed the wall for support. My panties were soaking wet and my entire body trembled from the sensual escapade. Daxon knew he held all the power over me and he proved it. I could no longer deny what he did to me, and I wanted so much more. I craved it.

I wanted daddy to take me right here.

The vibrations ended, and I put the cell phone back in my pocket. I ignored Dylan and didn't give a fuck. All I wanted to do was fuck Mr. Daxon Stark right here on this hallway floor. And I didn't give a damn who found us.

I reached out for him, but he backed away from me. He released me from his sensual hold, and I wanted nothing more than to tuck my way back inside. For him to take me in his arms and never let me go.

But his eyes turned cold.

He put up the annoyed front like he always did with me and licked his lower lip. His teeth clenched it within their grasp and he grabbed the decoration samples. He brought them to me and put them back in my hands.

"You make me do shit I shouldn't do." Daxon whispered huskily and touched my lips. "But I can't deny the monster that's inside me when it comes to you, princess."

His fingers dropped from my lips, and he turned his back to me. All I could do was stand there and watch him walk away. But the elevator gave one final ding.

And Dylan got off of it.

Daxon looked at him and Dylan peered back. He held his cell phone in his hand and that's when I remembered his call. The one that made me tumble over the edge of ecstasy.

"Dylan..." I said as soon as I found my voice and pushed the shock of him aside. "You're late again, darling."

He looked away from his father and walked towards me. "And I was trying to call you. Why the hell weren't you picking up?"

My eyes shot to Daxon, and he peered back at me. There was no fear on his face. No shame in what he had just done with his son's fiancé. But instead, desperation to cover it up.

"Oh, that's my fault son." Daxon announced as he stepped forward and patted his son's shoulder. "Your fiancée was showing me the pictures of..."

"Decoration samples..." I interrupted as I finished his sentence and covered up the bold-faced lie. "For our wedding, darling. Remember? The one that you're late for."

"Yes, I know and I'm sorry." He apologized as he kissed my cheek and put his arm around me. "I fell behind with work."

I knew it was complete and utter bullshit. He fell into bed with his lover. Again.

Who was I to judge when I was climaxing in his father's arms?

Daxon looked at us, and his face was expressionless. He continued to play this game with me, and I always fell right into it. He wanted to make me jealous, and it worked. I did the same thing, and it sent him over the edge. Enough so, his wicked torment with me continued, and here we were. But I wasn't finished with him just yet.

"Your father brought back a fabulous-looking woman from a lunch date earlier. She screamed marriage potential." I said as I changed the subject and knew it would strike a nerve.

"Oh, really?" Dylan asked as he raised an eyebrow and looked at his father. "This one wasn't just for pleasure?"

"They always are, son." He glared as he looked at me and snapped. "I'm never settling down and have no plans to."

I raised an eyebrow and huffed. "Well, try it sometime. It's the best kind of pleasure to share with someone you love. It's something me and my fiancé will do tonight."

Suddenly, Dylan laughed and threw me off guard. His laughter echoed through the hallway and left me confused. He let go of me and put his hands up in front of him. This wasn't a joke, this was war.

Why the fuck was that so funny?

"Okay, as funny as this was, the tension between you two is too much. If Celeste and I are going to get married, you both need to learn how to get along with each other." Dylan announced with sincerity and got serious. "We can't have you getting into a fight in public because you're going to be family soon enough."

"How can I get along with an insufferable man like your father, who just thinks of himself?" I snapped and stood my ground. "I tolerate him as much as I can."

Daxon puffed out his chest and was ready to speak, but Dylan interrupted him. "And that's why I'm sending you both away on a trip together. You can bond and get whatever tension this is out before the wedding."

"But, Dylan I..." I argued.

"But son, she..." Daxon huffed.

"There are no arguments and you're both going." Dylan said firmly as he reached into his pocket and held out two tickets. "You leave first thing tomorrow for a beautiful cabin tucked away in the woods. No distractions. You can learn to rely on each other and get along. Understood?"

I sighed and took the ticket from his hand. "Understood."

Daxon cleared his throat and tucked the ticket into his suit jacket pocket. "Understood, son."

Daxon's eyes locked with mine and we couldn't stop our frustrated glare at each other. I knew he was thinking what I was thinking. This was a terrible idea.

TWENTY
Stuck Together

Dylan's plan to bring Daxon and I closer began, but he had no idea how close we'd actually gotten. The secret we've kept from him and the game we've played. But because of our heated tension, it has brought us to this moment.

Stuck on a first-class flight and headed straight for the mountains.

It was an early flight and Dylan couldn't see us off. We rode the limousine together in silence, and the awkwardness bit like a knife. No arguments, no disagreements, and no butting heads. But the tension still loomed in the air and was hard to ignore.

Neither one of us looked forward to this mini vacation to be friendly, but when it came down to it, it forced us to try. We were going to be stuck in a cabin up in the woods together, and Dylan insisted on pictures of us. He wanted to see our progress for himself. There was no way out of this and we could only get through it. Together.

I sighed as I tugged at my carry-on in the overhead cabinet, but it wouldn't budge. "Could this get any worse?"

"Do you need a hand, princess?" Daxon asked from beside me and leaned against the airplane seat. "As amusing as this is, Dylan is calling us in less than ten minutes to check in."

"I'm fine." I mumbled with stubbornness and pulled some more.

It must be stuck on something and if I was taller, this wouldn't be a problem. I didn't need his help, especially when these were his first words to me in hours. I wasn't in the mood for his stupid games.

I tugged harder with anger at this entire situation and the bag gave way with no warning. It rushed out of the compartment and flew straight at my face. I cried out in surprise and expected it to collide with my head. My eyes closed, and I braced myself for impact, but it never came.

I peeked through one eyelid, and I was floored. Daxon held my carry-on in his hands with a smirk on his much too handsome face. He was so close I could smell his expensive cologne I was able to recognize from all of our close encounters. I hated to admit it, but it was growing on me.

"Your stubbornness is going to get you nowhere except a spanking, young lady." Daxon breathed as his face turned serious and he peered down at me with intensity.

I raised my eyebrow and shot back. "And who's giving me a spanking? Would that be you, daddy?"

He got so close and his eyes smoldered. "Only if you're naughty, princess."

My pussy shivered at his husky words of promise and my panties grew wet. Daxon hated disobedience, and I wanted to break the rules. His eyes spoke to me, and my body wanted more. I pushed his limits, tested them. I wanted to see how far I could push him until he broke.

Suddenly, Daxon's cell phone chimed, and it stunned him back to reality as he passed my carry on into my arms. He pulled the phone out of his jacket pocket and we looked down at the screen. It was Dylan.

"Are you ready to play nice, princess?" Daxon asked as his eyebrow rose and he peered down at me.

"Do I really have a choice?" I snapped back as Daxon growled at me and hit the accept button.

Dylan's face appeared with him in his office chair and paperwork at his desk. He was back at the office and a place I longed to be. Anywhere other than here, trapped with the only man who got under my skin.

"There you both are." Dylan said as he smiled and wrote something on the paper in front of him. "How's it going so far? Are you both getting along?"

"It's going great, darling." I lied with a fake smile.

"Fantastic! The mountains should do you both good. It's cold, secluded and beautiful. It will bring you two closer." Dylan said with enthusiasm.

"That's just great!" I beamed with a fake front and cursed it all.

This was a horrible plan.

"Well, we just landed and the limousine will be waiting." Daxon said as he wanted to cut the call short and I secretly thanked him for it. "We'll be in touch, son."

"Okay, dad..." Dylan breathed as he picked up the phone and his face went blurry. "Take care of my future wife and don't forget to send me pictures of your progress."

"If there's any progress at all..." Daxon grumbled and didn't lie.

But we didn't need Dylan to know that.

I grabbed the phone from Daxon's hands and wobbled it. It made the screen fuzzy and our image unrecognizable. Daxon reached for it, but I fought him off.

"D-Dylan you... Breaking up..." I faked as the phone shook and I tried to wrap this horror show up. "We've got.... Go now... Bye."

I hit the end button before he could speak another word. We needed to keep this trip positive and Daxon just about ruined it. This entire situation had a bad ending written all over it and didn't need his truth leaking through now. The sooner this was over, the better for us all.

"What the hell was that all about, Celeste?" Daxon growled and grabbed his phone from my hands.

"We don't need you sneaking the truth in there. We need to fake it until we make it. Got it?" I snapped and pointed my index finger at him.

"You surprise me every day, princess." Daxon smirked as he looked at my finger and back at my face with enlightenment.

I cleared my throat. "Good, now let's go find our ride and get this show on the road."

I turned my back to him and felt his eyes on my backside. It blazed with heat and sizzled through my clothes. It travelled over my skin and left me bare. Naked for only him as I shivered under his stare, but didn't dare look back. I'd be lost in him, and I needed to stay focused. He could do me in and I knew it. I needed to make it out of this in one piece.

We got off the plane and went down the steps. A long limousine was on the airport tarmac and I knew it was our ride out of here. Our luxurious ride into the mountains was all set up by my future father-in-law's son. A getaway for two meant to bring us closer when we should be further apart. But fate had other plans.

I slide into the limousine and let the leather seat form to my backside. The smooth leather was a relief from the airplane seats. First class was lavish, but I hated the seats. There was only so much comfort someone could create on an aircraft. A smaller object up against gravity and an entire sky.

I closed my eyes to relax my mind and could hear Daxon talk to the driver with directions. I left him in charge of everything because I didn't want to be here, but someone had to be in on the plan. Someone had to know Dylan's instructions on how this would play out. He organized it after all and we just had to follow his plan. Follow through until it was all over and we could get back to our lives.

I felt him sit down on the seat beside me and heard his door slam shut. The trunk opened and weighed down a bit with the rest of our luggage, but soon closed shut. I blew out a breath and heard the engine come to life. I just had to tell myself this would all be over soon, but I knew I lied to myself. Everything about this was one big fat fake, and I was stuck right in the middle of it. Right along with my fiancé's father.

***

I tensely peered out the window as the limousine climbed the mountain side carefully. It took extra precaution, and the driver informed us of the narrow roadway before we hit it. I had a good view of the steep decline down the side of the mountain from my side of the limousine, but it wreaked havoc on my nerves.

"Why the hell did he have to pick a death trap?" I mumbled with unease as the limousine climbed higher and I played with my hands in my lap.

Daxon looked over at me and smugly smiled. "He's your fiancé."

"And he's your son." I snapped and returned the sarcasm.

He huffed, and I knew I had made my point. I expected him to argue with me as per usual, but he kept his mouth shut. It surprised me and I wanted to tease the issue just to get on his nerves. But I let it go. I took pride in the fact I had made him speechless for just this once.

Even though the view made me uneasy, the scenery was beautiful. It captivated me as we rode higher up the mountain and the snow lightly dusted the ground. But as we went higher, it got thicker on the landscape.

It blanketed the terrain, and everything was white. There was an odd color here and there, with the grey sky high above. Snow didn't drop from the sky, but it appeared it could open up at any moment. And from the way it looked, it would produce a heavy snowfall.

Soon the road stopped its continuous curve and straightened up into a line. We headed into a thick forest of trees covered with snow everywhere I looked. There wasn't a single vehicle in sight for miles, and it was very secluded. Just like Dylan had promised, and my stomach knotted at the thought. I knew it would be just the two of us, but figured there would be someone way out here. Dylan wasn't fucking around and he wanted us to focus with no other distractions. In any ideal dysfunctional relationship, this would make sense, but to add the pent-up sexual tension. It called for an avalanche down the rocky mountainside.

It was a very clear day for such a cloudy one as the limousine turned left and onto a single paved road. Up ahead, my eyes caught sight of a beautiful cabin right in the woods. The wooden log structure was stunning and vast, with enormous windows. It was an expensive appearance for a cabin in the woods and not all what I expected.

A small barn was off to the side of it and it made my mind turn as to what was inside. It wasn't like a usual farm barn, but sturdier. It was hardy and ready for the colder weather. The identical cabin next to it had no windows.

The limousine pulled up out front and put on the brakes as it gave my head a slight jerk. The driver opened Daxon's door and went to retrieve our luggage from the trunk. I was about to open my door when Daxon opened it for me and ushered me out of the vehicle.

The driver placed our luggage by the front door while I admired the structure's beauty. It was even more fabulous up close. Even though I hate the thought of spending one moment here with this egotistical asshole, I could get used to the seclusion.

I wandered over towards the luggage to get my stuff and heard the limousine pull away. My eyes narrowed as I looked towards three items and something was missing. There was my carry on, Daxon's carry on, and his luggage.

But where was mine?

"Um, where's all my stuff?" I asked as I pointed towards the pile and put my other hand on my hip.

"Yes, about that..." Daxon breathed as he took his carry on and unhooked the handle for his luggage. "We ran into a bit of a problem."

"A problem?" I asked with annoyance. "What problem, Daxon?"

"They couldn't locate your luggage at the airport when we landed." He admitted as he took out the key to unlock the cabin and put his hands out in front of him. "Your luggage got lost."

"Lost!" I exclaimed in disbelief. "This is just great!"

"Now, calm down, Celeste..." Daxon urged.

"Calm down?" I glared angrily and threw my hands up in the air. "We're both stuck here when neither one of us wants to be. To make matters worse, I have no clothes and it's freezing up here!"

I rubbed my arms with my hands and wished I hadn't worn my winter coat. I only had a long sleeve shirt on with jeans and now I cursed myself. They lost all my stuff except for the tiny bit I had packed in my carry on and I grabbed it with attitude.

"Don't worry, it will all work out." Daxon said as he tried to reassure me, but it didn't help.

"That's easy for you to say because you have all your damn luggage." I shot back. "Why didn't you tell me at the airport?"

"Because I knew you'd lose your shit like you just did." Daxon admitted as he shrugged his shoulders and came closer towards me.

"Well, no shit, daddy..." I mumbled with defeat.

"Listen, I laid into the driver and told him it's unacceptable." He sighed with understanding. "I told him to get the luggage to me right away or else he wouldn't have a job to go back to."

His words helped calm my angry unease. "Really? Did he say when it will be here?"

"He said no later than early tomorrow morning." Daxon explained.

I nodded my head and processed it. "Okay, thank you. I appreciate you standing up for me, Daxon."

I admitted my gratitude to him and laid my hand on his chest. He looked down at it and back into my eyes. His eyes swirled with something unreadable, and I wished I knew what he thought. My hand burned when I touched him and I wondered if he felt it, too. I quickly removed my hand from him and still couldn't believe he stuck up for me.

"Anything for you, princess." He whispered as he turned away from me and I could barely make out the words.

He unlocked the door, and we went inside. We stood there, side by side and took in our getaway. The living area was big and bright, but the floor to ceiling windows helped with that. The furnishings were all distinct tones of brown and gave it a true cabin vibe. I loved every bit, and the fireplace was huge. It stretched across the wall of the room and behind it was the modern kitchen. A huge island took over the middle with a sink right front and center. The gas stove was on the other side of the kitchen counter and they finished it in black sparkle granite. A built-in refrigerator and dishwasher matched the dark wood cabinets. It was a luxurious sight.

"I've got to hand it to my son..." Daxon breathed as he stood in the kitchen and took it all in. "This is really nice."

I followed him as he led the way back down a hallway towards bedrooms that we could choose from. I counted and there were at least five. Lots to pick from and I planned on picking the one farthest away from Daxon.

"I think you should take the one closest to the kitchen and I'll take the last one down the hall." I suggested as I looked at him and he looked back at me. "You know, maintain some distance?"

Daxon came closer, and it made me anxious. I swallowed hard and felt unsteady on my own two feet. His scent surrounded me and it mixed with the pine tree's sap from outside.

"It's a good idea, except for one problem." He mumbled as he tucked a strand of hair behind my ear and it made me shiver.

"Oh, ya? And what's that?" I asked as I licked my lips from the dry air and realized it was a mistake.

His eyes darted towards them. "We're all alone up here, princess. We should keep close because I couldn't let anything happen to you."

His admission threw me off-guard and I couldn't form a witty comeback even if I tried. His fingers caressed my cheek and trailed down my neckline. I quivered inside with lust at the remembrance of his tantalizing touch. I couldn't look away from his intensity even though I knew I should, but he captivated me. With him this close, there was no going back.

"Try as I might, princess, I can't stop thinking about you." Daxon whispered in the cabin's silence, and his thumb caught my bottom lip. "I can't fathom being away from these delicious lips."

Suddenly, Daxon's cell phone dinged, and I snapped out of his entrapment. I stepped back and pressed my lips together as I looked down towards the floor. He pulled me in and shared with me a truth I couldn't wrap my head around. Daxon still craved me as much as I did him, but it couldn't be and shouldn't be. We both knew it, too.

I glanced at him as he tore his eyes from me and peered down at his cellphone. "Dylan wants his first picture of us together."

I licked my lips at the remembrance of his touch and wanted to give in. I wanted to send my fiancé a quick snap of our lips locked together and get this all over with. All the lies, the secret acts, and false promises. I was tired of it. Damn it all to hell.

But I knew the stakes were too high. There was too much to lose. Too many hearts to break and too much truth to unfold.

The secrets continue.

I gave a small smile and straightened my stride over towards a fireplace in one bedroom. I could hear his curious footsteps behind me on the dark hardwood as he followed my lead and my gaze. The flames flicked and licked the glass. A red, orange and yellow glow.

"Why not right here?" I instructed as I pointed towards the fire and admired its beauty.

"It's cozy, comforting and a great way to show us getting along."

Daxon gave a brief nod and fell beside me. "Smile like you mean it."

I flung my arm over his shoulder in a friendly daughter-in-law stance and hoped for the best. I smiled up towards the camera as Daxon held the cellphone high and snapped a selfie to send. The photograph was cute and straight to the point. It showed us having a blast, even though the flames grew out of control between us.

I pulled away from Daxon as soon as it was over and gained some space. "So, I guess I'll take this room."

I dropped my carryon on the comforter and walked towards the window. The drawn curtains showed a gorgeous view, and it was breathtaking. Some snow dropped from the branches and fell to the earth below. It revealed green pine trees underneath and bare tree branches. I breathed in the woodsy smell and wished I was anywhere else but here. Only because his dark eyes drank me in from behind me.

I heard a zipper and spun around. Daxon laid out a long sleeve dress shirt on the bed. It was white, and I bet it smelled just like him.

"You can wear this for bed until your clothes arrive tomorrow morning." He instructed as he pointed at the neatly pressed shirt and looked at me.

"Okay..." I whispered with ease at his order. "Whatever daddy wants, daddy gets."

His eyes looked me over and my body melted under his stare. He didn't dare come any closer, and I was thankful he didn't because I couldn't take it. I knew he pictured me with only his dress shirt on. The coolness of it touched my skin as it flowed just past my tight ass and displayed my clean-shaven legs.

He cleared his throat and tore his eyes away from me. "I'll... Um... Take the next room beside yours, then?"

"Sounds like a plan." I smiled briefly, but pondered. "So, what happens next?"

Daxon looked down at his phone and asked me. "Do you like horses?"

"They are beautiful creatures." I answered his question.

"That's an excellent answer, because Dylan has horseback riding planned in the snow." Daxon explained as he tucked his phone away and turned his back to me.

"What?" I asked with disbelief.

I followed behind him to the next room and my nerves kicked back into high gear. Everything about this getaway has turned out to be an anxious wreck and my anxiety was at an all-time high. I had just about enough of Dylan's plans and was ready to forget the whole mess.

"You heard me right." Daxon said firmly as he laid his luggage on the floor beside the bed and turned to look at me. "Dylan wants us to go horseback riding together, princess."

"I'm not getting on a horse." I said stubbornly and crossed my arms in front of me. "This is absurd."

"So, you're telling me you've never been on a horse before?" Daxon said as he came closer and raised an eyebrow. "I figured my princess would've ridden before?"

I knew a challenge when I saw one and Daxon was setting one up. His demeanor oozed confidence, and he wanted to win the battle. But I would not let him have his way.

"Oh, get off your high horse and show me where these damn horses are." I snapped as I waved him through and followed him through the cabin.

We entered a foyer, and there were racks with extra winter coats. I took one since they lost mine with my luggage and grabbed a pair of riding gloves. I was sure I would need these, and they were very warm inside.

Daxon zipped up his coat, and we headed out the side door with the fancy barn within our sight. I pushed through the ankle-deep snow and hoped it didn't tumble into my boots. I tried to follow in his footsteps in the snow, but his strides were much larger than mine. His long legs swiftly made it through the snow and he pulled the locked latch open. The barn doors opened wide and two horses were inside their warm stalls. Straw hay laid at their feet and their stalls appeared to be spotless. The owner must've been here before our stay to ensure everything was ready for our arrival, and it impressed me.

"I expected to see shit in their stalls, if I'm being honest." I admitted as I watched Daxon work at getting the saddles ready and getting everything we needed.

Daxon laughed. "So, did I. Here, grab one."

I went to take the saddle, but retreated. "I don't know the first thing about riding a horse."

"Well, I guess you'll have to get on with me then." Daxon admitted as he opened one stall and hooked up a saddle to a white horse.

"What? No way." I grumbled as I shook my head and waved my hands in front of me.

"I'll teach you how to ride." Daxon offered as he held out his hand and offered to help me on the horse. "I won't bite. I'll even let you sit at the front."

I just shook my head repeatedly. "This is a bad idea."

"We need to get this picture for Dylan. What choice do you have?" Daxon urged as he grabbed my hand and pulled me towards the horse. "Come on, daddy's orders."

Daxon meant business and hoisted me up onto the horse's saddle in one swift motion. He lifted me like I was a feather and I gasped at his strength. I sat on top of the white creature and held on tight. I was frightened I'd fall, but Daxon hoisted himself up behind me and wrapped his powerful arms around me. He grabbed the reins and held them up towards me. He used one hand while the other wrapped around my waist and held me close so I wouldn't fall. I felt safe and protected within his embrace.

"I taught Dylan how to horseback ride when he was just a kid." He breathed in my ear as he steered the magnificent white creature out of the barn and into the snow.

The warmth of his breath against me made me relax into him and I loved the way his body felt up against mine. I shouldn't, but I couldn't help it. He was so close, and everything else melted away.

The horse trotted slowly through the snow, and Daxon directed it where he wanted it to go. I noticed he pulled the reins to instruct the animal on which direction to take. He was very good with the horse and a decent rider. I had to give him credit for where it was due. I knew absolutely nothing about horseback riding, but I was sure Daxon would teach me.

Daxon made a short clicking sound and gently kicked it with the back of his heel. The horse kicked into a higher gear and took off. My head jerked, and I held onto the reins with Daxon. The body of the horse moved below us as it galloped through the snow. It was unlike any other feeling I had experienced before. The wind whipped through my wavy hair and blew it back behind me. It moved faster as the trees went by and the speed was remarkable. Daxon still wrapped his arm tightly around me and held me close. His solid form was flush up against my back and our bodies moved like one with the rocking horse.

"Pull the reins to the left, princess." He breathed in my ear and put his hand over mine. "We're going to go deeper into the woods."

I did as he instructed and laughed as the wind changed direction as we moved. The horse picked up speed and its white coat moved with the wind speed. Not a single snowflake was in the air, but snow fell from the branches above. I wasn't afraid anymore and quickly got the hang of it.

"How do I make it go faster?" I asked over my shoulder.

He ran his hand up my thigh. "You squeeze your legs together and whip the reins."

The sensation of his hand on my thigh made me look down. He ran it along my inner thigh and stopped just before my sweet spot. He let his arm curve around me once again, and I did as he instructed.

My legs squeezed against the creature, and I whipped the reins. The horse picked up pace, and the world flew by. I did it again because my adrenaline raced and I couldn't get enough. The horse let out a short neigh, and I felt in complete control.

Daxon tightened his grip around me and gave a stern warning in my ear. "You're going too fast! Slow the damn horse down or else I'm taking over!"

But I refused to listen, and the reign took over. "Not this time, daddy. I'm in charge now."

Suddenly, out of nowhere, a deer cut out of the woods and spooked the horse. My eyes went agape as the deer got out of the way in time, but the horse wasn't so lucky. It halted abruptly and threw itself up onto its hind legs. Thrashing its forelegs up in the air with fear as I lost my grip and fell from the horse. I fell in slow motion with no time to think and nothing to grab onto but air.

And I hit the snow with a hard thump.

TWENTY-ONE
Punish Me

Daxon grabbed the reins of the horse as it let out a terrified neigh into the brisk air and the animal's forelegs fell to the ground. It had trouble calming down and Daxon pulled on the reins to gain back control. He redirected the spooked horse, and it trotted from side to side. He settled it down and could get the horse tied safely to a nearby tree.

"Celeste!" He cried out as he raced to my side to check on me and found me within the snowy ground.

I groaned, and snow covered my face as I felt him scoop me up into his protective arms. He wiped the snow from my face with his gloved hand and pushed my frozen hair back with a shaky hand. I blinked several times as the world stopped spinning and his face came into view. I was unsure if he was worried about me or if he caught a chill until I saw his eyes.

The concern he held for me swirled within them and he stroked my cheek. "Are you okay?"

His voice trembled with fear, and his worry for me threw me for a loop. One minute we were butting heads and the next it forced us to get close. Revealing his true nature and the genuine feelings he held for me.

"I-I'm okay, just shaken up." I admitted.

But confused as fuck.

I wanted to stand, but my legs wouldn't work. The shock kicked in and everything was freezing. My body vibrated within his arms and I was frozen. The wet snow that covered me was now frozen on my body and parts of my exposed skin. My teeth chattered together from the sudden temperature drop and I was sure my lips would turn blue.

"We've got to head back and get you warmed up." He said with worry and lifted me up into his arms. "It's okay, princess. I've got you."

His strength held me tight as he untied the horse from the tree and talked to it softly. "It's okay, boy..."

The soothing tone of it kept the horse relaxed as he hoisted us both up and we sat on top of the horse. He held me close, and I buried my frozen face against his warmth. He tucked me safely away in his embrace and kicked the horse with the back of his heel. We took off as the wind whistled in my ears and the air was even colder. My teeth chattered as I held on tightly and he gave the reins a yank. The horse jolted ahead faster, and the world flew by as I peeked out beneath his embrace.

It was snowing.

White snowflakes fell from the grey sky as they had opened up and gave away mother nature's gift. The surprise of a snowfall and it got heavier as we went. The cold flakes touched my face, but hurt as they came down faster with our increased speed. But I needed to get warm, and being out in this blizzard wasn't helping.

The blustered flurries raged on and covered my eyes until I couldn't see. The thick white mass was wet on my face and accumulated quickly. I tried to tuck myself in closer to his warmth, but it was no use.

"D-Daxon, I'm scared..." I whispered as my teeth chattered and I vibrated against his body. "I-I'm so cold."

"I know, princess!" He exclaimed over the winds that blew and pulled me closer to help shield me from the storm. "Hold on, we're almost there!"

His words tried to soothe me, but it wasn't enough. I was so unbelievably cold. I had never been this chilled in my entire life and time wasn't on my side. It seemed to drag on as I tried to remember how far we galloped into the snowy woods, but I couldn't. I had lost track of time with him and it was so much fun until it wasn't.

The horse slowed down as Daxon guided the horse past evergreen trees and a familiar barn came into view. It was smaller, but came closer with each stride of the horse's legs. I felt relieved we made it back, and we weren't lost.

Daxon wiped off his face of the access snow and steered the horse through the barn doors. I knew I should've felt the warmth, but with my temperature drop I couldn't. The heat should be there, but I just couldn't feel it yet.

"I-I'm numb, Daxon..." I stumbled to get the words out. "S-so c-cold."

He got the white beauty into its stall, and he brought us down from the horse. He grabbed a blanket from nearby and laid me down inside it. It wrapped around me as my body trembled and hay got in my hair, but I didn't care. I just needed to get warmed up and Daxon tried everything in his power to do so.

The blanket covered me as he carried me out of the barn and into the blizzard. He shielded me from the worst as he pushed on and locked up the barn. He raced across to the side of the house as my body bounced with his and he got me inside. I peeked through the blanket as his chest puffed against me and he dashed for the nearest bedroom.

The lights weren't on and it was dim inside the room from the snow cover outside. It blanketed the windows and blocked any light from coming through, but the fire within the bedroom blazed. It created a dim glow as it hit the bed sheets and Daxon sat me down.

"We need to get you warmed up." Daxon said as he took my head in his hands and cupped my face. "Do you trust me, princess?"

I searched his eyes for the strength I needed and found it within them as I whispered. "Yes."

He helped me out of my clothes. The wet layers shed from me, and he tossed them in front of the fire on the floor. He didn't waste a second and raced to get my temperature back up. The only thing he left on was my tan bra and panties to match. He peeled back the sheets and laid me inside them. They covered me from head to toe and I listened to a rustling sound. A flurry of unfamiliar sounds and a race against time. But soon he pulled back the sheets and got underneath with me.

In only his boxer briefs.

He pulled the sheets over our heads and moved in closer. His skin was on mine as he pulled me closer and he surrounded us in darkness. The blackness let up a bit as our eyes adjusted to the change and I could see him reach out towards me.

He brushed strands of hair behind my ears and breathed. "Turn around, princess."

I obeyed and turned so my backside was towards him. He got even closer to me and wrapped his body around mine. I could slowly feel his heat mingle with my chilled being and I shivered against him.

"We need to bring up your body heat so you don't go into shock." Daxon explained into my ear as his hands wrapped around me and the heat rose between us.

He caressed my arms I had pulled into my body and tucked myself into the fetal position. He covered me like a warm blanket and tucked me in. Even though we were already underneath sheets and a comforter.

I closed my eyes and trembled, but it slowly subsided. The fear had once consumed me, but went away and my body relaxed against his. My body heat steadily rose and with it an arousal took over me. It shouldn't, but I couldn't help it with him this close. So, close it connected us as one to mix our temperatures and become the same heat.

He moved slightly and brushed my hair away from my ear. His fingers sweetly touched my earlobe and his warm, labored breath caressed the side of my face. My skin burned where his eyes searched me, and tingles formed over me. I noticed his nearness and got lost in him like I normally did. Daxon just affected me in ways no other man could, and I couldn't get enough of him.

I heard him clear his throat, and he whispered in my ear. "Do you feel better now, princess?"

And I responded. "I always feel better in your arms, daddy."

His fingertip brushed my ear and circled it. "I don't like it when you disobey me, princess."

His other hand ran down the side of my body, and electricity coursed through me. My breath hitched right along with his as he discovered me and the moment spun out of control. His hand landed on my ass cheek and his fingers circled it. I couldn't deny him, and he didn't want me to.

His words of being disobedient echoed in my head and I remembered the way I acted on the horse. I didn't listen to him and was reckless. It caused an accident that shouldn't have happened if I had only listened to him. But I didn't and now a threat loomed between us.

I peered over my shoulder and asked softly. "What are you going to do about it, daddy?"

He growled with need from behind me at my defiance, and his fingers bit into the flesh on my ass. It bubbled with sultry heat and I knew a punishment was coming. But I wanted it more than anything.

I wanted to see daddy at his worst.

Immediately, he peeled back the sheets, and a warmth coated the air. It blew my hair to the side as he kneeled on the bed and flung me over his lap. I gasped at the assertiveness of him and red fiery lust seared through me. The unknown of what he was about to do coursed through me and my adrenaline ran wild.

He ran his hands along my flesh and tortured me with his touch. The caress of passion as the flames grew higher between us and his one hand rested on the small of my back. It made circles there as his other hand ran up my quivering thigh and made it to its destination.

Right on my ass.

His breath quivered from above me with passionate excitement. "I'm going to spank you for being a very naughty girl."

My breath caught as I braced myself for his punishment and closed my eyes. I wasn't afraid, but completely aroused. I wanted it. He wanted to do whatever he wanted to me and I...

He slapped my ass as pain seared across my ass cheek and I jolted to his scorched touch. A whimper escaped me with the next one and I ached my back with the sensation. He tortured me and I heard him groan from above me. He was in complete control and in all his glory. But it was the most sexist thing in the world.

"Oh, my dearest daughter-in-law, you've been so unruly." He breathed as his hand ran over the redness on my flesh and he let out a moan. "But so have I when it comes to you, princess."

He spanked me again and again as the fire burned through me. My panties were wet from the lustful mistreatment and I clenched the bed sheets. I whimpered into them and bit them to help conceal my cry of painful passion.

"Are you going to do that again, princess?" He growled.

"No." I said as I repeatedly shook my head.

My pussy clenched together with a slap, and I gasped when he grabbed the back of my neck. He pulled it upwards and towards his eyes that met mine as they glowed. His stare drank me in and my eyes reflected the same desire he felt. Raw, undeniable, torturous lust.

"Take off your panties and sit on my lap." He breathed heavily into my face. "Now, princess."

I didn't waste any time and followed his demand. My panties were soaked, and I didn't dare to defy daddy. I tossed them aside and sat on his lap. My backside was towards him with my long waves of black hair tumbling down my back. He groaned at the sight of me and his dick pulsated against my ass. His massive cock was hard and waited for me. But I shivered with passionate anticipation of what he was going to do next.

His hands touched my back on each side and ran down it. The skin tingled with want and my breath hitched. His caress spiraled me out of control as he stopped at my ass cheek and squeezed my plump ass into his powerful grasp.

"Oh, please, daddy, please..." I begged him with a moan of passion.

"I know what you want, young lady." Daxon groaned as he grabbed my hair and yanked it backwards. "But you didn't listen to daddy and I'm very frustrated."

"I'm sorry..." I whimpered.

He pressed his cock firmly up against me and rubbed my ass with it. "Do you see what you do to me, princess?"

"Yes, I do." I breathed.

His cock dry humped my plump ass and the silk fabric of his briefs slid against me. I moaned at the pleasure of it all and he yanked my hair again. I gasped for him, he groaned and his breath picked up pace. My pussy got wetter at just the friction of his uncontrollable need.

He stopped and slightly pushed me forward, but struck my ass again. My plumpness jiggled at the force and I cried out at the pain. He spanked me again and again. I gasped, moaned, and arched my back. The mix of pleasure with torment. My cunt got wet with each slap and my heavy breaths mixed with sounds of my flesh. It lost me in the desire and it stung me, but I loved it.

He pulled my hair again and breathed in my ear. "Touch yourself, princess."

He spanked me again, and I whimpered as I bit my lip. I followed his instructions and touched my wet clit. My finger slid around in small circles and he released my hair. His hands ran up my thighs until they landed on my hips and stopped. He squeezed them as my pleasure took over and I moved my hips. He groaned from behind me and watched my torturous rhythm he wanted to see.

My behind thrust against his firm cock with each circle of my clit, but it wasn't enough. I needed more and dipped two fingers inside my juicy pussy. I brought them in and out of me as my walls clenched around them. My climax was extremely close because of his wicked game.

But the pleasure mixed with pain when he spanked me again.

"Oh!" I whimpered.

And he growled at me. "I want your sweet juices to spill all over daddy's lap."

His words built me higher, and I circled my clit faster. He pressed my ass up against his cock and moved my hips. His groans mixed with my moans of pleasured delight. He brought me higher as my fingers worked inside me and I bit my lip again.

The pleasure rose higher and higher. The flames grew brighter and brighter. And I tossed my head back at my earth-shattering release.

"Oh, daddy!" I cried out as my ass rocked against his cock and beams of light twinkled in my eyes.

"That's my good girl." He moaned from behind me.

I came down from my climax and felt his cock rage below me. He ran his hands down to my thighs and pinched their plumpness. I knew he wasn't done with me yet.

"I think my dirty girl needs a shower." He whispered as he brushed my hair aside and ran his lips up my neck.

"Oh, yes, daddy, please." I begged him and fell under his spell.

He grabbed my hand and brought my fingers to his mouth. I watched in agony as his eyes locked with mine and his tongue swirled over my juices. He licked them and sucked them into his mouth. His tongue flicked inside and I moaned for him.

He released them and licked his lips clean. "My sweet young lady."

His hungry stare tore into me and his lips found mine. The kiss was passionate. It was full of greed and it intoxicated me. I drank him in as his air mixed with mine and our salvia mingled into one. His French Kiss I could never get enough of and his skilled tongue worked with my own. It swirled and glided smoothly inside of me. He made me whole, wanted and completely his.

With one swift motion, he lifted me from the bed and against his muscular chest. My hands landed on his brawny pec's and ran over the hair there. They ran down his sides to his muscular torso, and my nails bit into him. He growled into me and jolted me upwards. My legs hugged him as he got off the bed and carried me towards the luxurious bathroom.

We kissed with a wild frenzy and couldn't get enough of each other. My hands found his salt and pepper hair. My fingers wove into it and clenched the silky stands. He hissed as my thumbs played with his earlobes and his cock throbbed against me. I couldn't help it when my hips moved with a mind of their own and rotated against his firmness. He loved every second as he slapped my ass and I bounced to his beat. Squealed in his arms as he continued to kiss down my cheek and towards my neckline. His tongue lapped over it as I heard the water hiss and the warmth of it grazed my backside.

My legs unwrapped themselves from around him and fell to the cool, tiled floor. His mouth worked its way to my cleavage and his hands found the clasp of my bra. He undid it with my tits free to be pleased, and my bra fell to the floor.

"Oh, yes..." I sighed with pleasure.

He consumed my breast and took it inside his mouth. His tongue lapped over it and teased my nipple. He made it fully erect and pointed right at him. My nipples ached for him as he nibbled, licked, and sucked each one. He took his time and pleased them until I begged him for more.

My back arched to give him full exposure as he toyed with me and I backed up into the shower. The warm beads fell over my body and mixed with the warmth I already felt inside. My passion flickered with a need that seared through every fiber of my being. I burned like a fiery flame and waited to be blown out.

He released my pleasured tits and stood back to look at me. His eyes starved for me as he pulled down his boxer briefs and threw them aside. They never left my body as

I backed up and he moved forward. The water sprinkled down, but it didn't stop his approach. He was a hungry man who wanted me, and his magnificent cock was full of his seed. It pulsated under the trickle of the rainfall shower and my eyes grew wide with want. I wanted his cock buried deep inside. So deep that when he came, it would make me come too.

My backside hit the cool, clear glass of the shower, and a whimper escaped me. He darted towards me like a dog in heat and panted in my face. His one arm rested against the glass over the top of my head and his other ran down my body. Over my neck, grazed my erect mounds, past my navel, and his fingers found my clit. He slapped it and I cried out as he snatched my lower lip with his teeth. My breath hitched as he slapped it again and I reached out to touch him, but he wouldn't let me. He wanted to please me and tease me. Mr. Daxon Stark made me his dirty little secret.

"Turn around, my sweet princess." He breathed against my lip as they quivered just for him. "Daddy wants to take you from behind."

I spun around because my pussy ached for him. It begged me to give into his every need and let him have all the control. He was a man who thrived on power and I wanted him to own me.

He groaned from behind me as my hands braced against the crisp glass and my hot breath fogged it up. Each breath I panted with the desired anticipation of his thirst for me, and I wanted nothing more than for him to plunge himself inside of me. To dive deep into my pussy hole and bury himself inside.

His hand ran down my wet hair, and he curled it into his fist. He pulled it backwards as I whimpered and he ran his other hand down my arched backside. He took his time as he played with me and took in the beauty of his princess. All wet and ready for him to bang.

His cock teased my entrance. He dragged the tip of himself over it and grazed my ass. His other hand rested on my left hip and the water ran down his back. Daddy was a wet beast, ready to claim his princess.

"Fuck me, daddy." I hissed with pleasure.

And he drove right into me.

His dick pounded into my pussy at full force. He didn't let up as I squealed and my hands slipped on the glass. I tried to grab something, anything to hold on to as his power raged into me, but there was nothing. He banged his dick into my juicy pussy as my left cheek met the glass and my breath fogged it up. His force was so strong I couldn't stop myself from crying out for more.

The pleasure he inflicted on me was profound and unlike anything I'd ever felt before. The sweet sound of wet flesh smacked together and echoed inside the shower. It mixed with my moans of delight as I fell deeper into his grasp and he pressed me up against the glass. Fucked me hardcore as everything spun and it lost me in him.

He grunted with each thrust as his pace slowed, but he dove deep inside me. Buried his dick within me, just like I wanted him to. My pussy walls wrapped themselves around him and clenched his throbbing cock with each wave of pleasure.

He yanked my head backwards with one swift pull of my hair and whispered in my ear. "You're mine, princess."

I looked back at him as the heat sizzled between us, and we locked eyes. "Yes, daddy, I'm all yours."

It sent him over the edge as he pounded into me and didn't lose momentum. I cried out for him with a long squeal of his name and he growled from above me. His cock pulsated, and I knew his seed was coming. He couldn't hold it back as his release took over his face, and he filled me up. The force of his pounds set me tumbling over the edge and my climax rang out.

"Oh, fuck, daddy!" I cried with passion.

"Oh, fuck, Celeste..." He groaned my name with lust.

Bright stars filled my eyes as I panted my release and he still beat into me. He kept going until I was complete and pulled his hard cock from me. I felt his seed drip down the sides of my pussy lips as he kissed my mouth and didn't stop. I was taken by him and he wound up in me. We couldn't get enough of each other and didn't want this moment to end.

I hated to admit it, but Dylan's plan had worked. He brought us to this place for us to get closer, but for a very different reason. He wanted us to get along and work together. We'd done just that and so much more. But as he carried me back to the bedroom, my heart sang.

My heartbeat for him and I wanted nothing but him. I wanted my fiancé's father to be mine. My heart belonged to him and I could never get it back. I didn't want it back because this getaway brought me closer to him.

He laid me back down on the bed and covered me with the sheets. The tenderness of it seared through my soul as he touched my cheek and his eyes searched mine. I wanted them to tell me he felt it too, but it never came. But I knew as he laid down beside me and squeezed my hand tight, I had fallen in love with him.

And it terrified me.

TWENTY-TWO

Game Over

The next morning, I woke up to a bright light streaming through the curtains. I shielded it with my hands and rubbed my eyes. I slept like a baby.

I stretched out my arms and expected to feel him beside me, but he was gone. The side of the bed where he had laid before I fell asleep was cold and it reminded me of the first time we were intimate. I had sworn to myself never again, but here I was. In bed, craving his cock once again.

But this time, I was in love.

Love didn't happen at first sight. It didn't even come after, but the attraction ran wild. The game he played with me twisted me within it and tangled me to no point of return. Doomed to fall for him from the beginning. But my heart didn't know it until it had already happened.

He was all I could think about. All I wanted, and all I needed. He couldn't see it. I wasn't even sure I wanted him to because of the rejection. Daxon was all about his business and nothing else. He loved his son, but that was it. He could never love me.

I pondered where he was as I grabbed the shirt he left out for me and put it over my naked body. Our night of passion was too much for me to take and I had fallen asleep bare beneath the bed sheets. I didn't even know if he had stayed in bed with me, but I doubted it. Daxon didn't do commitments, and he stayed as far away from it as possible.

His tragic past had made sure of it.

I slowly made my way out of the bedroom and ran my hands through my messy hair. I had no choice with no luggage. My legs were wobbly from last night, and my pussy was sore from his intoxicating sex. But it was the best sex of my life.

Hell, both times were.

I smiled to myself and saw movement in the kitchen. To my surprise, there was Daxon and he was cooking. The delicious smell of breakfast filled my nose, and I sniffed freshly made waffles. But with it, a hint of greasy bacon and eggs.

"What are you doing?" I smiled as I leaned against a beam in the kitchen and watched him work.

I admired the way he looked in a black apron with no shirt on. The way he swayed this way and that. His perfect ass hugged tightly underneath blue jeans and he tucked a dish towel in his back pocket. He moved around the kitchen like a chef who knew what he was doing and I never knew this side of him existed.

I had to remind myself he raised a child practically on his own. He was a hot single dad who lived his life alone, and the only thing he cared for was his son through all those years. Therefore, he'd have to take care of him, feed him, do homework with him, bathe him and tuck him into bed. He'd have to do all of it on his own.

No wonder he knew his way around the kitchen.

"What does it look like?" Daxon said as he flipped an egg with the frying pan and looked right at home. "I'm making us breakfast."

"Yes, but why?" I asked as I went closer and leaned over the island with my hands cupping my face. "It's not like we like each other."

I was trying to get a reaction from him. To test him. I tried to see what his answer would be, but I feared I already knew the response. There was no us and there could never be.

He stopped and looked at me. His eyes went straight towards my cleavage and he licked his bottom lip. His top teeth grabbed it and curled it into his mouth as he watched me. He drank me in and I didn't want him to spit me back out. I wanted to stay in him forever.

"Dylan instructed me to make us breakfast." Daxon admitted as he took his spatula and ran it down my neck.

It teased my neckline, and I bit my lip with need. He turned me on in an instant and he didn't even have to do anything. Just use a kitchen utensil to increase the heat that already bubbled inside me.

"Oh, yes, we don't want to disappoint him with our progress." I whispered, and it came out like a purr.

"My shirt looks good on you, princess." Daxon stated as his eyes teased me and he loved what he saw.

The hard metal touched my cleavage, and he pushed the opening aside to reveal one erect, rosy bud. Ready just for him, and I heard a groan come from deep inside him. It erupted to the surface and escaped his lips. His eyes told me he wanted to pounce, but for some unknown reason, he held back.

"And that apron suits you well, daddy." I teased.

But he pulled the spatula back.

He cleared his throat. "We should get a picture for Dylan. He is expecting one."

"Right..." I mumbled with disappointment. "Can't forget about that."

My shoulders slumped as I walked around the island and in front of the stove with Daxon. He held up his cell phone for a selfie and I plastered on a fake smile. The picture he snapped was cute, but a total lie. Everything about this was a complete shame. Except for my broken heart.

Suddenly, the front doorbell rang, and I was relieved. I needed a distraction and hurried for the front door. I felt underdressed answering it, but someone had to. Maybe it was my lost luggage?

My hand grasped the doorknob, and I gave it a hard tug. The chilly morning air filled the entryway and my wavy locks slightly blew with it. A man dressed in normal clothes was present with my luggage right beside him.

"I have luggage for a Celeste Lovette?" The gentleman said as he looked down at his paperwork and back at me.

"That would be me." I beamed with happiness and took my luggage handle.

"I'm sorry for the slight delay." He apologized.

"Not a problem. Have a good day." I said as I brought my luggage inside and closed the door to his slight nod.

I hurried it through the entryway and into the kitchen. "Look what finally arrived!"

I presented him with my luggage and felt excited. He flashed me a dashing smile and I could've melted. He was so incredibly handsome. All in his own silver fox way.

"That's great because breakfast is served." He announced as he laid a waffle on a plate and pushed it towards me.

I sat down on the fancy stool and dug into it at the island. The waffles were delicious, with just the right amount of butter and maple syrup. It coated my hungry stomach and built up the energy I lost last night.

Daxon ate while he cooked, and I couldn't help but watch him. He was in his element and it looked damn good on him. He served me bacon and eggs on another plate, but chewed on a crunchy piece of meat. The sink filled up with soapy water and he did the dishes. He got his hands wet and scrubbed the frying pan he no longer needed. He washed all the dishes except mine and turned around to look at me.

His face grew serious and unreadable. "A limousine should be here shortly. You can stay if you wish, but I have to leave."

My eyes searched him with questions, but I received no answer. "Why? I thought we were staying for a few days? Dylan planned this entire trip and..."

"Well, plans change and I have to work." He snapped at me bitterly.

"Okay, but what about Dylan? He'll wonder why you left." I explained and pleaded with him to stay. "He wants us to get along and we're supposed to fake it till we make it, remember?"

"I think we've gotten along a little too well." Daxon said sternly with his voice on edge. "I think we've proved our point."

I knew exactly where he was going with this. He referred to our night together as a mistake, and it was his way of creating that wall he had built up so high. A wall around his heart that no one could break because it broke a long time ago.

I understood and nodded my head. "I'll get dressed and be ready to go."

But it shattered my heart into a million pieces.

I pushed away my food. "I've suddenly lost my appetite."

I left the room and pulled my luggage behind me. It felt as heavy as my broken heart. I had gone and fallen for a man who could never return my feelings. But it stung so badly.

How could I let this happen?

Now, I had to agree to a loveless marriage and try to maintain some sort of normal with Daxon around. He was Dylan's father, and I had no idea how I was going to make it work. But I had no choice.

I got dressed as quickly as I could with the bit of notice of our departure and gathered all my belongings. I brushed my hair and tied it up in a messy bun. The world felt like it was ending and I was on the borderline of tears. They stung my eyes and wanted to fall, but I didn't let them. I had to remain strong and push forward. I had to draw a line somewhere for myself and for my sanity.

I needed to end this secret affair once and for all.

I blew out the breath I held and headed for the front door. Our getaway was over, and so were our secret moments together. He needed to keep his distance from me so this could be bearable. I needed him to stop this game we fell into so my heart would stop breaking.

Daxon stood beside the long limousine stretched out near the front of the cabin. The sunlight glistened in his salt and pepper hair. I wanted to run my fingers through it, wrap my hands around the nape of his neck, and kiss him senseless. But I ignored my wishful thoughts and plastered on a fake smile just for him.

I gave my luggage and carry-on to the driver. Daxon opened the door for me, but I stopped in front of him and looked him straight in the eyes. He peered back at me with unreadable cold eyes, the same old ruthless man I met just over a year ago. He hadn't changed and never could. Not even for me.

"This twisted game we've been playing is over, Daxon." I told him as my heart broke and I held up my fake composure. "We can't keep having sex behind Dylan's back. It's wrong and we need to move on because I'm marrying your son. I was never yours to begin with."

I stepped forward to get in the limousine, but he grabbed my wrist. My eyes shot towards his and they blazed at me with dominance. My pussy pulsated at his thirst for lust. But that's all he appeared to think of me.

"You're just a young fuck like all the rest." Daxon responded harshly. "And you know you want it."

The pad of his thumb caressed my palm and sent shivers through me. I wanted to give in to him, but my heart was on the line. I needed to think with my head and not my pussy.

"No, Daxon, it's over." I glared as I pulled my hand out of reach and got inside the limousine. "Our game is over."

I ignored him and didn't look his way. My body wanted to defy me and leap into his arms one more time. But he was all over the place and a hot mess.

"The game is never over, princess." He breathed with power and slammed the door shut.

He climbed in the other side and remained silent beside me. It was going to be another plane ride home in quietness. The loneliness would set in and I'd crave his closeness. But nothing would save my heartbreak, not even his unloving heart.

I wish I had never fallen for such a cold and heartless man.

TWENTY-THREE

Sickness

Two long weeks had passed since my getaway with Mr. Daxon Stark and I had tried to avoid him at all costs. It was hard with family get together or anything to do with the business and I tried my best. But Daxon never promised to go along with the plan.

He didn't help with his long, unwavering gaze at me or his daring good looks. He knew how to stray me along and tempt me to play. I didn't give in, but I knew deep down it was only a matter of time.

The clock was ticking, and Daxon would be right there when the opportunity struck. He'd be there to pull me back into his twisted fate because that was what we did. We torment and taunt one another. We couldn't help ourselves because our attraction spiraled out of control and had a need of its own. A thirst to bring us together in the worst way possible. Caught up in secrets and deceit. A game where there was no escape, not until the truth came out. And it could never be.

I walked towards the bathroom and grabbed the doorframe. A sudden unease fell over me and I was queasy. My legs shook as I held myself up and touched the back of my hand to my mouth. My stomach turned and the world spun. I held the door frame tighter as my breath hitched and my heartbeat faster.

I was going to be sick.

I let go of the doorframe and knew I needed the toilet. I hurried as I made my way towards it and lifted the seat. My head heaved as the contents of my last meal spilled into the water below, and I leaned against the toilet. My tummy groaned, and the dizziness subsided, along with the need to throw up.

I held my hand over my weak stomach and my head fell against the wall as I sat there. My thoughts ran to this past week and how sick I had felt. The dizziness, bloated belly and my extreme hunger, but throw it all back up again. Not to mention my tender breasts. I was so tired with low energy and it just made little sense.

"I just want to get back to normal." I sighed to myself, with no one else here.

I was alone again while Dylan had to work long hours. I used to believe him and blame Daxon for all his time away from me, but it just wasn't the case. Now I knew the truth. I knew Dylan was with his lover. I was in a loveless relationship and it got lonely sometimes.

I stood up when I felt more like myself and went to the sink. The sound of rushing water filled my ears, and I splashed it onto my face. The coolness of the beads trickled over it and fell back down the drain. And I patted my face clean.

That felt much better.

My eyes caught something on the vanity over the toilet, and my mind raced. I felt a panic rush through me as I grabbed my unopened box of tampons and stared at it. I couldn't believe I never even noticed. All my unusual symptoms and now this. I was late for my period and the unopened box was my clear sign.

I always bought a new box for every period because it usually gave me the right amount for each one. Last period, I used the entire box and bought this one for my next cycle. The next one that hadn't come yet and was overdue.

Oh, my god...

As I walked out of the bathroom, I put the box back in its place and my hands shook. I grabbed my purse, warm jacket for the chilly evening, and left the penthouse. I hurried towards the street and knew exactly where I needed to go to get answers.

My heels clicked along the paved sidewalk as I laid eyes on my destination. It was a short walk away from home and I knew I could make it in time before it closed. I had the strength to get there on my own and the uncertainty would help guide me there.

My anxiety pumped through me as I pulled open the pharmacy door and made my way inside. I never had to look for this before and had no idea where to start. So, I made my way down each long aisle and felt like it took me a lifetime. The need for an answer was what I sought, and time just ticked by while I searched.

I almost caved and asked someone, but refused because I didn't want anyone to know. I was simply buying it for someone else and not for myself was the lie I'd tell someone if they asked. More lies to pile on top of the rest of this big mess.

I reached an aisle with condoms, lubricants, and pregnancy tests. It was a strange combination to have all together, and the view made me stop to think. Condoms lead to pleasure and lubricants help with pleasure, but pregnancy tests confirm a pregnancy.

Why were they even here?

Who thought this was ever a good idea?

I guess if the condoms fail and the lubricants help move the process along, one would need a pregnancy test. So, someone would need a pregnancy test. But I never would've thought to look here, of all places.

I shook my head and quickly picked one up. It didn't matter which one I chose, because they all did the same thing. They all tested for the pregnancy hormone. I didn't want to be caught with this in my hands. I needed to get out of here as fast as possible.

I turned around with the test in my hand and placed it behind my back. I took a few steps and stopped. My heart pounded wildly in my chest and felt like it climbed up my throat. I thought I'd choke on it with surprise at who I saw in front of me.

Daxon Stark.

"Celeste? What are you doing here?" He asked me as he came down the aisle and stood in front of me.

I looked at him with shock, and my anxiety ran wild. It pumped through me and took me for a ride. My palms grew sweaty as I held the pregnancy test against my back and kept it out of sight. At least I hoped I did.

I couldn't believe out of all the people he was here right now. It was late and a last-minute stop for me. He couldn't possibly have a good reason for being here.

"I-I came here to pick up a prescription for myself." I stammered out and lied through my teeth.

"Are you okay?" He asked as he stepped forward with concern and I stepped back. "You look a little pale."

I pulled myself together because I had no other choice. "I'm fine. You just startled me. I didn't expect to see you here."

Which was the truth and not a boldfaced lie. Unlike all the other ones I told, and it included our recent affair together. Our intimate encounters could've landed me here.

"It was a last-minute stop for me." Daxon admitted.

I grew curious. "Why are you here, Daxon?"

He simply pointed at the lubricant bottles, all neatly lined up on the shelf. The stakes were too high for me to laugh at him. I was impatient and needed to get out of here. I need to get away from him before he figured out the truth.

My heartbeat was so loud it thudded in my ears. The anxiousness of the situation was out of control and I felt beads of sweat produced on my forehead. I was so worried I'd make a slip and I had to keep this a secret. It had to stay hidden from him because he couldn't figure out I might be pregnant.

I masked the emotions that ran wild inside and put on a fake face of sarcasm. I picked up a lube bottle with my free hand and held it out towards him. He looked down at it and back at me. My idea worked and drew his attention away from the object I hid behind my back.

"So, you're going to use this to squirt on your latest hook up?" I asked and disguised my secret.

He took the bottle from my hand, stepped closer and looked me straight in the eyes. "No, it's for me to jerk off while I think of you, princess."

His admission rang out over top of my wild heart. It slowed, but steadied as the temperature grew hotter between us and the familiar attraction sparked to life. The sweatiness went away and a cool calm ran over me as his breath blew into my face. It took me from eager to turned on in seconds and made me forget why I was here.

His eyes roamed down my body, and it tingled with every look. He was hot, horny, and I knew his cock pulsated against his pants. I was sure of it.

The air between us was thick, and he was dead serious. His last-minute stop was because of me. He needed a release since he couldn't have me.

I watched him as he licked his lower lip and his teeth took it into his mouth. A sexy habit he always did with me. And it suited him well because it made me hot.

He reached out, let go of his lip, flicked my jacket collar and hissed at me with lust. "It was good seeing you, Celeste."

He left me there in the aisle, completely consumed by him. I watched him go with long strides of confidence in his step as he made his way to the checkout and didn't look back. I almost expected him to, but this was all part of his game. His turn to make me lust after him and want more.

Well, it worked.

I was hot and bothered. Ready to give into temptation even though I knew the stakes were too high. And if he kept this up, I might just break.

He kept his back to me as he held the lube he would use to masturbate to the thought of me and took it to the nearest cashier. He paid for it with cash and left the store. But tossed it in his jacket pocket and away he went.

I soaked my panties from the heated encounter. Turned on, but also terrified. He could've seen the truth. I might be pregnant and he could very well be the father.

But I got lucky.

When my feet could finally move, I headed for the same cashier Daxon did. I just wanted to get out of here before any other unexpected occurrences. The woman behind the register looked at me while I paid with cash. I knew the reels ran in her mind as she tried to piece together if the pregnancy test was for me. Her suspicion made me nervous, and I grabbed the box before the receipt was printed. I just needed to get out of there because everything caved in.

My legs hurried back to the penthouse with the pregnancy test tucked inside my jacket. It remained out of sight from suspicious eyes and I needed nothing leaked to the media. This story was big, but it would be even bigger than many realized. And the media would have a field day out of it.

I opened the door and wanted to be sure no one was home. "Dylan, darling! I'm home!"

There was no answer, and I let out a sigh of relief. Even though it hadn't even been an hour since I had realized I could be pregnant, the worry ate at me. I had to find out and put this all behind me.

"There's no way I'm pregnant." I convinced myself as I headed for the bathroom and threw my jacket on the couch.

My purse fell on the countertop, and I closed the bathroom door behind me. I peered down at the dreadful instructions and cursed myself for being in this position. I knew I should've played it safe with both men, but my sexual need came before all else. It was reckless, and I paid the price.

After opening the box, I took out the thin pregnancy test. I inspected it because I had never had to use one before. The lid came off and I walked towards the toilet. I couldn't believe that such a small thing could change a woman's life in just an instant.

I pulled down my pants and panties. Thoughts weighed heavy on my mind as I peed on the stick and tried to hope for the best. A positive outcome was that I wasn't pregnant because I wasn't ready. I wasn't ready to be a mother, and a baby didn't deserve that. It deserved certainty, support and proper care. I wasn't even sure I could do that for a little human being.

I wrapped up what I needed to do and set the timer for two minutes. The test laid on the counter as I paced the floor and chewed on the inside of my cheeks. My nerves ran wild, and I played with my hands. I couldn't bring myself to look at the test because I knew it might already hold my answer. An answer with my future on the line and anything was possible.

Even a baby.

My fate was in the hands of this tiny pregnancy test, and I waited for it to reveal the truth. I waited to find out if I could go back to the way things were or if I needed to make a doctor's appointment to confirm the pregnancy. All things that came with bringing a child into this world and what comes next.

Suddenly, the timer beeped and startled me back to reality. I fumbled to stop it with my finger, pushing the button, and I tossed my cell phone on the counter. My eyes intently diverted the test, and I shook my hands to calm my nerves.

"Just breathe. It's going to be okay, Celeste. You aren't pregnant and can't be, it's just a..." I breathed to myself as I looked at it and couldn't finish my rant.

Two little pink lines were right in sight. They were bright, bold lines on the indicator and I couldn't believe my eyes. I was in shock and the truth was undeniable.

I was pregnant.

But I didn't know what to do about it.

This wasn't part of the plan and wasn't supposed to happen like this. I was supposed to get married. Dylan wasn't interested in me and we could've tried the in vitro fertilization route. But it looked like that wasn't going to happen.

I couldn't be pregnant right now. Not with everything going on and all the lies. This isn't the way I'd raise a baby.

My body went into panic mode and my head felt like it would explode. My mind went crazy, and I needed to do something before I made this situation worse. I had to calm down and pull myself together, but I needed to tell someone. I need to get this off my chest.

I grabbed my cell phone as my breath shook with anxiousness and my fingers trembled on the screen. I pressed on Paisley's number and waited for her face to appear. It rang and rang. But each one sent my nerves through the roof.

Suddenly, my best friend's face appeared. My breath quickened and I couldn't contain it. I couldn't fathom what was happening, and everything just changed in an instant.

"Celeste? What's wrong?" Paisley asked immediately as she took in my frazzled demeanor and was concerned.

"I didn't know what else to do." I admitted as I tried to gain control of myself and took some deep breaths.

"You didn't know what to do about what, sweetie?" Paisley asked, puzzled by my craziness.

"I have something to tell you." I breathed as I held up the pregnancy test without another moment's hesitation and waited for her reaction. "I'm pregnant."

Shock took over Paisley's face. "Is that what I think it is?"

I looked over at the test that held all the truth and back at Paisley. "Yes, Pais, it's exactly what you think it is."

"You're pregnant? Oh my god! Congratulations!" Paisley announced as her mouth went agape and she bounced with joy. "Oh, I bet Dylan is just over the moon!"

I put the pregnancy test down and frowned. "He doesn't know."

Paisley immediately stopped the celebration and narrowed her eyes. "And why doesn't he know, Celeste?"

I blew out a long breath and knew it was time to come clean. "Because I just found out, and he may not be the father."

Paisley stared at me wide eyed and said, "What did you just say?"

And I repeated. "My fiancé might not be the father of this baby."

I let her sink it in. It took several moments as I watched her face change from shock and then back to normal. Her mind processed everything and tried to grasp the reality of the situation. The same way I tried to do, but I freaked out instead.

Finally, Paisley breathed. "Oh, my god... I knew something was going on."

I squinted my eyes and shook my head with confusion. "What are you talking about?"

She pointed her finger at me with suspicion. "This has something to do with that night you stayed in the presidential suite with Dylan's father, doesn't it?"

I didn't speak a word, but knew she was piecing the puzzle together as we spoke. She knew me better than most people and it surprised me I kept the truth from her this long. Paisley was anything but polite. She was a nosy genius.

She got closer to the screen and whispered to me. "Girl, did you sleep with his dad?"

I bit my bottom lip, closed my eyes and spoke the truth. "Yes, I slept with him."

I opened my eyes and felt a weight lifted off my shoulders. The truth felt great to let out, but there was still so much to be told. This didn't even graze the surface.

"I knew it!" Paisley exclaimed and smiled. "I just knew something more went on! Why the hell didn't you tell me?"

"Because it was wrong, and I wanted to forget it happened." I admitted and hung my head in shame. "I swore to myself it wouldn't happen again. But then Dylan booked us a surprise getaway to make us get along. We were all alone at a cabin in the woods and the temptation was just too high and..."

Paisley cut me off. "You had sex with him again?"

I gazed up at her with defeat and admitted my double betrayal. "Yes, I did."

"This is quite the mess you've got yourself mixed in, Celeste." Paisley breathed as she shook her head and looked me straight in the eyes. "But you need to come clean and tell them the truth."

I repeatedly shook my head with fright. "No, no, they can't find out. This could destroy everything. The company, Daxon's life, Dylan's secret and so much..."

Paisley stopped me. "What do you mean by Dylan's secret?"

Oh, no, I let it slip.

I wasn't supposed to tell anyone and now it was too late. She wouldn't let this go and would pry it from me till the bitter end. I couldn't keep it from her now.

So, I filled her in. "That night when I slept with Daxon, I caught Dylan in bed with another man. He made me swear I wouldn't tell his father because it could ruin everything but now I'm going to be in a loveless marriage for the rest of my life."

The look of shock came back to life on Paisley's face. Her freckles even glowed along with it and made her entire appearance light up like a Christmas tree. She couldn't believe it as much as I couldn't when I caught him in the act. I could still remember the embarrassment and anger that took over me. I didn't know if I could ever get over it, but I had to move on.

"Do one thing for me?" I asked with certainty. "Swear to me, you won't tell a soul. You can't speak a word about my pregnancy, Dylan, or that I slept with my fiancé's father."

Paisley exhaled and looked me in the eye. "I respect your decision and our friendship. I won't tell a soul."

"Oh, thank god..." I breathed a sigh of relief.

"I don't like this. I have a bad feeling about it." Paisley admitted with the look of worry on her face and shook her head.

But the damage was done.

Everything needed to be kept secret, and that was the way it'd stay. This pregnancy would remain hidden for as long as possible and I need to figure out what to do. Even though I had a terrible feeling about it, too.

TWENTY-FOUR

Anniversary

I walked into the plain white painted waiting room and patients waited to be seen. Some were on their cell phones killing time and others had their noses stuck in a magazine. But I didn't want to be here.

I wanted to be anywhere other than here as I made myself head up towards the secretary to register. I half smiled at her and she asked me to pee in a cup. She handed me the hard plastic with my name on the label and an orange lid. I took it and followed the directions to the bathroom behind me.

The door opened with a loud squeak and others peered my way. They looked at the cup in my hands and I felt caught. The truth was exposed, and my cheeks burned bright red as I quickly closed the door behind me.

My embarrassment faded away as I exhaled. I had a more pressing issue to deal with today. I opened the tiny cup, but the seal broke and I was relieved knowing this was a sterile test. No reason to second guess the result and the answer would be clear.

I peed into the cup that sealed my fate and was lucky not to pee on my hand. This task was harder than I thought and the skill to get my pee directly into it took effort. But I did it and the sample was ready.

I washed my hands and looked at myself in the mirror. My eyes had bags underneath them from the lack of sleep, and my makeup was a quick fix. I ran my fingers through my hair and straightened my back. I was ready to get this over with.

I left the bathroom, and to my surprise, heard my name. "The doctor will see you now."

I nodded my head and handed the secretary my fate. She took it and dropped it off in the lab as we walked by on the way to the room. The thin hallway wasn't comforting and the single room had a chair I sat down in while I waited for the doctor's arrival. But my nerves went into overdrive.

Those two pink lines had sent me tossing and turning since they showed up. I slept in bed alone while Dylan slept on the couch. We hadn't been in the same bed since I found him with his lover. We'd barely spoken to each other except for wedding plans or business. Everything else was completely off the table, and I was grateful for the distance. Especially with this latest development.

I still held onto hope the pregnancy test was a mistake. An unthinkable and terrible mistake. I found out it was possible because I had read about it online. False positive home pregnancy tests were a thing, and I crossed my fingers that it could be the case for me. I didn't need a baby right now, and none of us did. No one needed this mess. I had a wedding to plan and secrets to uphold. I didn't have time for another one.

Suddenly, there was a soft tap at the door, and it opened. I looked over to see a short, plump woman with round black frames and curly black hair. Her fancy name tag had the name Erin on it.

She glanced at me briefly and took a seat in front of me. "I'm Erin, and I'll be reading your results today. Can you tell me what brings you in?"

She cut straight to the point, and I admired that. I didn't want to be here, and I had never been here before. I was always very healthy and never had health problems. No reason to visit the doctors here in the city until now.

"Well, I have been feeling unwell for a few days and getting sick." I breathed as my anxiety took over and I fidgeted with my hands in my seat. "I'm normally healthy and it was odd."

The doctor looked at her chart. "Can you describe the symptoms you have been experiencing?"

I answered her question in a soft tone. "Tender breasts, hungry all the time, vomiting, dizziness, bloated stomach and exhausted."

She jotted it down on the chart and I heard the pen scribble. The room was silent and if a pin were to drop, anyone would hear it. It made my nerves even worse, and I realized this was hard to do alone. But I had no other choice.

She stopped the pen and asked. "Did you notice a late period, by chance?"

I replied. "Yes, I figured I'm at least a week late and I took a pregnancy test. It was positive, but there must be a mistake."

She took off her glasses, laid them on the table and her eyes looked into mine. "I'm afraid there's no mistake."

I blinked repeatedly and asked. "What do you mean?"

"The urine culture we used to detect pregnancy came back positive. You are expecting a baby." She explained as the chair swiveled closer towards me and she clasped her hands together. "But the questions now are how far along are you and is your body healthy enough to carry this baby to full-term?"

I sat there and took in the news. I knew, and the odds were against me. Those two pink lines were right, and I was pregnant. But I had no clue who the father was.

Erin put her glasses back on and wrote on the paper in front of her. She tore it off and looked at me with the note in her hand. Loneliness set in, and I had no idea what came next. I felt like the world had slipped out from underneath me and left me behind.

She passed the note to me. "I want you to take this out to my secretary. She will order blood work and I will get you scheduled for your first ultrasound."

I took the instructions and peered down at the paper. This was the next step, and it gave me slight relief. But I still had a long journey ahead of me.

I laid my hand on my belly with the baby that grew inside and I couldn't believe this had happened. A tiny human being grew inside me. It ate everything I did and breathed the same air as me. We shared so much and yet I felt unattached to it. But my body connected us as one.

"Do you think I can do this?" I asked with uncertainty.

She smiled and laid her hand on top of mine. "I know you can, Celeste. A woman's body holds so much power and this baby is a gift. Congratulations on your pregnancy."

She let go of me, tucked her chart under her arm, and left the room. I sat there stunned and let the reality of my situation sink in. I had to change my life and bring a child into this world. A tiny little baby that would depend on me for everything. I was going to be a mother. Whether or not I wanted to be.

***

I arrived home at the penthouse and dropped my keys onto the side table. They made a loud clunk. The pregnancy exhausted me from the afternoon and took off my heels as I fell back onto the couch. I needed to rest my aching feet and my hand fell onto my stomach. But my mind wandered to my stroll I had through the park on this glorious afternoon.

I needed to clear my head, and the day was beautiful for a walk through the park. I realized I had to think like a parent and what better place to go than the park? This baby was coming, and it was now a fact.

This tiny being grew arms, legs and organs. It had a cute little button nose, gorgeous eyes, a sophisticated mouth and silky hair. It would have its own personality and genetics, just like mine. This baby was mine, and I had helped create it. But so had its father.

The one that remained unknown. Two possible options with an impossible outcome. I had to keep it a secret for as long as I could. Too much harm came from this pregnancy and the damage was irreversible. I didn't need it and this baby that grew inside of me didn't deserve it. I had to protect my child from the truth and I was keeping it from its father because the risk was too high.

I watched children play in the park with their parents. A family swung their young daughter on the swing and her blonde hair blew in the breeze. The mother was at the front and snapped pictures of the precious memory. The father pushed his little girl, and she giggled with glee.

I wished I could give my baby that. I wanted so much to give it the love it deserved, but it seemed impossible. There were too many lies, my secret affair with my fiancé's dad and a soon to be loveless marriage. All in front of the public eye and they could rip us to shreds in a heartbeat.

I barely held on as it was and with a healthy pregnancy, it would be too much to take. The stress was a risk I couldn't afford and my baby needed more from me. I had to live with the life I had created for myself, but I would not let my baby suffer because of my actions.

Suddenly, I heard movement from down the hallway and I snapped back to reality. Dylan came around the corner and it surprised me because he was home early. I didn't even realize he was here. He usually worked late, and I knew what that meant. His lover had other plans.

"Where have you been?" He looked at her with judgement. "I've been trying to reach you."

The morning had brought a lot of tension and I forgot to turn on my cell phone. "I must've forgotten to turn on my cell phone, darling. I didn't realize."

Dylan snapped. "Well, you should know better. Business is important and you're my fiancée. We have an image to uphold."

And boy, I knew it.

I had kept so many secrets just for the sake of the company and I was sick of it. The business wasn't even part of my family, but it would be, and that was the only reason I put up with this madhouse. I wanted out, but it was too late for that now. My child's father could be in this very room and it tied us together for the rest of our lives, even if he wasn't.

But he doesn't even know it.

"An extremely fake one." I snapped back and didn't look at him.

He came closer and pointed a finger at my hand on my belly. "Are you okay?"

His concern touched me when he had chosen not to use his ignorance, but I wished he hadn't noticed. I had forgotten my hand was on my stomach that grew with a baby. And a high possibility of being his child, but I quickly removed it.

It was a shock to the system, but I straightened my posture. The truth was a secret, and it needed to stay that way. Even though I wanted to lay down and sleep the day away from exhaustion. But he couldn't even get the hunch I was expecting, and it had to stay like this at all costs.

I raised my nose in the air and held it together. "I'm fine."

"Well, that's good, because I need you to be ready in an hour for our client's twentieth wedding anniversary." He huffed and made his way towards the refrigerator. "You made quite the impression on her and invited us as guests."

I fondly remembered the client as Beverly. A pleasant older woman and wise beyond her years. The business dinner had been quite the occasion, and the deal was quite the celebration. D.S. Industries rose to the top because of it and it would be an honor to attend. I just wish I felt better and didn't drag my feet through the entire event.

"I will be ready in an hour, darling." I beamed with fakeness and he knew it.

He just didn't know the truth about why.

He closed the fridge door and looked at my appearance. "Make sure you wear something far more suitable for the occasion. We wouldn't want people to gossip, darling."

I rolled my eyes at him and snapped. "I wouldn't dream of it."

***

We arrived at the spectacular occasion dressed to impress. Dylan wore a red suit with a bow tie to match the color of my attire and led the way. My arm looped through his and he acted like a true gentleman. Handsome as ever, with his brown hair combed to the side and deep eyes that shimmered. But I knew it was just that.

It was all an act.

He took me through double doors and into a palace suited for royalty. The castle walls shimmered with a gold touch and they set gigantic statues up for shock value. Enormous chandeliers hung from overhead and sparkled with the bright light. Anyone who set foot inside was treated like royalty, and it was an event like no other. Servers walked around with champagne and Dylan snagged one. He sipped the bubbling liquid and admired the view.

But someone caught his attention.

A man snagged his eye as his gaze roamed his backside, and I didn't know how I never noticed it before. All the signs were there, but I had refused to follow them. If I did, maybe I wouldn't be in this mess. I'd have a business degree finished and I could be at the top of my game, but I chose this life. I had to finish it and see where it led me.

And so far, straight to this party.

Pregnant and very alone. In a loveless relationship and soon to tie the knot. Hopelessly in love with a man I couldn't have, because he made himself unavailable long ago.

And he stood right across from me.

Daxon watched me from across the crowded room, but I held my head high. I kept my composure together because I couldn't afford to fall apart. He deserved to squirm, and I dressed myself to make his cock hard.

I wore a red sequined ball gown, and it had fantastic cleavage. It spilled out over the top of the feathered trim and I pulled my hair back in a sleek, high ponytail. Bright red lipstick was on my plump lips because it was my fiancé's favorite and this evening was all about appearance.

An engaged couple in love.

But it couldn't be further from the truth.

I whispered to Dylan. "I didn't know daddy dearest would be here?"

"And why the hell not?" Dylan answered back in a low tone. "He runs the company, and it's good for business."

We wandered closer towards Daxon, and my eyes fell on his date. She came over to him with two glasses of sparkling champagne and a gorgeous young smile. But his eyes shimmered at me just like the chandelier light, and it made me sizzle.

His gorgeous date hung off his arm, but I knew it was all for show. A show for me or for everyone, but it didn't matter.

I knew I was the one he longed for because he had made it known.

He played a good game, but his cock had won the trophy. It triumphed over all else, and I knew how much he craved me. It was the same need I held deep within me. The same hunger we both starved for and it was for each other. Daxon wanted fantastic sex, but I wanted more. He couldn't give me that, but it didn't mean I couldn't tease him.

Only for one night.

"Come on, let's dance." I encouraged Dylan with a smile and took his hand.

He raised his eyebrows with surprise and tilted his head to his side. He went in the direction of the dance floor and we grew closer. Our closeness made my body cringe, but it was all for show. A show for the public eye and my show for his father.

Our bodies swayed to the rhythm of the music, and he whispered in my ear. "It's about time you want to leave a lasting impression, darling. What's come over you?"

I tilted my head to the side with a devilish smirk. "Let's just say your dad got under my skin."

Dylan laughed it off and thought nothing of it. He viewed it as my annoyance for his rude father, but it was now the opposite. An attraction that burned bright and never went out.

We spun across the floor as we moved to a slower beat and all eyes were on us. We made the impression Dylan wanted and my plan had worked. Daxon's eyes caught Dylan's hand as he held the small of my back and brought me closer. Jealous flames sparked to life within his heated gaze and flicked his frustration with me.

He joined us on the dance floor with his date. His hands were on her and travelled lower to her ass. My head spun with hot envy and I wanted it to be me. His eyes caught mine across the dance floor and gleamed with challenge. I accepted his dare, and he tried to show us up. But I wouldn't have it.

"Dip me, darling." I whispered in Dylan's ear as my hands squeezed his broad shoulders and I held on tight.

He did as instructed and my head flung backwards. The tip of my ponytail touched the floor, and he swung me to the right side. My eyes caught Daxon's surprised look and his wicked smirk took over. He knew the game was on.

In one swift motion, Dylan brought me back up flush to his chest, and we breathed heavily. My hips swayed to the beat as it picked up rhythm and the band knew to play faster. I was tightly against his body and his hand took mine. He twirled me outwards and spun me back into his embrace. I smiled at our dance of excellence and peered over Dylan's shoulder.

His dad moved his date closer towards us and ran his hands down the sides of her body. An intoxicating move that made me shiver and wish his hands were on me. He stopped at her hips and grabbed her hand. Her hair flicked in the air as he spun her in circles and her dress blew with it. He paused as his hands grabbed her hips once more and he threw her with ease into the air.

The coward gasped at his display as he balanced her with strength and held her steady high above his head. She was stiff and the chandelier light beamed behind her. He tossed her body upwards, and she spun in the air. The sight was a spectacular show no one expected as he caught her in his arms and the crowd broke out in a cheer.

He carried her with grace and let her body slide down his own until her heels met with the floor. His nostrils extended with each big breath he took and he held her close. But his eyes locked on my surprised face and he knew he had won this round.

Dylan led the way and brought us closer to the couple. I dreaded every second as his eyes never left mine and I took in his attire. He was gorgeous in a silver tux with black dress shoes and it matched his hair perfectly. His wicked smirk made me wet, and I knew he looked this good just for me.

"Could I take your partner for a spin?" Dylan asked as he looked at Daxon's date and admired her. "That dance was quite impressive."

Daxon's date threw her head back and giggled with flattery. "Absolutely."

Daxon made no fuss and handed her to Dylan. He let go of me as we exchanged partners and Daxon wrapped one arm around me. His other hand intertwined with mine and he pulled me flush up against him.

"Alone at long last, princess." He beamed with victory.

His eyes shone at me like he had won his prize. A bright, sparkling trophy all dressed in red. A dance with a monster wrapped up in darkness. But the darkness was me.

The pad of his thumb caressed the back of my hand, and we moved together in unison. My being no longer cringed with regret, but scorched with heat. A wicked flame that never burnt out as we fell into step with one another and created a beat of our own.

The world stood still. Time froze as we weaved through it and broke all boundaries. Our forbidden dance grew heavier as our breath mingled and our faces were inches apart. But his eyes captivated me and drew me in.

Their different hues of brown blazed with passion as he looked back at me and burned a hole straight into my heart. It burst wide open and welcomed him inside. But I knew he wouldn't enter even though I longed for it.

His need was only sexual, and that was all he had to give. I had to accept it, but it still sliced like a knife. But my emotions needed to remain in check.

He was my future father-in-law, after all. We too had an image to uphold, and too many eyes were on us. And I needed to snap out of it.

"Well, what are you waiting for, daddy?" I breathed against his face. "Show me your moves, old man."

My tease had done the trick, as he groaned with annoyance. He blasted me back into reality as our legs moved in overtime and he flung me outward. He twirled me back into his sphere as my ponytail flew through the air. My tits pressed flush up against his chest as his heart hammered inside it and he dipped me backwards. My head flew back, and I saw the eyes of the crowd. We enchanted them and I was stuck within his beat.

He pulled me back into him, and I wrapped my hands behind his neck. His hands ran down my sides and rested at my hips, but I felt his willpower torture him. He wanted to venture lower and touch my most intimate places. But he used restraint with the public eye on us.

"You torture me, princess." Daxon growled against my cheek. "The monster inside me wants to come out and play."

Our foreheads touched, and I sighed. "And how would it amuse itself?"

Daxon licked his lower lip and bit it with need. "It would take your tightness and taunt it until it explodes."

I whimpered at the thought and bit my lip. His eyes caught the movement and his lips came closer. It was a need we couldn't deny, and our adrenaline raced. My heartbeat clouded my ears, and I wanted nothing more than his mouth on mine. I masked my judgement with desire and we were about to give into temptation.

Screw it all to hell.

"What a performance!" Beverly beamed from beside us.

We broke apart and stared at one another. Our breath was heavy, and the flame burnt out. We had almost engaged in the unthinkable. Almost showing our true thirst for one another. We almost broke all the rules and gave into temptation. In front of everyone.

"Would you care to dance, Beverly?" Daxon asked as he lent her his hand and got back into character.

"You don't mind if I steal him from you, dear?" Beverly asked sweetly and touched my shoulder.

"No, he's all yours." I replied as I swallowed hard and choked down my emotion.

She took his hand and as he led her away from me; she shouted with delight. "I'm so happy you could make it!"

"I wish I felt the same..." I breathed to myself as I watched them spin away and I felt unsteady on my feet.

The sudden change of pace threw me off, or maybe it was because he wasn't beside me. I let myself get carried away and got lost in our game. The same game I vowed to not get involved in again, but I couldn't help myself. I couldn't keep myself from him.

He had played his pieces right and made his checkmate. The game lived on, but it was all about to change. I was pregnant, and that changed everything.

TWENTY-FIVE

Pantry

Hours turned into days, and days turned into weeks. Time moved on and my belly grew each day. It expanded and turned into more than just bloat. It grew firmer with my baby inside and created a protective barrier for it.

The doctor's appointments impeded wedding planning and had to be a priority. My child came over everything else. Wedding plans could wait and if we had to push the big day, we would. This baby wasn't going to wait and be here in less than nine months.

The blood work came back great, and I was in the best shape to carry a pregnancy to full-term. I booked the first ultrasound for nine weeks along and I couldn't wait to see my baby. To view what it looked like inside of me and get its first picture. Too bad I had to do it alone.

My clothes grew tighter, and it was harder to conceal the pregnancy. I wore fancy baggy clothes to keep up my image and dresses with more room. My bra size expanded, and I had to hit the store. My hair grew thicker, and I loved the new shape. But my stomach still heaved from the morning sickness and I hated it.

It always showed up whenever it felt like it, and I hated every moment. It made no sense why a woman's body would be so hungry yet so sick all at the same time. And today I was starving.

I hit up the restaurant across the street from D.S. Industries. It wasn't far from my penthouse, just in case this meal turned into a disaster. But I felt fine, and it was one of my better days.

Plus, I hadn't eaten out much and was dying for a meaty cheeseburger. Tomatoes, pickles, onions, lettuce, mustard and ketchup. I needed a good meal and today felt like the day.

When the food arrived, I stuffed my face like there was no tomorrow. My intense hunger took over, and it was all I wanted. My cravings were crazy, and I ordered a milkshake to add to the mix. I was pregnant after all and eating for two. I indulged in whatever food I wanted, and no one could say a damn thing.

The food was delicious, and I savored the taste inside my mouth. I sat back and rubbed my full belly. But it gargled with unease.

Oh, no...

I had overdone it and panic took over. My palm grew sweaty, and I knew I needed to get home. My cry for food was replaced by fear of vomiting all over myself.

I couldn't wait for the bill and placed a fifty on the table. It would be more than enough to cover my single meal and give a generous tip. The food hit my stomach and didn't waste any time, but I was queasy as soon as I stood. The floor rocked from side to side as I stumbled for the door and a dreadful burp escaped me. It was loud and obnoxious. I was sure someone at the far side of the restaurant could hear it.

And a jerk joked with a laugh. "It's a little too early to be drinking there, sweetheart."

I wanted to blast him with my middle finger, but it was no use and I struggled for the door instead. My foot tripped over a table leg and I fell onto it. Luckily, it was an empty table no one used, and I was thankful for that. I didn't need this to turn into an even bigger mess than it already was.

But someone touched my arm.

"Celeste?" A deep tone said with concern.

Something blurred my vision as I turned to look and stood from the table. It was no use, and I was far too weak. This morning sickness just didn't want to give up.

"I got you, princess." He breathed as his arms scooped me up, and he carried me out of the restaurant.

I knew that voice anywhere. The smooth, deep tone of command and power. But it was his nickname for me that gave him away.

It was Daxon.

"I don't know what the hell is wrong, but I'm getting you home, Celeste." He breathed as I laid my head against his chest and listened to his heartbeat.

He peered down at me with worry in his eyes and back towards his mission. Cars loudly honked from around us as his long strides stepped into the busy traffic and he carried me through the street. He didn't waste a moment and halted traffic with me in his arms.

It pissed people off, and I could hear their angry threats, but he paid no attention. I was his top priority, and he wanted to get me back home. He protected me in his embrace from all else, and nothing else mattered to him. Just me.

He finally made it across the street and hurried towards the penthouse. I heard him curse as my limp body laid in his arms and wondered if he feared the worst. But I simply had no strength to go on.

My venture turned into a disaster and I felt like utter shit. I should've eaten at home, but I figured I was out of the woods for the day. I felt fine and ready to tackle a nice hot meal. But this baby had other plans.

And I was about to throw up.

"I think I'm going to be sick..." I muttered as my hand flew to my mouth and I held it back.

"Christ..." He groaned with displeasure.

Black dots danced before my eyes as he found my keys in my purse and opened the front door. It opened with a thud and he didn't waste a second. He kept going and headed straight for the bathroom. The bile pushed up into my throat just as he sat me down in front of the toilet and I released the contents of my meal into it.

"It's okay, sweetie, let it all out." Daxon breathed as he sat behind me and held my hair back.

My nauseous stomach let up and Daxon's caress soothed my backside. He ran his hand in slow circles as I leaned against the toilet and waited for some strength to come back. He just sat there behind me in silence and listened to my body relax.

Daxon, recently the man who was my enemy. The man who I thought wanted me gone. A man so cruel and ruthless who only put his business first. But yet so kind, thoughtful and complex.

There was so much more to Daxon Stark and I saw it first hand as he handed me a towel to clean my mouth. He let go of my hair and brushed the strands behind my ears. His hands cupped my face as I tried to turn away, and he made me look at him. His kind eyes shone into my soul, and I never wanted to come back from it. I could stay lost in them forever because this was the man Daxon truly was. And he was incredible.

The pads of his thumbs caressed my face, and I was sure my breath stank, but he didn't care. He laid his forehead against mine and the quietness was everything. He was everything, and he softly brushed my lips.

"Feel better, princess?" He asked me against my mouth.

"Yes, much better." I breathed against his lips.

He pulled back and scooped me back into his arms. "Good, because I'm staying whether you like it or not."

I wanted to refuse and put up a fight, but I didn't have the strength for it. I didn't care to be alone when I was like this, and it would be nice to have company. Being pregnant and sick was a chore. The extra help would be nice.

"Okay, daddy." I giggled softly as he laid me on the couch and covered me with a blanket.

"I wonder why you are so sick?" Daxon pondered as he stood up straight and looked down at me. "It has to be the food at that greasy restaurant. I'll put in a complaint first thing in the morning."

His concern was touching, but I knew the true reason for this dreadful sickness. The sickness would soon go away and turn into back pain. Next, would come swollen feet and the need for this baby out of me. But he couldn't know the truth.

No one could.

"No, don't worry about it." I sighed and lied to him. "It's probably just a bug I picked up."

"Well, regardless, I'm staying here until you're better and I'm going to make you some peppermint tea." He said with determination and headed towards the kitchen. "Where do you keep your tea bags?"

I heard cupboards open and shut. A rustle of utensils and random sounds from the kitchen behind me. He tried to navigate my kitchen with a mission to soothe my queasy belly, and it was the sweetest thing.

I giggled and answered without another thought. "They are in the pantry."

The pantry...

Oh, no!

My brain reeled into overdrive and pushed my pregnancy brain aside. The lack of sleep and sickness had finally taken its toll. I had forgotten about my prenatal vitamins in the pantry and Daxon was about to stumble upon them.

I threw the blanket aside and shot off the couch. I rounded around it to confront him and steer him away from the one thing that could give this pregnancy away. He couldn't learn the truth and I needed to hide it at all costs. Not like this.

"You know I think I made a mistake and..." I blurted out in panic.

But it was too late.

There was Daxon, and he held the bottle of prenatal vitamins in his hand. He looked down at them as he read the label and the surprise sank in. He peered in my direction and back at the bottle of supplements to help with the baby's development. The prenatal vitamins I took to help me have a safe and healthy pregnancy.

"Why the hell are these in your pantry?" He asked as he stepped closer to me and narrowed his eyes.

"I-I..." I stammered, but no words came out.

He caught me, and the secret was up. There was no way out of it and no matter what lie I came up with, he knew the truth. Daxon Stark wasn't stupid and far from it. He was wise and had already had a child. He knew exactly what those meant.

"You're pregnant?" He breathed in disbelief and looked down at my swollen belly.

"Yes, I am." I sighed and held my breath.

"How could you keep this from me?" Daxon asked as he walked closer still and fell to his knees.

His reaction shocked me as his hands touched my belly, and the moment was tender. He caressed my swollen skin and my hands found his hair. They ran through the silky strands and tears touched my eyes. The delicate moment had touched me in a way I never thought possible because I didn't realize he was capable. Capable of caring for this baby and it wasn't even born yet.

"I kept it a secret because of all the lives it could ruin. Yours, Dylan's, and our image in the public eye." I admitted as he looked up at me and his eyes narrowed. "This baby might not be yours. It could be your son's."

The reality of the situation hit him like a brick wall. He blinked several times, and the tenderness was over. He removed his hands from my stomach and stood. His hands went into his pockets, he gave me space and a sharp look came back to his eyes. He closed himself off once again, but I wanted him to open back up to me. To us and our potential child together. But that reality was uncertain, and he knew that.

So, he gave me space.

"How far along are you?" He asked with ease.

"I'm about seven weeks along, according to all the tests so far." I breathed as I took the prenatal vitamins and hid them back in the pantry.

"Christ, Celeste, you were so sick, and you were just going to keep it from everyone?" Daxon snapped with concern.

"I had little choice." The air became tense, and I snapped back. "I slept with you and your son. It could ruin everything if the truth came out."

"And you thought this was the best idea?" Daxon sighed as he ran his hands through his hair and he grabbed my shoulders. "This was the worst idea you've had, princess."

I held his intense stare. "Oh, ya? Do you have a better one?"

Daxon looked back at me, but didn't speak a word. He knew there was no better idea except for the truth. A truth that could shatter our lives in an instant and he knew deep down I tried to save us. I tried to spare us all from unwanted heartache.

He let me go and backed away, but the door clicked behind me. I spun around and saw Dylan. His eyes found mine, but I knew they fell on his father over my shoulder. Shit was about to all go to hell and there was no turning back now.

"Dad? What are you doing here?" Dylan asked his father, and his eyebrows knitted together.

I turned my head to look at Daxon, and he looked back at me. His eyes swirled with uncertainty and I caught his hands diving into his pockets. He was nervous, and he had every right to be.

"Celeste was feeling under the weather and I brought her home." He answered and kept his uneasiness in check.

I quickly added. "I was at the restaurant across the street and felt sick. Your father helped me home, darling."

Dylan dropped his belongings in the chair and came to my side. He took my face in his hands and kissed my forehead. It was the sweetest gesture he had shown me in quite a while.

"Darling, what's going on? You look pale." He asked as his eyes searched my face and he caressed my cheek with his thumb. "Tell me what's going on."

At that very moment, I knew it was time. It was time to kill two birds with one stone. I had kept this secret for as long as I could and I would've kept it longer if I could, but this was it. Daxon knew and Dylan would too. It was time for the truth.

Well, some of it at least.

I saw Daxon move towards the door to escape the private moment. His hand touched the doorknob, and I wished he would stay. But I understood his reason to flee.

"I'm pregnant." I blurted out the truth and looked Dylan right in the eyes.

He stood there with his mouth agape. No words tumbled out, and it shocked him. He didn't move, but his face suddenly changed to pure happiness.

"You're pregnant?" He belted out, lifted me up, and spun me around. "Did you hear that, dad? We're having a baby!"

Dylan stopped spinning me and I looked over at Daxon, whose hand fell from the doorknob. He looked shocked, and he didn't expect me to tell Dylan like this. I didn't expect any of it to go like this, but I figured it was time.

Daxon's shock turned into joy as he looked his son's way and beamed brightly. "Congratulations, you two. I'm going to be a grandfather!"

Or father.

Dylan put me down and went over to his father. He grabbed him and pulled him into a big hug. Daxon patted his back, peered at me over his shoulder, and his eyes locked onto mine with fright. But his face spoke it all.

What the hell were we going to do now?

TWENTY-SIX
Paternity

Two weeks passed by, and Dylan had been more supportive than usual. He was around more and much more involved. It all came as a surprise I tried to get used to, but while Dylan hadn't been around, his father had.

With Dylan around more, Daxon had kept his distance. I was pregnant, and it changed everything. He knew it could be his son's child, and I knew it weighed heavily on his decision. We still had to play the part. I was the happy pregnant fiancé and Daxon was a joyous grandpa to be. Even though we both knew the paternity of the baby could change everything. We still had to act like everything was normal, even when it wasn't.

And that played with my heart.

It still belonged to Daxon, no matter what. He was the man who tempted me with his games and I fell for him. I fell hard.

This baby could very well be his. He could be the father and Daxon knew it. But we had to be sure.

Until then, Daxon had kept his distance and let Dylan partake in all the moments of becoming a father. Dylan would talk to the baby over my stomach, he'd get the food I was craving and help me when I felt sick. It was great with him by my side, but I wished he could've been like this just for me. He had asked me to marry him, to be his wife, and this was the way he was supposed to be. Not gone and his time surrounded by his lover. But his homosexuality had kept him from me and I knew this was all for the child growing inside of me.

Dylan was gay, and I wished he never dragged me into it. He made me his trophy just to carry around on his arm. I wished he didn't lead me to believe we were meant to be when he knew it was all wrong. I was the entire package to conceal his truth that was inside. A man and his lover. His ultimate secret.

But now I kept it a secret. One that could change the course of all our lives. The real paternity of my child.

And today was a tremendous day.

Today, I will get to see my baby for the first time. It was a nine-week ultrasound to check on the pregnancy and hear its heartbeat. To finally meet my little one for the first time.

But Daxon would be there.

Dylan had insisted and wanted his dad present. The glad grandfather to be. He wanted Daxon to be there for every scan, because he knew it would mean the world to him. Under different circumstances it would, but this situation was different and Dylan didn't know that.

He didn't realize there was a huge chance that his dad was the father. I slept with his dad and he didn't know I did the unthinkable. He had no idea his own father went behind his back and had sex with his fiancé. Multiple times, for that matter, and I fell in love with him. I wanted him to be mine. Heart, body and soul. But he never could be and it broke my heart.

Tears stung my eyes as we waited in the dimly lit room for the ultrasound technician to join us. Dylan stood beside the bed and Daxon had his arms crossed by the door. My eyes met him from across the room and I knew he was uncomfortable, but only I could sense it. He kept it hidden for his son's sake and to conceal the truth. We faked it until we made it because it was all we could do until we knew the truth.

"Are you okay?" Dylan asked as he wiped a tear from my cheek that had escaped. "You're emotional, darling?"

I wiped my eyes and plastered on a fake smile. "I'm just so excited to see the baby."

And I was.

I was also heartbroken because the man who could be the father wasn't available. He was off limits and forbidden. I was angry at myself for giving in and I let this happen. This should have been one of the happiest moments of my life, and it felt unbearable.

I should know with absolute certainty who the father was. We should be here content and overjoyed. So excited to see our little one that grew inside of me and it should be all we could think about. But instead, we had uncertainty looming over our heads.

"I am too..." Dylan admitted with a huge smile and looked at his father. "How are you holding up, grandpa?"

Daxon's gorgeous smile lit up the room. "Splendid, son."

There was a soft tap at the door, and a thin woman walked into the room. Daxon moved in closer to get out of the way, but retreated towards the door and leaned against the frame. He looked awkward and like he wanted to be anywhere other than here. I could imagine he wished to be in the arms of another woman and fucking her brains out to forget I ever existed. This turned his life upside down thanks to our never-ending attraction. I knew he wanted it to never happen, but the temptation was too much. It was out of our control and still was.

"Good afternoon. I'll be your ultrasound technician today." She said politely in a soft manner. "I assume this is all family here?"

"Yes, this is my fiancé and his father." I answered with my anxiety over a notch.

"Okay, so father to be and grandpa to be. Nice to meet you both." She said with a smile.

I pulled my eyes away from Daxon and focused on the technician. She put on some clear gloves and sat beside my bed in front of the ultrasound machine. The screen was already on and she tilted it for everyone to see. She got the probe ready and squirted some clear blue jelly from a bottle onto it.

She held it up and pushed a button in front of her. "Are you ready to meet your baby?"

I took a deep breath and blew it out. "As ready as I'll ever be."

"Could you lift your shirt just below your bra?" She asked.

I followed her instructions and pulled it up. My fingers tucked the fabric underneath my bra to keep it out of the way. I wanted nothing to screw this up. I needed to be sure my baby was going to be healthy. My life may be crazy, but my pregnancy didn't have to be.

"Is this good enough?" I asked with uncertainty.

She nodded her head and said. "Now this jelly might be a little cold, so just bear with me."

The probe touched my warm belly, and I jerked a little. The slight chill from the jelly gave me a bit of a shock, but as she moved it around, it warmed up. She pressed in certain areas and gave me the urge to urinate, but I held it in. They instructed me to drink lots of water hours before my appointment and not to pee. And the need to use the bathroom was strong.

Suddenly, I heard a sound beat so loudly beside me and it made me raise my head. I tilted it to view the screen and didn't know what I was looking at. I saw two black sacs and the sound from the machine was getting stronger. It sounded like two different beats very close to each other and I became nervous.

"What is that sound?" I asked as my palms grew sweaty and I looked at the technician.

"That is the sound of your baby's heartbeat." She answered, but appeared puzzled.

She pressed a button several times and moved the probe to the right of my belly. She searched for things I didn't understand and wished I could. This was my baby, and I needed to be sure he or she was going to be okay.

"Is something wrong?" Dylan asked as he picked up on my tension and touched my leg.

"I just have to be certain..." She breathed as she moved the probe again and to the left side of my stomach.

"Certain of what?" Daxon asked impatiently, and I could hear the worry in his voice.

I looked up at him and the concern he held for me was there. The distress that something could be wrong with the baby. It swirled around in his eyes as he stepped closer and touched my ankle. The instinctive need was there to touch me and it was the closest part of me he could touch.

"I had to be certain there were two babies and not just one." She replied with a smile and looked down at me. "You're having twins, Celeste."

"What?" I breathed in disbelief.

She pointed at the screen. "See these two black sacs? Each one is for a different baby. You are having fraternal twins and these are your babies moving inside their own placenta."

Tears blurred my vision and streamed down my face. I couldn't believe my eyes as I followed her instructions and realized it was true. I was having twins.

Two babies with two unique personalities. Two heartbeats with two passions for life. And two babies that would look the same.

"I can't believe this." Dylan whispered from beside me. "We're having twins."

He looked at the screen and couldn't take his eyes away from the babies. We could see their little blobs move, but nothing more. I couldn't understand anything else I saw and fell in love with their heartbeats. It was the most precious sound I could ever imagine. I knew they were alive and everything was going to be okay. I felt it deep down inside.

My eyes caught Daxon's, and they shimmered in the light. He didn't look at the babies and only at me. I knew he couldn't believe it and was just as shocked as everyone else.

But pure relief fell over him and his emotions got the best of him.

He squeezed my ankle and smiled, but wiped his eyes of the powerful emotions he felt inside. They pushed past his breaking point and he gave into them. But we knew everything was going to be alright.

"You're going to be an amazing mother to these precious babies, Celeste." Daxon breathed as he smiled and his words tugged at my heart. "They are lucky to have you."

"And they are lucky to have you too, Daxon." I breathed as the words escaped my lips and I couldn't take them back.

But I didn't want to.

It was the whole truth. Nothing but the truth. So, help me if I can't help myself.

Dylan grabbed my hand and his father's. "They are lucky to have all of us."

We both looked at Dylan and we all connected as one. The family would grow. These twins would bond us together for the rest of our lives. But we just didn't know how, and Dylan had no idea the truth was just around the corner.

And I didn't know if he would ever find out.

***

Several weeks passed, and I hit fourteen weeks into my pregnancy. I didn't think my belly could get any bigger, but it did, and I didn't think it could stretch anymore. My clothes didn't fit the way I hoped, and a shopping trip was in order. My morning sickness had settled, and I was more at ease. I slept better and could eat anything I wanted. I enjoyed my pregnancy, and it was a high note.

But today I was nervous.

We went behind Dylan's back and had a paternity test done at thirteen weeks pregnant. Daxon ordered it and wanted it done immediately. It was invasive, but would provide us with the truth, and we were ready to take that risk.

The test was called Chorionic Villus Sampling. I had to go to a special lab, and a doctor used a needle to take a small tissue sample from my uterine wall through the cervix. They took that fluid sample and would compare the DNA to Daxon's.

Dylan didn't even need to be involved because if Daxon wasn't the father, then we knew he was. It was simple, but terrifying. These results held my future in its scientific grasp and without it I wouldn't know the answer. The truth we both sought.

Who was the father?

Daxon told me the results of the paternity test were ready. He held the answer within an envelope and he wanted me to meet him at his office. We'd do this in secret with no one else around. The same way everything else was going so far. Strictly confidential.

My nerves kicked into overdrive when I saw his office door closed and knew he was just on the other side. I knew he waited for me with the same anxiousness I felt pushing at the surface and it needed air. We needed to breathe and let the truth sink in.

Was Daxon the father, or was his son?

"You can do this, Celeste..." I breathed as I held a hand over my belly and tapped on his door.

Immediately, the door opened and Daxon stood on the other side. His hair was a disheveled mess, like he had run his hands through it multiple times and some pieces stood up. I wanted to touch him and fix it, but I knew it wasn't the time.

So, I let out a nervous laugh instead.

"Seriously?" Daxon asked with an annoyed look. "There's nothing funny about this situation, princess."

"You don't have to remind me, daddy." I huffed and closed the door behind me. "Did you look inside the envelope yet?"

He shook his head. "I couldn't bring myself to without you."

My heart skipped a beat, and I looked at the plain white envelope in his hands. He wanted me to be with him when he found out. And I couldn't wait another second.

"Well, I'm here now." I sighed as I plucked it out of his hands and peered down at my fate. "Let's get this over with."

I opened the flap of the white paper and pulled out the result inside. They folded it into three and blank on the backside. I turned it over and unfolded it.

"Wait..." Daxon blurted out and his hand touched mine.

His eyes caught mine. The deep hues of brown shone against the light and burned deep into my soul. He stared at me with such intensity it made my heart pound in my ears and my toes curled in my shoes.

"What is it?" I asked with curiosity.

The pad of his thumb caressed my hand, and he whispered. "No matter what the result is, you'll always be mine. Mine to tempt, mine to play with and mine to cherish."

I swallowed hard and knew it was true. I was his, and I knew it from the moment this game between us started. The tug of war for power pulled me in and I fell for him.

He let me go, and I opened the paper with the fine print, staring me right back in the face. The result we both sought was 99.9 percent accurate. The bold black print stated that Daxon Stark was indeed the father and everything was about to change.

"You're the father, Daxon." I breathed with certainty as my eyes shimmered with happiness at the twins' father. "These babies are yours."

I laid his hand on my stomach as he read the result on the paper, and his eyes shimmered just like mine. He looked at me and down at his hand on my belly. He caressed it softly and tucked the paper into his suit pocket. His eyes met mine again after he hid it away.

But they turned cold.

"I will care for our children, provide them with all they need. We will co-parent, but we can be nothing more, princess." Daxon said in a businesslike manner and he let go of my stomach. "And for the sake of my company, we will let my son believe he is the father of the twins. Do you understand?"

He broke eye contact with me and walked to the tall office window. He looked out at the view in all his closed off glory and I wanted to hate him. I wanted to hurt him and hit him to make him see what he was doing was wrong. But my heart ached for him.

This ruthless, icy, bitter man. My soon to be father-in-law. The father of my children.

And I agreed with the monster before me. "I understand, daddy."

TWENTY-SEVEN

Dinner is Served

I got ready in a tight purple dress that sparkled and cut off just above my knees. The occasion was special and I haven't worn a dress like this since I fell pregnant. It showed off my bump, but everyone knew about the pregnancy. It no longer remained a secret, and the media grabbed onto it like a piranha. They ate away at it and attacked it until it was old news.

I fluffed my wavy hair over my shoulders and puckered my lips together. The pink lip gloss shimmered in the reflection and my hands fell on my belly. I looked so cute in this dress with my noticeable small bump, but a sweet touch. A pregnant wife to be and it suited me well. I never thought I could do this, but I was, and I looked damn good doing it.

"Darling, hurry or we will be late for dinner!" Dylan called from the main room and I grabbed my purse from the table.

"I'm coming!" I answered back and hurried across the floor to get my heels on.

"You aren't seriously going to wear those, are you?" Dylan asked with disagreement.

"I'm pregnant, not dead, Dylan." I muttered and put the purple heels on.

I walked past him with grace even though my feet hurt and I knew I couldn't continue to wear them after this evening. My feet were now swelling from the extra weight and a few changes needed to be made. But tonight was special.

It was a celebration for my babies.

Dylan had made the arrangements because he was a proud dad to be and he wanted us all to celebrate our family. It was getting bigger, and he decided a celebratory dinner was in order. Just myself, him, and his father. All a family unit, together to ring in our pregnancy.

It was the first time I'd been close to Daxon since we received the result of the paternity test. He had kept his distance, but remained close. He'd watch and react from the sidelines. But he never interfered even though he knew these babies were his.

His icy haughty demeanor was back, and he'd built up those walls. I hated every minute, but if this was how he wanted to deal with it. Then that was on him. My babies were with me. I had a pregnancy to get through, and I certainly didn't have the energy to babysit him. I didn't have time to question his choice. It was done, and it had to stay this way. It was the best for him, the company, and Dylan's secret.

Dylan being my babies' father was the best outcome for everyone. I had to continue telling myself that because deep down; it felt like I was drowning. We sank deeper into all the lies and scandal of it all. I couldn't catch my breath as it all consumed me whole, and I felt like I'd never be the same.

Dylan was gay. I had an affair with his father. And I was pregnant with Daxon's twins.

What more could go wrong?

The walk was a short one to the fancy restaurant of Dylan's choosing and the brightly lit sign shined down on the sidewalk. My heels clicked along the pavement as I came along the side of the building and Dylan touched my side. He loved to put up the image of a true gentleman in case there were any cameras nearby. Daddy had taught him well.

He held the door for me, and we made our way inside. I set foot into the main area and Daxon was there. His brawny figure stood out and stole my breath away from his handsome good looks. He slightly tilted his head to the side and his eyes roamed down the front of my dress. He gave his lower lip a quick bite and pressed his lips together. The way he looked at me made me sizzle, and I felt like the sexiest woman alive.

"Hello, daddy dearest." I teased as I looked around and raised an eyebrow at him. "You didn't bring a date this time?"

He huffed. "There was no need."

I squared him up, and my mind reeled. No date for daddy meant he was through with making me jealous. I pondered what his next move would be, but maybe there wasn't one any longer. Now that I was pregnant with his children. Deep down, I was truly and utterly his.

"I would rather that, since this is a family celebration." Dylan admitted as he rubbed my belly and beamed proudly.

Daxon's gaze landed on the gesture and only I could tell he didn't like it. I knew it should be him who did this and not his son, but this was what he wanted. He wanted our affair to stay hidden and Dylan to carry on as the father. He wanted to pose no risk to his business, and Dylan wanted to stay in the closet. It was a win for all, but it sure as hell didn't look like it.

Daxon tore his eyes from my stomach and cleared his throat. "Shall we begin?"

"Yes, we should." I nodded and didn't hesitate with the change of pace.

Daxon led the way towards a high-top seated table with fancy fabric grey colored chairs. They had bigger legs on them to match the height of the table. It was perfect for my bigger belly and much better than a lower seat.

"I thought this would suit you much better." Daxon said as he referred to the babies and pulled out my seat.

"It definitely does." I breathed as I sat in my seat and he tucked in my chair. "Thank you, daddy."

He was so close his face touched my hair and I heard him breathe in the smell of me. It made me shudder at the thought of what I do to him, and he touched my shoulder. I glanced up at him and his eyes shone at me with desire. It was a simple gesture that appeared innocent, but it was bad as hell. He and I both knew what his touch did to me. It set me on fire with a flame that flickered only for him.

"So, what's on the menu for this evening?" Dylan muttered from beside me as he opened his menu and didn't notice a thing.

I touched Daxon's hand and pushed it away. If I didn't, I was afraid he wouldn't let go. His need to be close to me was so strong I could taste it, but we couldn't afford to slip up. We were in public where anyone could notice and Dylan might catch on. We couldn't risk it, and my eyes flickered at him with warning as he rounded the table and took his seat on the other side.

The server came around and we ordered our drinks. I got a tall glass of orange juice with pulp and the men received their finest bottle of red wine. It was a celebration after all, even though I couldn't drink.

"So, Celeste and I have been talking..." Dylan said as he opened the wine bottle and poured his father a glass. "We've been discussing the children's future and school options."

"And?" Daxon asked as he raised the wineglass to his mouth and took a sip of the red liquid.

"We want our children to attend a normal public school in the city." Dylan announced with happiness.

Daxon choked on his drink and barked an order. "No, absolutely not. It should be a private school. They need to be educated in a strict environment and learn from the best because one of them will take over the business one day."

"What's wrong with a public school?" I asked in frustration.

"It lacks the proper education." Daxon replied.

"Well, I beg to differ." I argued and crossed my arms in front of me. "I think nothing is wrong with a public school and we can find the best one to send them to."

Daxon slammed his hand down on the table and glared at me from across it. "These are my grandchildren and I have a say in what happens with their education."

"Dad, just calm down. There's no need to get so upset." Dylan added as he shrugged his shoulders and looked around.

Daxon caused a scene, and people were staring. We didn't need this kind of attention, not here and not this evening. This was supposed to be a celebration, not a public show. I hadn't realized Daxon would be this upset about the children just going to school. This would be harder than I ever imagined.

Daxon was truly upset, and he had every right to be because he was their father. I now see I should've at least discussed this with him first in private or gave him a heads up. But Dylan had brought it up and agreed with me.

An education at a public school was much more rewarding than a private one. Dylan had attended private school and hated it. The loneliness and need to succeed outweighed everything. Dylan never truly got to be a kid, and he didn't want that for his children. He wanted something different for them. But he didn't realize these weren't his babies.

Until it changed and the truth came to light, Dylan could do what he thought was best for his kids. This was the way Daxon wanted it and the way it would stay. It wouldn't change because Daxon would do anything for his company. He'd even let his own son raise his children.

I looked at Daxon, who became angered by the situation and softened my eyes. He needed to calm down and see reason. He was a hard man to break through, but I knew there was a way it could be done. I could reason with him and win. Or I could distract him and triumph.

"My dear future father-in-law, surely you can see these are our children. They are not yours and we, as their parents, will let them go to whatever school we choose." I breathed as my eyes pleaded with him to let this go.

"But these are my grandchildren, Celeste." Daxon hissed, and he couldn't let it go.

"We know that, father and we respect that you want to have a huge part in their lives, but you aren't their parent." Dylan added as he looked over at me and took my hand with a smile. "We are."

I smiled at his gesture, but my heart broke for Daxon. These were his children, and he viewed everything from the sidelines. It broke me inside and I could see how much these babies meant to him. For him to just step aside and let it happen must slice away at his heart piece by piece.

I looked away from Dylan and my eyes landed on Daxon from across the table. I could tell he barely held it together, but he was about to explode. We needed a change in plans, something to throw him off and have him settle down. He'd blow it all to hell and the truth would ruin us all.

It was time for a distraction.

My eyes darted around in a hurry for some sort of solution and landed on my full glass of orange juice. Dylan and Daxon were too busy arguing about the difference in school boards to notice my plan. I flung my hand out and hit the freshly squeezed orange juice. The cold drink spilled across the table and straight into Daxon's lap.

He gave a shocked face from the chill of it and stared down at the liquid all over his expensive suit. He looked up at me as I rounded the table with a fabric napkin that I got from my lap. I got to his side and dabbed away at the mess as I tried to clean it up.

"Goddamnit, Celeste! Why do you always have to be so clumsy?" Dylan cried out in disgust.

I fired a glare his way and wanted to tell him to go fuck himself, but I bit my tongue. "I'm sorry, darling, but it must be a slip up because of the pregnancy."

I looked away and at Daxon as I heard his son huff. His eyes met mine while I patted his lap, but the napkin slipped lower and he didn't stop me. Instead, his brown haze darkened and lust swirled around inside.

I realized Dylan couldn't notice anything because the table was higher up and the seats lower. Temptation kicked into high gear and I continued to dab, but something grew inside his pants. It caused me to look down and move the napkin aside with my curiosity in overdrive. Curiosity killed the cat, but my pussy was very much alive and wet. He was rock solid, and it was all because of me.

My eyes zoned in on the bulge in his pants and my sexual needs from this pregnancy intensified. My hormones went into overdrive and I realized I hadn't had sex since I found out I was pregnant. But he sat there all hot and bothered, but did something to me.

It made me want to be a very naughty future daughter-in-law.

Daddy called for me and I wanted it just as much.

I let my hand slide down his shaft and I squeezed him. He held in his need for me as his breath sucked in. I knew it took all his willpower not to take me in his arms and fuck me at the dinner table.

Daxon blew out a deep breath and looked over at his son. I kept up the distraction, stroked his cock and knew it would appear I cleaned up my mess. But what a messy situation it was.

I knew Daxon would force me to stop if the stakes were too high. He'd push me aside if Dylan grew suspicious, but it never happened and I kept up my risky tease. Daxon's breath caught in my hair and he quickly brushed it behind my ear. A low moan escaped from deep inside him and he puffed out labored breaths of air. He kept quiet as my adrenaline went into overdrive and I knew someone could catch us at any moment. No sex could do something to a pregnant woman, and it brought out the wickedness in me. But I was far too aroused to care.

Suddenly, Dylan's cell phone rang, and it brought me back to the present. I stopped my torment of his throbbing dick and rested my hand on his lap. My eyes landed on Dylan and I thought the truth was out. But he simply answered his phone and stood up from his seat.

"I got to take this..." Dylan said as he pointed and barely looked at us as he left the table.

I blew out the breath I held and sat back in the chair. I relaxed beside Daxon and couldn't believe I had just done that. It was far too risky, and I clearly wasn't in the right state of mind. This pregnancy was a sham, and it made me into a madwoman.

"What the hell are we doing?" I sighed as I looked over at him and met his eyes.

His gaze gleamed with lust, and he smirked. "What we always do, princess."

His hand fell into my lap and his fingers roamed down my purple dress. They got to the edge, and he hiked it up with his fingers crawling upwards underneath it. He kept going up my inner thigh and my temperature rose with each new pace.

"What are you doing?" I gasped.

He squeezed my thigh and whispered in my ear. "I'm continuing the wicked game you started."

My skin tingled with want as he skillfully tortured my flesh and made me want more. He made me want all he offered and my body couldn't deny him. I shouldn't, I swore I wouldn't, but daddy made me naughty.

I knew he did this on purpose and it was all part of the plan. It unfolded into a secretive passion as his fingers snuck in behind my wet panties and found my clit. He circled them around and lit the match. But my world burst into flames.

"I love touching you, but you know what I love more?" He whispered into my ear.

"What?" I softly gasped.

"I love to watch you squirm, princess." He said as he sat back in his chair and watched me.

My head spun with pure bliss, and my back arched against the chair. I kept my eyes open and the dim lights swirled with little stars. My hands clenched the sides on the seat and my fingernails dug into the fabric. His torturous taunt did me over and I found my ass move in my seat. It slowly circled with his pace and pressed my clit closer towards his movement. My climax grew fast because of the thrill of being caught. Each breath I took came out more like a slight pant as I tried to contain myself against the pleasure building inside.

He massaged, flicked and teased me. The sensation grew throughout me, and I knew my release was just around the corner. My rhythm picked up when no one was watching except his lustful stare, and it pleased him. I caught him as he rubbed himself out of the corner of my eye and I wanted to help him, but the risk was too much.

"Oh..." I softly groaned as he patted my clit and I clenched my eyes closed.

My climax was so close I could scream, and he circled faster. I had ridden my release out for as long as it could and was right at the edge. I braced my back against the chair and my hands found the wood of the table. As the bright stars formed, I clung onto it, but I didn't want to cry out and I...

A throat cleared, and I heard Dylan's voice. "Sorry that took so long, but business comes first. Right, dad?"

My eyes shot open, and I crossed my legs. He scared me right back to reality as the stars vanished and my head cleared. I pushed Daxon's hand aside and looked at Dylan. He sat in his seat and fixed his tie before he took his seat. His eyes fell on his dad and I blew out my unsteady breath. I couldn't speak, and Dylan had almost had us. Another second and Dylan would've caught me lost in pure sexual foreplay with his father.

Daxon swallowed hard and answered. "Right, son. Business before pleasure."

Daxon stole a quick glance at me, and I found my voice. "Excuse me, gentleman. I need to use the ladies' room."

"I need to clean this mess up. I'll be right back, son." Daxon announced as I heard him from behind me and walked away from the table.

I left before I got a response because I needed to breathe. I need to think straight and I couldn't do it with Daxon around. He made me wild and crazy, but it was the most passion I had ever felt. He made me live again.

But I couldn't continue like this.

This was too much, and we almost got caught. I did things I never would do with him, and there was too much at stake. Too much to risk to be so stupid and foolish. It needed to end.

I got to the bathroom and saw the men's restroom first. My heels continued for the ladies' room, but an arm wrapped around my round waist. It pulled me backwards with a swift movement and through a door. I gasped as my back hit a stall in the bathroom and I stared into Daxon's uneasy eyes. He puffed, and it fanned my face.

"What on earth has gotten into you, Daxon?" I asked in a bewildered state and pushed against his broad shoulders.

He didn't budge, and his eyes changed from unease to passion within seconds. I set him aflame, and he was ready to devour me on the spot. Right here in the men's restroom.

"You've gotten into me, princess." He breathed as his eyes blazed into mine and wouldn't let me go. "And daddy wants more."

I pushed him once more, and he backed up. "Well, daddy can't have more because this is over. We can't keep doing this. Your son almost caught us together."

He moved toward me and I moved back. Daxon Stark was a hungry beast, and he wanted what he craved the most. Me.

"It's not over and it never will be, princess." Daxon demanded as he shut the stall door closed behind him and picked me up off the ground.

I gasped as he sat me on the toilet's closed lid and my eyes were on the bulge I created inside his pants. A groan escaped him at the sight of me when I looked up at him. I should be afraid, but I wasn't. He made me hot, wet and horny. His broad figure of power loomed over me and it turned me on.

I never broke eye contact with him as he unzipped his pants and his massive cock sprang free. I knew what he needed and gave him a taste. He moaned from above after I licked the head of his dick. Passion seared through him and it made me wetter than ever. I slid my tongue down the side of him and back until I took him inside my mouth. My mouth took all of him and he grabbed my hair. He bobbed my head back and forth as I gagged on his cock. The head of him hit the back of my throat and he released himself from me with a wicked grin.

"Enough foreplay, young lady." Daxon growled as he bent down and pulled down my panties. "It's time to make you scream."

He cupped his hands under my ass and lifted me into his arms. I hung onto the back of his neck as he pressed me up against the bathroom stall, but my dress hitched up. And his massive cock slid right inside me.

"Oh, Daxon..." I moaned into his shoulder as he bounced me and the bathroom stall groaned.

With each bounce, his dick hit deep inside me and my head leaned back against the cool stall. His manly hands squeezed my ass cheeks as he pounded into me and my nails bit into his neck. Our breath panted as we bounced in desire against one another. The sound of his balls slapped against me and made my head spin.

I was out of control and alive in his arms. Wrapped up in a pure passion with him and I never wanted it to stop. I couldn't ever deny daddy when he wanted to rail the pure shit out of me.

"Oh, yes!" I screamed, just like he promised.

My climax came quickly and strong. Stars hit my eyes, and the world faded away. It tore through me as he kept driving into my core and his cock throbbed inside me. It twitched as his seed spilled from him and he came right along with me. Our need for one another was far too strong to hold back anymore.

"Fuck, Celeste..." He growled as his warmth filled inside me and his body let go.

We came down from our quickie in the bathroom and he set me back on my feet. We heard nothing but our unsteady puffs and Daxon passed me my panties. He brushed my hair behind my ears and kissed my forehead. But I didn't speak a word.

The moment didn't need it, and everything was spoken. Daxon could never let me go. He couldn't let the sex go and these babies were his. He'd try with all his might to have the last word and I'd just have to deal with it.

Once I got balanced again with the world below my feet, I put my panties back on. Daxon looked at me one last time before he turned his back and opened the stall door. He walked out first and held out his hand. I took it, but he didn't tightly squeeze it like he usually did. I found it odd and stepped out beside him as my eyes landed on someone I wished I'd never seen.

Dylan stood there, and his nostrils flared with red, furious rage. "You son of a bitch!"

And he lunged straight for his father.

TWENTY-EIGHT
Caught in Desire

Dylan's powerful attack connected with his father, and he grabbed his shirt collar. Daxon grunted with surprise after Dylan pressed him up against the stall with a hard thud. He was caught off guard and never expected his son to find out like this. He never wanted him to see the truth, but now he had, and it was too late.

"This is what you two have been doing?" Dylan glared into his father's eyes. "Screwing each other behind my back?"

"Dylan, please let your father go!" I shouted as I touched him, but he nudged me away.

I backed up out of fear for the babies. I needed to protect them. All I could do was watch on in horror at a father and son at each other's throats. But it was all because of me.

I came into their lives, and now I was tearing them apart. This should've never happened and I should've stayed away. The attraction for Daxon I could've stopped, but I gave in and now their relationship paid the price.

Dylan choked his father and Daxon pushed back against him as he tried to get air. His hands pressed into Dylan's face and pulled the skin of his cheeks back. Dylan never let up and growled with rage as he pressed his hands tighter around his father's throat.

"Dylan, stop! You're hurting him!" I shouted and watched on in terror.

Somehow, Daxon gained power back at my words and pushed his son off of him. He bent over and held his knees as he gasped for breath. He coughed and breathed in the air as I let out a sigh of relief. But Dylan's eyes stared at my pregnant belly.

"Are those two beautiful babies even mine?" Dylan asked as tears blurred his eyes and he looked up at me. "Is my dad the father?"

"Yes, Dylan. Your dad is the father of the babies growing inside me." I admitted as tears streamed down my face and I felt like this was the end.

We were doomed, and the truth was out. Everything I had worked so hard to hide finished in the blink of an eye. Dylan had caught us in the act. He heard me scream his father's name in our moment of passion. He had heard his father pound into me and give into his need.

"Son, I never meant you harm. I never should've touched her." Daxon admitted as he stood tall and gave into his faults. "But the monster inside me needed her."

"You both led me to believe a lie." Dylan hissed as he pointed his finger at us and it stung. "You made me believe I was going to be a father. How could you?"

"I'm so sorry, son, but there was no other choice. The company was at stake and I..." Daxon said.

"Fuck the company! It's my company too and you should've told me the truth!" Dylan shouted as his anger turned into an uncontrollable urge to strike, and he raised his fist at his father. "How could you do this to me, dad?"

I cried out in protest, but Dylan brought his fist down and Daxon braced himself for the punch. Daxon knew he deserved it and he wouldn't fight back. He brought on everything he was about to receive, but the hit never came. Dylan's fist stopped right beside Daxon's cheek and shook with anger.

Daxon's eyes shone with emotion, and his voice trembled. "I'm a selfish asshole. You deserved none of this. I'm so sorry, son."

Dylan slammed his hand into the stall behind Daxon's head and the loud thud startled me. He released his father and Daxon saw the terror upon my face. He immediately came to my side and touched my cheek. His caress soothed me, but it was short-lived as Dylan let out a groan of rage and came after his father again.

This time, his arm wrapped around his neck and pulled him away from me. Dylan couldn't handle his father touching me after what he had done. He squeezed his arm around his father's neck and the grip tightened around his throat. Daxon pulled at his arm with all he had, but it wasn't enough for his fit of rage.

"Dylan, please stop! Stop it, Dylan!" I cried out as I sobbed and watched Daxon's eyes blink.

He tried to stay conscious, but Dylan's choke hold closed off his oxygen. Daxon watched me as his body gave up the fight and his eyes closed. I screamed in horror as my worst fear had come true. This would end badly. It would end with Dylan killing his father.

My screams turned to agony as pain seared through me, and I bent over. It came in waves through my body and hurt from my belly to my cervix. Everything cramped up and the pain made me clench my stomach. Something was wrong.

"The babies, something is wrong with the babies..." I groaned as I reached down and touched my panties.

My hand was bright red.

Suddenly, Dylan released his father and heavily breathed against the stall. Daxon fell to the floor and crawled towards my feet. Deep breaths puffed into his lungs as he made it to me and touched my belly. It was rock hard as Daxon stared up at me with blood-shot eyes and worry.

He choked out. "Dylan, help me..."

Dylan was in shock at what he had done and just stood there with a blank stare. His father's words didn't register. Not until Daxon stumbled to his feet with the energy he had left and grabbed Dylan.

"For fuck's sake, son! Pull yourself together!" Daxon yelled at him and shook his shoulders. "Celeste needs our help! We need to work together and get her to the hospital right now!"

Dylan snapped out of it, and his eyes locked on his father's face. His lips pressed together, and he pushed his dad off of him. He walked towards the bathroom entrance and I thought he would leave. But he opened the door and looked straight at his dad.

"Carry her to my car. It's parked out front." Dylan ordered.

Daxon picked me up into his safe embrace, and my head leaned into him. The pain seared through my belly, but I had to stay calm. I couldn't fear the worst and had to remain strong for my babies. They depended on me and my body to protect them. To keep them safe and I felt like I had failed them. I squeezed my eyes shut at the next wave of pain and

Daxon carried me from the scene that changed my future forever.

***

I laid in a hospital bed with clean white sheets and a fluffy pillow behind my head. I was alone in a room with a warm sheet over top of me to help soothe my nerves. The obstetrician on call in the emergency department worked fast and found the reason for my pain. She took bloodwork and gave me a pelvic exam. She even gave me an ultrasound to check on the babies and thank God they were okay.

The bleeding and cramping were associated with stress. I was under too much worry and uncertainty. It needed to get under control or the babies and my life could both be at risk. Something needed to change.

I thought for sure I was in some form of labor, but it was too soon. It was just a false alarm and because of high stress. But it hit both father and son very hard.

The truth was out and Dylan was no longer the father. Dylan was going to have siblings. He had to wrap his mind around the fact he would no longer be a dad and I understood it took time. He would need that, but we still had one big problem, and that was the company.

Dylan and Daxon both left me alone to relax while they came to a solution. We all knew there had to be some sort of common ground for the company, but for the babies' sake as well. A tough decision had to be made, and we'd live with it for the rest of our lives. But if Dylan wouldn't go along with a plan, we were toast.

I couldn't imagine him not, considering the secret he kept from his father. The secret I knew, and he wanted me to keep. A truth I kept from Daxon, because I had no other choice. Unless I wanted to ruin him and all he had worked for.

Suddenly, the door groaned as it opened and Daxon came inside. Dylan joined in behind him and didn't appear pleased. He'd just found out his fiancé was banging his dad, and they were having children together.

Why would he be thrilled?

I didn't expect him to be, nor did I expect he'd understand. Daxon had shown me more attention than he ever did, and I knew the real reason. He never loved me and played me to help him keep his secret affair hidden. He had used me in the worst way and I didn't sleep with his father for revenge. I slept with him because I wanted to. He made me feel alive again. He challenged me like no one else had and made me see I wanted more for myself.

I wanted love, and I wanted him.

Daxon made me love him even when I was too bullheaded to see the truth. The truth of how I felt inside and I could love a man who was a monster. But his past broke him and needed time to heal.

Daxon felt something for me and I knew it. It was there in the way he looked at me, touched me and cared for me. I was the naughty one who wouldn't back down to him and challenged him. It pushed us closer and into each other's arms. And I fell hard for him.

But he doesn't return my love.

And it hurts.

These babies were the only thing that held us all together at this point. Without them, we'd probably go our separate ways and my heart would be with Daxon forever. Lost and for no one else.

I rubbed my belly and was happy they were here. With them, I stood a chance to be close to the man I loved. We stood a chance to be a family. I had to hope for the best.

Dylan closed the door behind him and looked at me. "We have a few minutes to talk before the doctor comes back."

Daxon came over and laid his hand on mine. "You're going to be discharged, princess. The babies are okay to come home."

Daxon caressed my hand with the pad of his thumb over my belly, but he looked at his son on the other side of the bed. He pressed his lips together, and I knew something was wrong. I knew that look all too well on Daxon Stark and it was the look of frustration. We had a problem.

"What is it? Are there more tests before I can go home?" I asked with a puzzled look.

"No, darling... Celeste, the babies are fine and you are okay." Dylan said sternly and had a hard time keeping eye contact. "But with the amount of stress you've been under, we shouldn't live under the same roof anymore. I'm getting you your own place and..."

"But Dylan, the penthouse is my home." I sighed with sadness.

"But it was mine first and with you screwing my dad behind my back and..." Dylan said harshly and ran his hands through his hair. "See? This is why you need to go. It's not good for the babies and they are innocent in all this."

"Dylan has agreed it's best for everyone that we need to continue on with the lie." Daxon said in a matter-of-fact tone and looked at his son. "He will continue to play the part of being the babies' father for the sake of the company."

I hated the idea, but I don't have a choice. Dylan's secret needed to stay buried and Daxon's company was on the line. It could all come crashing down without this lie.

"But won't the tabloid's find out if we aren't living together anymore?" I asked with uncertainty.

"You just let Dylan and I worry about that, princess." Daxon said reassuringly.

"Okay, but where am I going to go?" I asked, with worry about my children. "We had a plan and now it's gone."

"You will stay with me." Daxon ordered as he stood up and put his hands in his pockets.

I quickly sat up and shook my head. "The hell I will."

"And why not?" Daxon argued.

"Because it's a terrible idea." I explained as I became frustrated with his never-ending demands and flung the sheet aside.

"I think it's a good idea since he is the twins' father." Dylan admitted.

"Stay out of it." Daxon barked at his son.

"What? Like you stayed out of my engagement?" Dylan shot back with a glare.

"An engagement that is still happening, but it's postponed because of the pregnancy complications." Daxon ordered as he looked from his son and towards me. "This marriage will still go on."

His words stung, but he was right. I doomed myself to be in a loveless marriage and the man who got me pregnant wanted that. He wanted his son to put a ring on my finger that symbolized everything I wanted from him. But he can never give me.

So, I snapped back. "Fine, but I'm not moving in with you."

Daxon stepped forward and grabbed my chin. He tilted my face up to meet his determined eyes, and they glimmered with challenge. He licked his lip and bit it as his frustration rose with me. I could tell he wanted to do bad things to me, but Dylan was right there.

When did that stop him?

"I'll carry you into my house kicking and screaming if I have to." Daxon hissed.

I pushed his hand off my chin and walked away from him. "You're not the boss of me, Daxon."

"But he is the father of your babies." Dylan interrupted.

"Dylan, I'm sorry for everything that happened, but you really need to mind your own business right now." I snapped and lost my cool with him.

"Oh, right, I'm not on daddy duty right now." Dylan said as he threw his hands up in the air and raised his eyebrows. "Good luck with the mom-to-be, but I'm out of here."

Just like that, Dylan left the room, and I was alone with his father. A man who wanted control and everything his way. And right now, he wanted his babies.

"Come and stay with me, Celeste." Daxon pleaded as he stepped closer and knelt down on his knees. "We can't be together, but I have an obligation to my children and I won't have them anywhere other than my home."

His hands laid on either side of my belly and he pressed his ear up against it. He listened to them move and he could hear my heartbeat. It beat for him and longed for him. Everything in me craved him, but he only wanted my children.

"But what about me, Daxon?" I sighed with emotion.

He looked up at me and his eyes shone with something I couldn't describe, but it wasn't for me. It was for the babies as he looked back at my stomach and he slowly stroked it. His touch was everything to me and everything I wanted him to give me. But it was all for our children.

He looked at my stomach with adoration and whispered to them. "You are my obligation and you are a part of mommy. You will all live with daddy so I can take care of you. Mommy just needs to agree."

His love for them was pure. It was the truest thing out of this whole mess and he wanted to give my children that. He wanted to cherish them like they were the most important things in the world. I couldn't take that away from them. Our children deserve everything. I just had to push my love for him aside and do what was right. I had to let Daxon be their father.

I touched his gorgeous hair, and he looked up at me. His eyes were no longer frustrated and pleaded with me to agree. He needed this, and I wanted it deep down. But my heart would always ache for him.

I smiled and whispered. "Okay, we will move in with you."

"Really?" He asked with excitement and looked down at my belly. "Mommy has finally come to her senses."

I giggled and pushed his hair aside. He got to his feet with a huge smile and lifted me off the floor. It swept me up in him as he kissed my forehead and his eyes locked on my mouth. He wanted to kiss me and I wanted it more than anything, but we've learned from our mistake. Anyone could walk in here at any moment.

I cleared my throat and spoke. "This is for our children and we should stick to that from now on."

Daxon placed me back on my feet and breathed. "We can try, but we both know it won't last, princess."

He was right.

No matter how much we tried, the temptation was too strong. It pulled us together, and we always gave into it. We lit the match and created a fire. But it never burnt out.

We were going to be living under the same roof and around each other every day. I had to learn to resist him and I knew he would tempt me because he always did. He was reckless, powerful, and undeniable. Living with Daxon Stark was my next challenge, and I knew he'd want to break all the rules.

TWENTY-NINE

Care for Us

The doctor discharged me with a warning. Be more careful about the well-being of myself and my children. This pregnancy could turn into a high-risk situation if I didn't proceed with caution and lower my stress level. I took this seriously because my children depended on it. I promised her I would, and I convinced her enough to let me go home.

But I was on my way to a new home.

Daxon Stark's home. Our new home together with our children. A place to call home.

The limousine ride to Daxon's house was a longer one. Busy city streets flew by and the horns honked in the distance. The city lights turned into stop signs and the tall buildings became trees.

We exited the city and rode along the outskirts of it. A freshly paved road with a smooth ride through the forest. The greenery was beautiful and the smell of fresh air came through the limousine vents. Living in the city for so long made me forget how gorgeous the outside was.

Our ride slowed down and turned left onto a single road with lovely, flowered trees leading down it. We kept going until a modern mansion came into view between them. They revealed a place with tons of windows and different levels. The home was extravagant and I couldn't believe my eyes.

"Is this your place?" I breathed in the breathtaking view.

"Yes, we are here, princess." Daxon said with certainty. "Welcome to your new home."

He reached out and took my hand in his. I looked down at the sweet gesture as he squeezed it with reassurance and I peered up into his serious eyes. They shimmered with joy at my approval of his home. I smiled at him with gratefulness, and his kindness shone through. It was a new side to him I had never seen before, but it suited him well. His entire face lit up and his handsome features stood out.

Mr. Cold, dark and infuriating, had a happy side.

The limousine pulled up out front and halted for us to depart. Daxon opened his door and pulled my hand to join him. He stood up and helped me out of the vehicle with his eyes never leaving me. I had to make sure I was capable, and he had to be sure of it. He wanted nothing to happen to me and the babies. His protection of us made me secure in my decision to come home with him. He'd keep us safe because we were his number one priority.

"I'll have all your belongings from the penthouse delivered here, and you won't have to lift a finger." He assured me as he kissed my knuckles and my belly warmed inside. "I'll take care of everything, princess."

This new side to Daxon Stark was a new beginning for us and my heart pounded for him when it shouldn't. My mind raced at the idea he could change his mind. With us here, he could finally see we could be a family. This was a chance I willed myself to take. It could change everything.

My eyes shimmered up at him with gratitude. "You don't have to do that, daddy."

"I'll do anything for you, princess." He whispered as he brought my hands to my swollen belly and he rubbed it tenderly. "You're the mother of my children and I'd go to the ends of the earth for them."

I gazed down at our tender moment and it was perfect. His masculine hands covered mine and caressed me along with our babies that grew inside me. He wanted to protect us, saving us from all harm, and he wanted to do it together. This couldn't get any better.

Suddenly, I felt a kick from inside me. Its force pushed my skin outwards as it stretched and my belly vibrated from the motion. It surprised me and caused me to blink repeatedly at the strange new feeling. But I knew exactly what it meant, and it warmed my heart with pure happiness.

"Did you feel that?" Daxon asked with surprise.

"Yes, I did, Daxon." I smiled brightly with joy.

Daxon looked up at me with disbelief as it happened again and with much more force this time. It made us laugh in joy and Daxon got down on his knees. The ground was still damp from the early evening air, but he didn't care. All he cared about was his babies. The ones that kicked for the first time from inside of me and we got to experience the precious moment together.

"We feel you little ones and we can't wait to meet you, too." Daxon breathed as he spoke to his children and took in everything. "Isn't that right, mommy?"

My eyes glistened with love, and I whispered. "That's right, daddy."

Daxon stood up with a newfound passion in him for his children and scooped me off my feet. The unexpected motion made me giggle with delight as he carried me to his home and the limousine drove away. He didn't waste one moment as he opened the front door with ease and brought me inside. The door closed behind him and he set me back on my feet.

I gazed around with curiosity at his home, and it was everything I pictured it would be. Dark wood floors, white painted walls and deeper toned furniture. It all fit his darker side. But the windows were everywhere I looked, and it was a touch I didn't expect.

Everything was modern and up to date with an enormous flat screen television in the living area. The long fireplace was a nice fit to set the mood for those cozy nights. A long staircase led to the upstairs and Daxon waved his hand as he encouraged me to follow him. He took the lead as he guided me further into his magnificent mansion, which I could now call home. The hallway was tall with lights that hung down from the ceiling and the windows kept going. He'd need a cleaner every week just to keep up, but I knew he could afford it.

I followed him into an enormous bedroom with a king-sized bed up against a vast window. Trees filled my view, and it was the prettiest sight to see. It was like a work of art behind the bed, but it wasn't on a canvas and it was the real deal. Everything about this room was delightfully overdone, but I loved it.

"This will be your room..." He breathed from a door frame further into the room. "It's perfect for my princess."

He walked through the doorframe and I grew curious. I ventured further to discover a bright white bathroom with floor tiles and they sparkled with the light. A large bathtub laid in front of a window with claws that dug into the tiles. An enclosed glass shower was behind it with a rainfall shower head and a big vanity with a sink on the other side. This master bathroom was every woman's dream.

But it was mine.

"I don't know what to say..." I breathed as I touched the porcelain and took it all in.

"You don't have to say anything at all, princess." Daxon breathed as he turned on the water for the bathtub and felt the warm beads. "This is all yours."

He stood up and walked over to me. His hand touched my shoulder as he walked around me and to my backside. His fingers found the zipper at the back of my dress and pulled it down. I let him do as he wished because I was far too tired from the nightmare we had just been through. The stress had been too much, and it was time to relax. I just needed to let him take over and help me undress.

"What are you doing, Daxon?" I asked with curiosity.

"Well, the doctor said a bath would help you relax and stop the bleeding." He answered as he let the purple dress fall to the floor and I stepped out of it. "I'm just following instructions."

I heard a rustle of fabric and turned around to look at him. He had taken off his shirt and his brawny familiar chest was in front of me. But he wasn't naked and kept his pants on.

"Doctor's orders, right?" I asked playfully.

"Right." He answered and unclasped my bra.

The garment fell to the floor and my oversized breast spilled free. They were full of breast milk and were getting ready to feed our babies. My veins were more noticeable, and my perky nipples pierced the air. I heard Daxon suck in a breath at my beauty, but he never touched them. He left them alone and bent down in front of me as he pulled down my panties. They came off easily, and I stood naked in front of him, but not at all awkward. I knew he loved my body and the way it changed. I carried his children and I was their mother. And his eyes showed me how much he still wanted me.

No matter what.

He reached out and touched my belly with tenderness. "Does it hurt?"

"No..." I whispered at his gentle affection. "But you don't have to stay. I can..."

"Shh, princess." He shushed me with his finger against my lips. "Daddy is going to take care of you."

He let his finger drop from my lips and carefully lifted me up into his embrace. He carried me over to the large white bathtub and put me inside the water. The warmth of it surrounded me and I sat up straight with my legs crossed. I heard him turn off the water behind me and I placed my hands on the side of the porcelain tub. The coolness of it grazed my nipples, and I looked up at him. He was impressive, massive, and powerful above me. But I felt like his queen.

"I know how to bathe myself." I said as he looked down at me and stirred all my emotions. "You really don't have to stay."

"Move over, princess." He demanded as he licked his lower lip and bit it. "Because I'm getting in too."

I blinked repeatedly and moved aside, but argued. "But you still have pants on?"

He slid into the water behind me with his legs on either side of my body. I looked over my shoulder at him as my wet hair floated in the water and he gave me a small smile. He didn't speak as he leaned back against the tub and motioned for me to lay back.

I gave his perfect chest one last look before laying back against it. The back of my head tucked into his shoulder and it felt like home. My legs sprawled out in front of me and floated with the water. He held me close and his hands found my warm belly. It poked out over the top of the surface with beads of water on it and his hands gently caressed it. The motion was soft, soothing, and relaxing. He put me at ease, kept me safe in his arms, and cared for me. I knew he would always put my children first.

Suddenly, he hummed a sweet tune in my ear. The vibration of it rumbled down my backside as it played from inside of him and echoed inside the bathroom. It should have shocked me by coming from someone so cold and dark, but it didn't. His tune relaxed me and my eyes drifted shut.

All I could feel was him. All I could think about was him. And all I wanted was him.

Everything fell away, and I dreamt of only him.

***

I woke up with a big stretch and an enormous yawn. I rubbed my eyes and blinked at the bright light that steamed through. It was brighter than I remembered, and that's when I realized I wasn't in my bed. It was a new bed, an enormous bed and an extremely soft bed.

I blocked the light with my hand until my vision adjusted and remembered everything. Dylan had caught us, but he almost killed his father out of a blind rage. It was like he had an out-of-body experience and something evil took over him. Something vengeful, but wicked with the devil. The stress of it was too much and my biggest fear happened.

I could've lost my babies.

But they were okay.

They were healthy and kicking up a storm. Daxon had stepped up to the plate as their father and welcomed us into his home. He had shown me a protective side of him I had never seen. A side so sweet and caring, I knew my children were in more than excellent hands. They were in their loving father's hands.

Light from the morning laid across the bed, and I saw clothes inside the closet. It was open, and I recognized dresses inside it. I threw back the sheets and made my way towards it. My hands ran over the clothes that hung from the hangers and I noticed they were all mine. Daxon had already moved me in without me even noticing. I slept through everything.

I smiled as I grabbed a cozy dress from the closet and wandered into the bathroom. It was spotless, with everything cleaned up from last night. There was no water in the tub or clothes on the floor. But my makeup, toilettes and everything I needed was here.

He had taken care of everything, and I didn't have to lift a finger. He had done as promised, and his actions surprised me. I shouldn't be when he was a man of money and could get what he wanted done in no time. But it was the thought that counted.

He could've easily left it for Dylan to deliver, and I probably wouldn't have my stuff for weeks. He could've let me fend for myself, but he'd promised me differently. And I saw Daxon Stark was a man of his word.

I smiled as I got dressed and brushed my hair. The smooth waves bounced with each stroke as I took an elastic and put it up into a bun. I wanted my hair to be neat today and not unruly. Yesterday was a shit show, and I didn't want another day like it. Certainly not today.

I brushed my teeth and put on some light makeup. My reflection glowed back at me from rest and relaxation. I felt content from the care I had received from a man I never expected it from. And I could thank Daxon for that.

I smiled as I strolled out of the bathroom and made my way towards the staircase. My nose sniffed the air as I hit the steps and the aroma was to die for. I let my nose lead the way as I hurried down the stairs and hit the main floor. It led me straight to the kitchen where I found Daxon hard at work without a shirt on and he made a wonderful breakfast. I noticed a trend with him not wearing a shirt while he cooked, but I could get used to it. A gorgeous bare chested middle-aged man working away in a kitchen to prepare a fabulous meal.

"Good morning, sleepyhead." Daxon smirked down at the bacon he made and it sizzled in response. "I see you found your stuff."

I rounded the island and sat on a bar stool. "I did."

He smiled at me as his eyes roamed over me and he breathed. "You look perfect for today."

I blushed at his compliment, but wondered. "What's today?"

"We're hitting the city and going shopping." Daxon explained as he got a plate and put some food on it.

"For what?" I asked with a scrunched-up face and an intrigued smile.

"For our babies, that will be here in a matter of weeks." He said as he put my plate in front of me and smiled a gorgeous smile. "Eat up, princess. You're going to need the energy."

I looked down at the delicious spread in front of me, and my mouth watered at the sight. An omelette with bacon on the side and he passed me a glass of freshly squeezed orange juice. My belly growled, and I knew the babies were hungry. But their daddy was about to solve that problem.

We ate with small talk about where we wanted to go and which store was best for baby products. He invested himself in their well-being and even named off some stores I already had in mind. But we came to an agreement on one place and I was excited.

We still had yet to purchase anything for these little ones and Daxon made it possible. He stepped up to the plate and took fatherhood seriously. His efforts somewhat surprised me because he had built his company from the ground up.

Daxon Stark meant business. But this business was a personal matter, and it was for his children.

"Well, that hit the spot." Daxon announced as he took our empty plates and put them in the dishwasher. "But we better get going before rush hour hits."

I nodded my head in agreement with a smile and Daxon led me towards his limousine parked out front. He had everything planned as he placed his hand on the small of my back and I got inside. Daxon Stark organized everything. He knew what he wanted and set it into motion. This was something I could get used to.

"What color scheme did you have in mind for the nursery?" Daxon asked me and took his seat.

"Well, I'm old-fashioned and it will depend on the babies gender." I replied.

"So, either blue or pink?" He asked as he straightened his jacket and relaxed in his seat.

"Yes. Or both." I responded with a smile and touched my belly.

He peered over at me and looked down at my stomach. His hand reached out to caress it and a baby kicked. We laughed at the sensation and got excited about what was to come. Our children were almost here and eagerness for their arrival was in full swing. But the pure adoration on his face meant everything to me, and it made my heart sing.

"Driver, take us to the city." Daxon instructed as he hollered to the front of the limousine, and it took off.

The drive to the urban area seemed shorter than the arrival to Daxon's house. The view changed from trees of green that loomed overhead to buildings that stretched for as far as the eye could see. Horns honked in the city, and it was a familiar place I didn't miss. Daxon's home was wonderful and nothing like here.

I missed it already.

The limousine halted outside of a lengthy mall and the place Daxon instructed the driver to go. The driver opened my door, and I made my exit. Daxon handed him some money with further orders and the driver nodded his head. He got back into the vehicle as the sunlight hit my skin and warmed me underneath its rays of light. It was a great day for good things ahead and it excited me to start.

Daxon came to my side, and we looked at the enormous poster of a mother holding her baby in her arms. She peered down at him with love and happiness. But the father stood over the mother's shoulder and protected them with a smile on his face.

"I wanted to give you a day of nothing but pure joy after what happened yesterday." Daxon admitted as he turned to look at me and his eyes shimmered. "But I realized I need it too. Just me and you, princess."

I pointed at my stomach and looked down at it. "And these little ones."

He tilted my chin upwards until I met his eyes, and he chuckled. "Yes, and them too."

His touch was tender and his energy intoxicating. It was incredible to see a different side to Daxon Stark. A lovable, adoring and sweet side. A man I wished could be this way for me, but I knew it was all for the babies inside of me. But deep down, I hoped it would change.

"You've surprised me, Daxon Stark." I sighed with a small smile.

"Have I? Well, there's much more where that came from." Daxon teased as he intertwined my hand with his and gave it a gentle squeeze. "Shall we get this shopping trip started?"

THIRTY
Gender Reveal

A few weeks passed, and the furniture for the nursery had arrived. It had been on backorder and there was a slight delay, but Daxon was on it every day. He called to ensure the delivery would be on its way because we had limited time to get the room ready before the little ones arrived. I had no reason to worry because he made sure everything was right. He took my stress level seriously and I got used to his security.

The movers brought the boxes up into the babies' room and placed them in the directed positions. I gave instructions while Daxon checked over each box and made sure everything was there. He was on building duty and determined to get everything ready.

I had a slight waddle in my step. My twenty-two-week belly walked the delivery men back to their truck and I thanked them for their time. The babies were right on track and everything fell into place. They were healthy and moved every day. Their energy brought a smile to my face, but made my lower back ache. Their little bodies grew, but the doctor projected them to be on the smaller side. It had worried Daxon, but the doctor assured him it was normal. They were twins and grew in the same womb. It was all part of the process.

I wandered back up the staircase at a slow pace and felt exhausted once I hit the top. It was turning into an everyday event and it got to where I couldn't wait to deliver these babies. My stomach stretched to the seams, my back hurt and my feet were swelling. I even had to wear breast pads to stop my boobs from leaking through my clothes. Everything prepared me for delivery and I was more than ready.

I shuffled across the floor as I made my way back towards the nursery to see what Daxon was up to. We had bought matching cribs, dressers, a rocker, two change tables, a double stroller, and a massive diaper bag. Diapers, wipes and diaper cream stacked up in the closet. There was enough for three months. We had everything we were going to need except babies' clothes. It was next on the list. But first we had to find out the babies' genders.

And it was happening in a few hours.

I was excited but anxious at the same time. This was an enormous step in the pregnancy and not all parents wanted to do it. Some preferred to wait until delivery to find out the sex, but we agreed to find out before. The preparations would come easier and the stress would be far less. I'd know their genders and be too busy getting everything ready for their big arrival.

I knew Daxon was beyond excited. It thrilled him. He went into full dad mode and wanted to pass the time by fixing up their nursery. He was going to get the items we already had organized and plans changed. His face lit up when he found out the furniture was to be delivered on the same day we were to find out the genders.

So, here we were with Daxon opening every item and me watching on the sidelines. I looked at him in his glory as he opened the cribs and got all the pieces together. It appeared to be a complex mess, and I was happy I sat this one out. But he was enthusiastic.

"I think we should put cribs over by the window. What do you think?" Daxon asked as he eyed up every likely position and moved around the room. "Or maybe here by the wall to keep them out of the sun?"

I giggled at his enthusiasm. "I'm sure we can get curtains to block out the sun."

"Right. I never thought of that." Daxon replied as he scratched his head and got to work. "I guess I'm getting ahead of myself, princess."

I smiled at him and breathed. "I think you are, but I like this side of you."

"Ya, right... This unorganized, jittery old mess." Daxon huffed.

"No, this take charge and impressive father vibe." I whispered in his ear and rubbed his tense shoulder blades. "You shouldn't be so hard on yourself, daddy."

Daxon relaxed at my touch as he knelt on the floor and I stood behind him. My fingers dug into his muscles and pressed out the tension. They rotated around the same area and pushed out hard tissue. The motion made it softer and workable as my fingers continued to move. The weight lifted off his shoulders and he kept going with the task at hand. He was determined to get the babies' nursery done in time and everything was plus two. Two of every item and one for each baby.

"Thanks, princess..." Daxon sighed as he loosened up and dove into his project.

I let go of his shoulders and went to the nearest wall. My back leaned against it and I watched him work. He started with the bases of each crib and worked his way up. They came into formation and everything became more real. Our babies would sleep inside them and grow until they outgrew them. Until they were ready for a bed set and the next steps of learning.

It was a surreal moment, and I found it entirely sweet how seriously Daxon took this. He worked so hard at everything he put his mind to and he did it for his children. He would be an amazing father to these little ones, and I was so lucky.

I ran my hand along the wall with no color on it and pushed myself off of it. A good half an hour had passed and Daxon was close to being finished with the cribs. But there was still much more to do.

I looked around the room with no paint color on the walls because we'd chosen to wait until we found out the sex of the babies. It was important to both of us and a big decision to make. Boxes needed to be recycled and pieces of furniture still had to be put together. It would all happen with time.

But the clock ticked down.

It was only a matter of weeks until they would make their grand appearance and today crept up on me. We'd scheduled this appointment weeks ago, but the reality of it hit me today. We'd find out who was cooking inside me and the next step was to figure out their names.

The excitement of it all was too much, and I'd lost track of time. I looked down at my wristwatch and knew we should head out. I didn't want to be late.

"Daxon, it's time." I breathed as I tapped my watch and looked at him. "We should get going."

"Let me get this last screw into place and..." Daxon groaned as he turned the screwdriver and the cherry wood crib stood up sturdy. "There! I finished the cribs."

He gazed at them with accomplishment. The pride on his face shone through and made him look so good I could kiss him. But a peck on the cheek would do.

"They look perfect." I beamed with excitement. "Now, onto everything else."

Daxon looked around the room with me and wrapped his arm around my back. He held me close and touched my belly. The gesture was tender and a warmth spread through me. I loved how much he loved our children. I just wished he could love me like that.

"Anything for my kids." Daxon breathed as he locked eyes with me and shot me a gorgeous smile. "Let's get out of here, princess."

We left the nursery together, and he led me downstairs. The limousine driver greeted us like clockwork and was there right on time. It was time to see the babies and find out their gender.

***

The room was chilly and matched the tone of my anxiety. It was all ready to go, and we just waited for the technician to arrive. Dylan sat this one out because he caught an awful cold. We thought about rescheduling because of the tabloids and their predator way, but we'd waited far too long. It was time. They could run their story and put their own spin on it. It didn't matter because no one knew the actual truth and Daxon wouldn't let anyone find out.

"You okay, princess?" Daxon asked sweetly as he took my hand and rubbed the pad of his thumb along it.

"I'm fine." I breathed as I laid on the table and waited for the technician to come in.

It was a lie, and I was anything but fine. I was all over the place. The excitement coursed through me and my nerves took over. I wanted to scream out of joy because this moment was here, but I could also do the opposite. Crying out of uncertainty from the time it took to receive an answer.

"Because I could always calm you down, young lady." Daxon claimed as his other hand ran up my thigh and tingled my skin. "You look way too good in that skirt today."

I pushed his hand away. "This isn't the time for games, daddy."

"As you wish, princess." Daxon breathed and tucked his hands into his pockets.

The temperature in the room turned up a notch with his request and it left me lost in it. It always did. It would be a pleasurable distraction until the technician came in, but it was too risky. We had already been down that road and couldn't afford someone stumbling on the truth. Our intimate encounter would make front page news and plastered all over social media. Daxon wasn't thinking clearly and someone had to.

And it was a good thing I did.

Because she just arrived.

"I'll be your technician for the visit." She announced as she took her seat and got jelly on the probe. "The father couldn't make it today?"

"No, he's sick with a cold." I said as I raised my blouse and tucked it under my bra. "So, the grandfather came for support."

"Oh, well, how wonderful you could make it. It's a pity the father couldn't because this is a big moment." She said with a smile and put the probe on my belly. "Just a cold touch here."

The usual chill from the jelly hit my skin, but didn't startle me like it normally does. My mind was elsewhere and lost in the unknown. I just sought two little answers.

What's the sex of these babies?

"We want to find out the gender of the babies." Daxon announced, but realized he shouldn't and tried to fix the situation. "Well, I know I do. How do you feel about it, Celeste?"

"Yes, it's solely your decision." The technician added. "Do you want to find out the sex of your twins?"

I took Daxon's hand and squeezed it. "I agree with Daxon, and we want to find out the genders."

He looked nervously down at me and realized he could've just blown our story to hell. I knew he needed my touch to calm him down and get us back on track. Get us to where we finally had the answers we came here for. He needed me as much as I needed him. We'd get through this together.

"Perfect because I have the gender of baby A." She announced with certainty. "Are you ready?"

"Yes..." I breathed.

"As ready as we'll ever be." Daxon sighed.

"Baby A's legs are wide open and pretty obvious it's a little boy." She revealed it with a smile on her face. "And as for baby B..."

She pressed the probe further to my left side and moved it around. The baby kicked and played with the movement on my stomach. It made me giggle with happiness from the news and overjoyed me as I watched the screen. Baby B was putting on quite the show.

"Yes, what's baby B going to be?" Daxon asked with anxious excitement and leaned in closer to me.

"Well, baby B is quite the little mover and your daughter is going to keep you busy." She said as she looked at me and took the probe off my belly. "Congratulations on having a baby boy and girl."

"I'm having a boy and a girl?" I asked in disbelief.

She smiled down at me and wiped the jelly off my belly. "Yes, you are, Celeste."

My heart hammered with happiness, and I couldn't believe the words she spoke. It was a boy. I could dress him in blue and he could play hockey. I was having a little girl. She could wear pink and become a ballerina. Hell, they could be whatever their little hearts desired.

"Oh, my gosh Daxon..." I cried with joy and held his hands in mine. "It's a boy and a girl. I can't believe it."

"Neither can I, princess." Daxon breathed in disbelief and squeezed my hands.

"I'll give you a moment and will be back with the twins' pictures." The technician said as she left the room and we were alone once again.

"A little boy and a little girl." I beamed up at Daxon as tears of happiness fell down my cheeks and his face was inches from mine. "Our babies together."

He kissed away my tears one by one and caressed my cheek. I leaned into his touch and met his eyes. They sizzled with want for me, but shimmered with love for his children. This moment was everything I could've asked for and it was a dream come true. A family I never expected and everything I could want. Only one thing was missing.

Daxon's love for me.

He kissed my forehead, and my heart swooned. I felt his passion and need to protect me, but I needed more from him. I hoped for more from him. These babies were only weeks away, and I wished something would change. And as I prayed for a miracle, he took my face in his hands.

His eyes shimmered with something I couldn't recognize, but I knew he was beyond happy. He was overjoyed by the news of our two precious ones we made together and he couldn't wait to meet them.

"Our future together, princess." Daxon breathed as his lips tenderly touched mine and I fell into him.

I lost my heart to him. He had me. He had all of me. My mind, body, and soul.

He broke the kiss and looked down at me like he wanted to speak more, but the door opened. The technician entered the room and pulled him back to reality. All that danced in his beautiful gaze was gone as he stepped away from me and let her hand me a strip of something. Something precious and it made my heart sing. A special gift just for us of our babies pictured on a strip of photo paper.

Our little boy with his legs open and a round head. Another with his thumb in his mouth. Our precious girl with her gymnastic movements made us laugh. One photograph she had her hand up and appeared to wave hello. It was a gift I won't ever forget.

I thought my heart was full. Extended from my love for their father, but I was wrong. Today, my heart grew two times bigger and with their love, I could do anything.

THIRTY-ONE
Tease

Weeks passed by since our gender appointment and the media was all over the news. Everyone knew I postponed my wedding to Dylan Stark because of the pregnancy. People also knew the gender of the babies and sent us gifts. All addressed to the penthouse, and Dylan grew frustrated with it. But that was too bad because he was the pretend daddy to be.

Everything had come together. The nursery was so close to being finished and all it needed was paint. Along with some decor on the walls. Hints of pink and blue throughout the room. We filled the closet with clothes for each baby and we didn't need anymore. We went a little crazy after we found out the genders and spent a day shopping for baby clothes. But it was so much fun.

Daxon looked through rows of clothes and got invested just as much as me. The joy filled his face and gave a lighter side to his harsh exterior. He has been so involved with everything it has changed him. I saw sides of Daxon Stark I had never seen before and it made me love him even more. We laughed, joked and enjoyed each other's company. It had been a great day.

And now it was time for grey paint.

Daxon did the painting job himself. He didn't want to hire anyone to do the job, and he wanted to put a personal touch to it. He wanted to tell his children that daddy did it just for them. Daxon didn't want me anywhere near it.

But I couldn't help myself.

He had chosen this weekend to do it while he had no work planned. I wanted to watch him and enjoy him. Lock in the memories of him and how much he cared. So, I didn't listen and crept up to the nursery.

I tiptoed as much as I could with my enormous belly and tried not to let the hardwood creak. I got to the door frame and peeked inside. He had a sweet side that I expected to be floored by. Instead, my body heated from the sexiness of him.

Daxon didn't have his shirt on, and he had his back turned towards me. His blue jeans hugged his perfectly tight ass and hung low on his hips. My gaze wandered up to the dip just above his waistband and the bit of hair there. The curve of his backside made my mouth water, and I wanted to crawl my hands up the fitness of it. I wanted to feel his heat come off his body as I made my way up to his broad shoulder blades. They held strength and moved with each stroke of the paintbrush. I had to clear my throat from all the pent-up sexual tension and he spun my way. I had startled him and a splash of grey paint hit his cheek, but he didn't flinch a muscle.

His eyes locked on my belly, and he warned. "You aren't supposed to be in here, young lady."

He stepped closer towards me with the paintbrush in his hand. His bare feet walked over the white sheets he had laid out on the floor. He looked over the covered furniture he had built with those powerful hands and it made me lick my lips. His power turned me on and I wanted to toy with him, even though I knew I shouldn't. I had danced with this monster for far too long and it made me want more. It made me want to give into our wicked game we played and the urgency pumped from within me.

I raised my eyebrow at him and teased him. "You know I don't like being told what to do, daddy."

"Paint fumes aren't good for the twins. I thought we discussed this." He argued as he grabbed my wrist and twirled me around. "Why do you always have to defy me, princess?"

My backside pressed up against his bare chest with my breasts rapidly rising and falling. The pent-up tension between us was close to bursting, but I held myself together. This was our twisted game after all and one I had started.

I ran my hand down his brawny arm and felt his toned veins underneath it. It made me shiver with need, but I kept on and grabbed onto his paintbrush. I pulled it from his hand when he least expected it and broke from his lustful embrace. I twirled around and playfully splashed grey paint on his chest. His reaction was full of surprise as he glared at me, but it soon turned to amusement when he saw the smile on my face.

"I defy you because you're way too serious sometimes and you should lighten up, daddy." I giggled as my smile widened and I handed him back the paintbrush.

I stood there and admired his handsome form. Grey paint on his sculpted cheekbone and a bit of shaded color covered his toned torso. He was a sight an artist could create and not be guilty of it. Daxon Stark was a magnificent-looking man. Even with a bit of grey paint.

"Anything for you, princess." He admitted with a smirk.

I licked my lips at the sight of him and breathed as I tossed my hair over my shoulder. "Well, I'm headed for a shower soon, but I think you might need one more than I do."

He licked his lower lip and flicked me a smile. It was a devilish look, and I knew he was up to something. But it wouldn't match what I had done.

I spun around and walked out of the room, but his voice echoed behind me. "Two can play this game, princess."

I was in a playful mood and answered back over my shoulder. "We'll see about that, daddy."

I continued down the hallway and didn't glance back. His stare burned into my backside the entire way, but I ignored him. I had won this match and my stomach grumbled. I craved a snack for my victory and a nice chocolate chip cookie would do the trick.

I headed downstairs for a quick bite to eat and found the pantry. Extra-large chocolate chip cookies wafted my nose and my mouth watered. I took two. One for baby A and one for baby B, I convinced myself as I bit into the first one.

The chocolate melted in my mouth and sent my taste buds into overdrive. With each bit, the babies kicked, and each jab made me giggle with delight. They grew more and more each day, but they squished in there. One baby sat on my bladder twenty-four-seven and the other one jabbed at my rib cage. It was a constant battle and one I never won. I always ended up exhausted and ready for them to come out. I just had to remind myself it could be any day now and to enjoy them protected inside of me while I still could.

I walked back up the stairs as I ate the last couple of bites and felt much better. More energetic than before as I hit the top floor and headed towards my bathroom. A nice, cold shower would do the trick and get my mind back on track. Not lost in Mr. Tall, dark and gorgeous.

I fussed with my wavy hair and walked into the bedroom. The adjoining bathroom caught my eye, and I made a puzzled look at the door. It was slightly ajar, and I didn't recall leaving it like that.

I slowly pushed it open and steam rose upward into my face. I swatted it away with my hand and it cleared. But my gaze landed on something far more interesting.

Daxon in the shower. His hand was around his firm cock as he leaned against the glass and fisted himself. He was masturbating in the shower.

My shower. The shower he knew I was going to use, but he beat me to it. Literally.

His eyes caught sight of me as he beat his gigantic dick and the sound of it echoed throughout the bathroom. The walls tossed around his groan as he pounded himself within his tight grasp and my body temperature rose. The sight of him getting off in my shower did me in, but I held back.

I needed to resist him and put up a fight. He wouldn't win, no matter how hard he tried. I moved in here for our babies. He didn't want to be with me. He wanted to have sex with me and I wanted that too, but I couldn't let him toy with my heart. I couldn't give in to him and I wouldn't. But my body sure begged me too.

So, I stood there and watched him. Watched him moan for me, pleasure himself for me and plead with me to give into temptation. It tempted me and turned me on, but I had to remain in control.

"You like what you see, princess?" He growled as he fisted his firmness and stared at me with lust. "This is all for you, darling. Come in here. Daddy wants to have his way with you."

But I defied him.

I refused to listen, and I knew it made daddy unhappy, but I didn't care. He didn't have control; I did. I wanted him to understand that.

"Not so fast, daddy." I breathed as I waved my index finger at him and leaned against the doorframe.

I bit my lower lip and teased my dress strap. It fell down my arm, and I did the same with the other one, but my dress fell to the floor. I looked down at it and stepped out of it, but kicked it aside with my big toe. I peered back at him with a naughty expression and his rapid breath fogged up the glass. He fisted himself faster as the water hit his backside and his wet hair was messy on top of his head. His body was gloriously aroused, and I wanted to give in, but I reminded myself what was at stake.

I kept my black bra on and played with the hem of my lace panties. They matched my bra and gave me a twist of seduction. I knew he loved the sight of me as his groans grew louder and it built him closer to climax. I teased the elastic and smirked wickedly his way. It snapped back against my skin and he growled at the tease.

I loved watching him beg. Craved, making him plead. But I enjoyed the sheer taunt of it all.

He was hot and bothered.

I loved to make him squirm.

"I'm wearing far too much, daddy." I breathed with playfulness.

"Yes, you are, princess." Daxon moaned.

I pulled my panties down to expose my cunt for his eyes only and took them in my grasp. I twirled the lace round my finger as he came out of the shower and water dripped from him. It fell to the floor and left a trail as he continued to beat himself. But I tossed my panties straight at him.

And he caught them in midair.

He stopped in front of me as his other hand held them in his grasp, and his skill surprised me. He took my panties and brought them to his nose as he sniffed at the smell of me. His behavior should disgust me, but it turned me on even more.

Daddy got off to the smell of my pussy.

He craved my cunt and his body shuddered as he watched me. I breathed rapidly right along with him as he inhaled my intoxicating scent one last time and held my panties at the tip of his cock. I watched his face change into pure release, but his deep haze never left my aroused body.

"Oh, my princess..." He groaned as he ejaculated his seed onto my panties.

It was the hottest thing I had ever seen.

His mouth was agape as he spilled himself all over it and I had a vivid image in my head. His hard cock pointed at my chest, and he gave me a shimmering pearl necklace. It made me ache for him. It made me want to crawl and plead for him to come once more. But I refrained and let my imagination run wild because this was war.

And I had just won the battle.

Daxon dropped my soaked panties to the ground. He leaned in close and his minty fresh breath caressed my face. It made me shiver and want a taste. But I held my ground and was about to declare victorious.

I played with him. Played him like a fiddle. And he came on my panties.

He ran his fingers up my arms and whispered. "Now, it's your turn, princess."

I looked down at my extremely used panties. His juice glimmered in the light and heat rose inside of me. The temptation was strong to give into him. Everything in me screamed to let go, and I cursed myself for denying him. But I smiled wickedly at him.

I leaned in, gave his earlobe a lick and whispered to him. "No, daddy. It looks like I won this round."

I stepped back and spun around. My ass was in clear view as it bounced just for him, and I walked away. But I gave it an extra sway, and he growled from behind me.

Victory was mine.

THIRTY-TWO

Heart Stopping Turn

"I have gifts for the babies and I'm dying to give them to them." Paisley announced through the phone line with excitement. "But I want to wait until they are born."

Joy spread through me at my best friend's eagerness for the twins' arrival. I was full term and Paisley called to catch up on the latest. She saw everything the tabloids posted, but knew to come to me for the truth. She knew the secrets and wouldn't believe the made up lies. Hell, they didn't even know the truth.

Dylan's father was actually the father of the twins. The hidden secret we had spent many times lost in each other's arms. The untold truth of Dylan's secret lover. A man.

I tried not to worry about it because stress wasn't good for the twins. They could come any day and nothing could impede a hopefully smooth delivery. My babies were healthy and strong, just like their father. They would be home in no time.

"I'm sure they are fabulous." I giggled at her willingness to be a part of their lives.

"They are! I have a cute pink dress for the girl and a sweet little tux to match for the boy." Paisley beamed through my ear. "But have you figured out their names yet?"

"We actually haven't. We can't agree on their names." I pouted. "I hope once I deliver them, we can come to an agreement after we see their sweet faces."

Another thing we couldn't decide on was our feelings for each other and it was depressing. I haven't told Daxon I was in love with him because he was reluctant. He firmly stated he couldn't give me his heart, and it has held me back. Deep down inside, I wonder if he knew how I felt, maybe it would change. He could open himself up to me and let me inside. We could be together and be a family.

"How is living with the famous billionaire bachelor Mr. Daxon Stark?" Paisley teased as she changed her tone and sarcasm filled her voice.

"It has been wonderful. He's been caring and attentive. He's going to be a great father, but..." I sighed as I looked down at my belly and rubbed the twins for comfort. "It feels like it's all for the babies and not for me. I just wish he could show me that kind of affection."

"Oh, I'm not so sure about that, Celeste. He moved you into his home and has done everything for you. He could've let you live in your own place and helped you. But a bachelor moved you in with him. It must mean there's something more?" Paisley said reassuringly.

"I don't know, Pais..." I sighed.

"Tell me one thing. Do you love him?" Paisley asked me, and I heard her suck in a breath.

My heart hammered in my chest. It felt like it would explode. Burst open with all the love I had for him. For a man I once viewed as the enemy and a cold-hearted bastard. He was far from it and a softie deep down. He was my everything.

"God help me, I love that man with all my heart." I admitted the truth.

"Then you've got to tell him, Celeste!" Paisley exclaimed as she let out her breath and excitement filled the phone.

Suddenly, I heard the front door open, and keys jiggled. Daxon was home from work. It was now or never. My best friend was right, and this was it. My future depended on it and my babies deserved a family.

"I've got to run, Pais, Daxon just walked in." I whispered into the phone and covered it with my hand. "Wish me luck."

"Good luck, love you and go get your man!" Paisley yelled with excitement in my ear and I hung up the phone.

It was the perfect moment to confess my love.

My heartbeat wildly in my chest, and I walked towards Daxon with a smile on my face. It excited me for what could be, but I was nervous about the unknown. He could very well shoot me down and leave me shattered. But this could be it.

This could be destiny.

"So, I wanted to take you to your favorite restaurant in the city for dinner before the baby's arrival." Daxon breathed as he grabbed my jacket and urged me over. "The limousine is outside and we better hurry before someone else takes our reservation."

His sweet gesture made my heart swell. He wanted to dine with me and feed me. But I needed to know the truth.

Did he love me too?

I let him put my jacket on as my arms fell into it and he buttoned it up over my swollen belly. He took the strap of my jacket and carefully tied it around the swell of my stomach. He passed me my purse, and I flung it over my shoulder.

His touch was tender and full of care. I loved it so much and could spend the rest of my life like this.

I stopped him and put my hand on his arm. "Daxon, wait..."

He gazed into my eyes and breathed. "What is it, princess?"

"I need to tell you something." I admitted as I looked down at his hand over mine and his thumb caressed me.

"Is something wrong? Is it the babies? Are you in pain? Should I..." Daxon asked with worry as a fear coated his eyes and he looked down at my stomach.

"No, no, the babies are fine." I interrupted and took his hands in mine. "It's about me, Daxon."

"You?" Daxon asked as he let go of my hands and cradled my face with his touch. "What's the matter, princess?"

My forehead leaned against his, and my voice came out in a whisper. "Nothing is wrong."

His lips sweetly brushed my cheek and kissed away a tear. "Then why are you crying?"

"Because I love you and want us to be a family." I confessed my devotion.

He froze and didn't speak a word. His eyes blinked repeatedly as my love for him sunk in and he processed the reality of it. I pulled my head back, his hands still cradled my face, and I tried to read his reaction, but I couldn't.

"Our children are almost here and I want us to be together." I added as my heart pounded and I waited for him to respond.

His hands dropped from my face, and he breathed. "I can't ever give you my heart. That side of me shut off long ago because it hurt too damn much. I can't go through that again. You need to accept that we can't ever be together, Celeste."

And he crushed my heart.

"What if I never can?" I asked with hurt.

He grew cold and ordered. "You will have to for our children."

I shook my head as he grew blurry, and my heart shattered into a million pieces. This couldn't end like this. I never wanted this. He rejected me and left me heartbroken.

How could he do this to me?

"And what about me, Daxon?" I raised my voice as the hurt and anger took over.

I barely recognized myself. This wasn't me. Lovesick and all alone.

But he wouldn't speak.

He just stood there. Emotionless, and closed off. This was Mr. Daxon Stark. I just lied to myself all along.

He backed away from me and wouldn't even acknowledge my existence. I had shared my heart with him, and he tore it to shreds in a matter of minutes. We played a game that I was sick of. I needed to get out of here.

I walked past him and snapped. "Don't follow me, Daxon."

I slammed the door shut behind me with all the hurt I felt inside. All the anger at myself for being so blind. I was a stupid woman forever believing he could love me back. I was just a twisted game he liked to play and toy with whenever he felt like it. But I deserved more, and so did my children.

They deserved to see their mother happy.

I got into the limousine that waited outside and informed the driver Mr. Stark wouldn't join us. The driver took off as the tears streamed down my face and I cursed myself for ever falling for a broken man. I couldn't change him and he never wanted me. The only thing he ever felt for me was lust and nothing more. Our disagreement had led to the end, and I was heartbroken.

I confessed my love for him and it meant nothing to him. He just needed me for sex and to carry his children. I just had to play a part. The same way his son played me, and I deserved more than that. I deserved a man devoted to me, who worshipped me and loved me.

And that man wasn't Daxon Stark.

Suddenly, my cell phone rang from inside my purse. The chime of it knocked me back into reality and I wiped my tears from my face. I knew I looked like a mess, but I didn't care. All I wanted was for him to love me and he never could. But he could call me on the phone.

I answered it with bitterness. "What do you want?"

He breathed. "I want you to come home, princess."

"Home? You are my home and you broke it." I cried out with hurt. "I can't come back because you don't love me. Daxon, I can't live like this anymore."

He pleaded with me. "Please, just come back so we can talk about this? You're the mother of my children and I have a responsibility..."

"And I have a responsibility to myself! I need to be happy and my children deserve to see me happy!" I shouted with anger. "What about me, Daxon?"

He voiced calmly. "I will take care of you and give you everything you need."

"How about your heart?" I pleaded, and my words fell to silence as I huffed. "Ya, that's what I thought."

Daxon blew out a breath of frustration and barked an order. "If you don't come home, I will find you and take you over my knee, young lady."

I knew my behavior annoyed him, but it was over. His usual tactic to get me to bend to his will was through. The game we played was done. It had cost me too much. I lost my heart.

"This game is officially over, Daxon. We're done." I snapped the final command.

Suddenly, there was a loud crash, and a force tossed me to the floor. It happened in the blink of an eye. But my world turned to darkness.

Except for his voice.

The man I loved with all my heart and soul shouted in fear. "Celeste? Princess, answer me? Celeste!"

And I faded away.

***

Beep, beep, beep...

My eyes fluttered, and everything was a blur. I couldn't collect my thoughts as the world spun, and I tried to see straight. I wanted to sit up and my body was far too weak. But I was comfortable.

Confusion took over, and I realized I was in bed. A hospital bed. Monitors calmly beeped, and I grew more aware of my surroundings.

I was in the hospital.

But there was an accident.

My vision cleared as I focused my eyes on someone beside me. The person held my hand and peered down at it. A tender caress tingled my skin, and I'd recognize his touch anywhere.

It was Daxon.

"W-what happened?" I choked out.

"Oh, thank god, you're awake." He rubbed his hand down his face. "You scared me so much, princess."

He took both my hands in his and kissed each one. His full lips brushed over my knuckles with care and I saw the scraps on them. His worn-down face looked into my eyes, but his eyes were full of concern.

But my hands touched my belly.

"The babies! Are they alright?" I asked with fright.

"They are just fine." Daxon breathed as he touched my swollen belly and smiled with relief. "They are strong, just like their mother."

I laid back against the pillow with relief. Our babies were okay. That was all I needed to hear. But then I remembered what happened.

"There was a loud crash and I couldn't see, but I heard you. I heard you shouting for me." I recalled and looked up at him with tears in my eyes. "You sounded so scared, and I wanted to answer you, but I couldn't. I..."

"I know, I know..." Daxon whispered as he leaned in and cupped my face. "I was, but it's okay now. You're alright and the twins are fine."

I remembered our disagreement and the last words I spoke to him. It all rushed back, and I just wanted to forget. Daxon didn't love me and I ended it.

"But everything isn't alright, Daxon." I whispered as tears fell down my cheeks and my being trembled with hurt. "You don't love me, and you never will."

"Oh, princess..." He breathed as he wiped my tears and his own eyes glistened. "I'm so sorry I hurt you."

"How could you?" I breathed.

"It scared me to love you, sweetheart." Daxon admitted as he stared into my eyes, and something awakened inside them. "But the accident happened. It knocked you unconscious, and it made me realize something."

"What?" I whispered.

"I feared losing you, princess." He breathed as his forehead touched mine and his hands cupped my belly. "And our precious little babies growing inside of you."

The tears fell from my eyes at an unstoppable pace, but I couldn't stop them. His admission took my broken heart and pieces it back together. What he had once shattered was now whole.

"You were?" I asked in a small voice.

"I love you, Celeste Lovette. I love you so damn much." Daxon whispered as his lips brushed mine and my heart melted for him. "I almost lost you, but it made me realize I can't live without you."

I cried tears of joy at his declaration of love, and he kissed me with passion. His protective arms wrapped around me, and I had never felt so whole. He made me complete. He was my missing piece.

"And I'm so in love with you." I mumbled with happiness against his lips and moved over on the bed. "Get up here, daddy."

We laughed as he cuddled up beside me and our babies laid in between us. There was just enough room for all of us and he caressed the hair from my face. His loving eyes gazed deep into my soul, and I couldn't believe he was all mine. I couldn't imagine my world without him.

"My wife lost her life, but I couldn't let that happen to you. You challenged me, beat me at my game and gave me your heart. You mean everything to me." Daxon breathed with love.

He brushed my hair behind my ear with the pad of his thumb caressing my cheek. His touch set me on fire and it never would burn out. Our flame was unstoppable, and so was our love.

But a thought stopped me in my tracks.

"What's next for us?" I asked with uncertainty.

"Well, I love you and I won't hide it anymore." He declared with a smile and left me breathless. "All our secrets will unfold and the truth will be told."

"Are you sure about this?" I asked with doubt. "It could ruin the company."

"Then so be it." He whispered with his face inches from mine. "I have a family to build and we have our entire future ahead of us."

My smile was unstoppable and our love unbreakable. My future was no longer bleak and shone with certainty. A certain reality with my children's father and our family. But as his lips caressed mine, one thought came to my mind.

Daddy completed me.

The End

Bonus Epilogue
Family

Our home was full of love, life, and happiness. Billionaire Mr. Daxon Stark's lonely life of freedom was now filled with family. A family that came together through business and it created true love. Love brought the truth to light when it wanted to stay hidden forever. But two precious children made it all happen.

Dylan Stark held his half-brother and sister in his arms. He lovingly looked down at them with a proud smile on his face and the babies cooed at him. They loved their big brother and their bond was like no other.

"I think Faith wants her mommy." Dylan announced as he passed my daughter to me and I took her into my arms.

Her deep brown eyes peered up at me with an innocence I vowed to protect. Her soft black hair matched my own and was out of control, but the cutest sight. She took my finger, and I cradled her close. The smell of her newborn baby scent still lingered, and I wished they could stay this small forever.

"And I think Damien wants his daddy." Dylan smiled as he passed his baby brother to his father.

Dylan stepped back and joined a man I knew from what now felt like so long ago. He joined hands with the same man I caught him in bed with. But it has changed my life for the better.

It no longer stung or felt vengeful. It was true and right. Dylan was now with the one he loved and no longer hidden in shame. His sexuality was out, and Dylan had come out of the closet. His lover wasn't just that, but a man he wanted to spend the rest of his life with and the ring on his fiancé's finger proved it.

We've put everything behind us. All the hurt, mistrust and we did it for the sake of our family. We've forgiven our mistakes and no longer live a lie.

Daxon smiled at Dylan with happiness, and he knew the truth. I'd convinced Dylan to come clean and told him his father wouldn't judge him like some dirty secret. He loved his children with all of his heart, and I knew deep down he would accept Dylan for who he truly was.

And I was right.

All he wanted was for Dylan to be happy. His love was no mistake, and he should be able to love who he wanted. His mother would've accepted it and he did too.

He was proud of Dylan and stood by his side when he revealed the truth to the world. Dylan expected backlash and judgement, but it was the complete opposite. Everyone accepted him for who he was and he became a role model for others. His strength had pushed many to come out and be true to themselves. We were all so proud of him.

But not all sincerity came easy.

It came as a shock.

We all thought D.S. Industries would tank. We thought it was the end of a business built from the ground up, but it was the complete opposite. It flourished.

When our forbidden relationship hit the tabloids it took off like wildfire. Mr. Daxon Stark was no longer a bachelor and took off the market. Everyone wanted to know more.

They raved to discover the woman who stole his heart and gave birth to his babies.

It was front page news.

I couldn't believe it, but the company took a slight hit. Our romance angered some that wanted Dylan and I married, but it wasn't possible. Our hearts belong elsewhere. But with me as the fresh face of D.S. Industries, the media ate it up.

I was the new inspiration for the company and my down-to-earth personality was a win for marketing. My face was everywhere, and it was a journey I never expected. I always wanted to run my company, but now we would run D.S. Industries together as a family.

And soon it would be permanent.

I peered down at the diamond ring that glistened with the light and my heart filled with love. My engagement ring was extravagant and told our story of passionate, forbidden love. A tale we never imagined would happen, but it did. And it was the best love story of all.

Behind every man was an extraordinary woman. I was his backbone, and he was in charge. But I was Daxon Stark's wife to be.

I gazed over at the man who won my heart and captured my soul. We played a tempting game, and it intoxicated us. It pulled us in, tortured our emotions, and played with our inner monster. It brought out the worst in us, but also our best.

Our twisted game clung on to the bitter end, but together we claimed victory. We held our trophies in our arms as their innocent eyes gazed up at us and we've conquered all.

Our hearts were full, and the battle was over. We had won the greatest award of all.

Our family.

Mister Lane – Book 5 Purchase

The steamy billionaire series continues with the second book of the Mister series. Mister Lane is now available for purchase.

Mister Lane - Book 5 Purchase[1]

She belongs to another man. He only wants her. Two hearts become one.

Matchmaker Brielle McKinsey's heading for divorce. A last attempt to save her marriage goes south when her husband leaves her at the airport. With the trip already booked, she boards the plane to find herself. Only to be seated next to a man with ocean blue eyes in first class.

Billionaire Baxter Lane of Lane's Lingerie is on vacation to unwind. His charm makes Brielle want to stay in paradise. Once he's had a taste of her, he can't stop. But she leaves him to head home and face reality.

Brielle's job is to find customers their soulmate. But with her business in trouble, and her wedding vows broken, her life is falling apart. Until destiny strolls in and her new client could be the one to save her from foreclosure, but there's a catch—he's the fling from her trip. And Mr. Lane needs a wife. Will fate meet its match?

1. https://mybook.to/MisterLane

Join and Follow the Author

Come join Breanne's Blazing Beauties readers group on Facebook! It's a place where you can talk about Breanne Bergie's books, get exclusive book teasers of upcoming releases and more! Don't miss out and send a request to join today!

Breanne's Blazing Beauties Readers Group[1]

Stay up to date and receive a free short story by author Breanne Bergie.

Please subscribe by going to Mrs.BreWrites Website[2]

Follow me at:

Facebook[3]

Instagram[4]

Twitter[5]

1. https://www.facebook.com/groups/1238819146535136
2. **http://mrsbrewrites.wixsite.com/mysite**
3. **http://facebook.com/MrsBreWrites**
4. **https://www.instagram.com/mrs.bre_writes/**
5. **https://twitter.com/MrsBre_Writes**

Printed in Dunstable, United Kingdom

81341432R00191